THE GAME OF LOVE

A Contemporary Sports Romance

K. ALEX WALKER

Copyright © 2014 by K. Alex Walker

All rights reserved, including the right of reproduction in whole or in part in any form. Without limiting the right under copyright reserved above, no part of this publication may be reproduced, stored in or introduced into a retrieval system, or transmitted, in any form by any means without the expressed written consent of the copyright owner.

Note from the author:
This is a work of fiction. Names, characters, places and incidents are either the product of the author's imagination or are used fictitiously, and any resemblance to actual persons, living or dead, business establishments, events, or locales is purely coincidental.

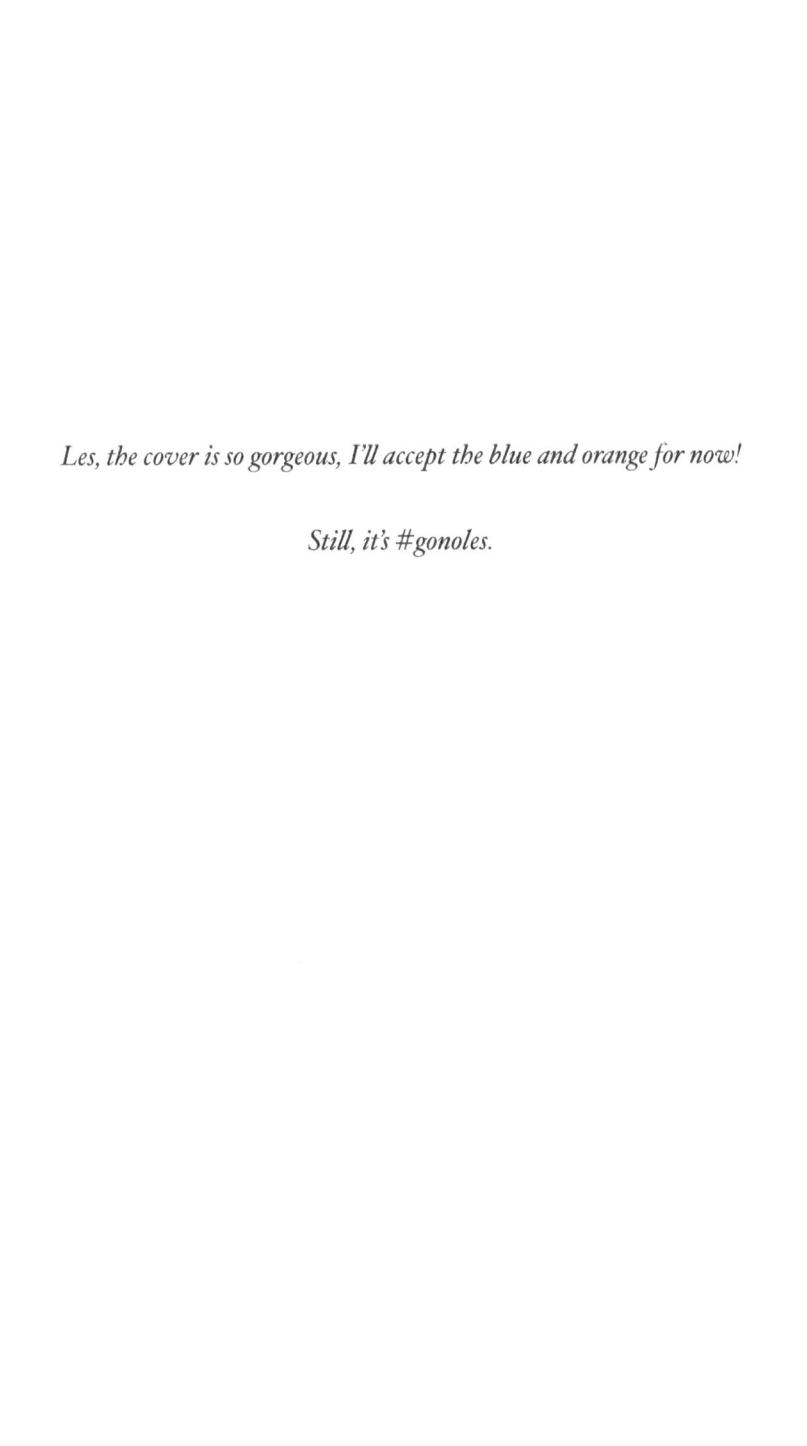

Les, the cover is so gorgeous, I'll accept the blue and orange for now!

Still, it's #gonoles.

Also by K. Alex Walker

The Game of Love

The Game of Love: Book I

The Game of Love: Book II

Angels and Assassins

The Wolf: Book I

The Protector: Book II

The Anarchist: Book III

A Fighting Chance - An Angels and Assassins Novella

More from K. Alex Walker

Fated - A Contemporary Erotic Romance

The Woman He Wanted

With A Kiss, I Die

The Gatekeeper - Coming This Fall (2019)

Chapter One

This is my last chance.

Austin Riley wiped his sweaty palms on his shorts. Rays of summer heat scorched the back of his neck. The crowd around him dissipated the closer he drew to the café where the love of his life worked. She didn't know she was the love of his life, and he was pretty sure she hated his guts with every fiber of her being, but that didn't stop him from trying. From flirting. From swallowing gallons of saliva as a blast of cold air hit him from the open café doors.

They would be leaving for college soon—him for Florida State University down south to play quarterback for the Seminoles while she headed to New York. It was the farthest they would ever be from each other, having both spent their entire lives in one of the smallest towns in North Carolina. There was also no guarantee they would return to Yearwood once they were done with college, so this would be the very last chance he had to tell her he loved her.

A heat wave had blanketed the town so the bakery café, although always busy, seemed to currently house every resident the town possessed. But he took his place in the quickly moving line that wrapped around and through the indoor tables and pretended to look at everything else but Sommer.

He'd heard things, *rumors* that it was possible Sommer was doing the same thing, pretending to be his enemy to hide the truth about what she felt for him. His mother had always taught him to disregard rumors, but this was one he hadn't. He couldn't. This was one he needed to be true.

"Hey, golden eyes."

There were still a couple people between him and the counter where she scooped colorful, frozen cream in cups and on cones, but she'd noticed him. Called out to him.

"Hey, Sommer."

She stared. He stared right back. Her lips parted. He swallowed. The few people fizzled down to none and then he was there, standing in front of her, the most beautiful girl in the world.

His gaze darted to the menu on the wall behind her. "Um...just vanilla."

She'd gone from staring to avoiding his gaze. He only knew because he was still staring. When she looked up at him to hand him his cone, he looked away.

"When are you leaving?" she asked. "For college, I mean."

"In a few days." His head bobbed to music that didn't exist. "You?"

"Same."

"Sommer—"

"Austin—"

He extended a hand. "You first."

"No." Her head shook, curls of dark hair wiggling with the movement. "You...go ahead."

Sommer, I love you. Everybody says we're too young to know that, to even understand love, but I've loved you since I could walk. I don't know what that means now that we won't be in the same elementary, middle, and high school like we've been our entire life, but I love you. And, one day, you'll be my wife.

"Sommer...good luck."

She licked her lips, searched his eyes. At least, it looked like she was searching his eyes. He only knew because he was *still staring*.

"Austin." She smiled. "You too."

He held up the cone. "Thanks, for this."

"You're welcome."

He lingered until he felt a slight shove in the back. The patron behind him—Mrs. Engleson, the infant teacher at the Yearwood preschool—grumbled for him to keep moving.

Austin made his way down to the end of the counter to pay for his ice cream. When he was finished, he headed for the doors, looking back one last time. Sommer was gone.

"You okay, Som?"

Sommer dabbed tears from the corners of her eyes. "Yeah, Mom. I just needed a quick break."

"I saw Austin leave," her mother said. "Did he say something to you?"

Not what I wish he'd said.

"He just wished me good luck."

Her mother's brow lifted into a skeptical arch. "Is that what's got you back here crying?"

"No ma'am." She swiped at her right eye. "Well, kind of. It's just hitting me that I'll be going away. But, I'll be fine, Mom."

Caroline Hayes leaned forward and pressed her lips against her daughter's forehead. "I know you will, sweetheart. But, are you *sure* that's all what's bothering you?"

No, Mom. I'm in love with Austin Riley and I wish the world worked in a way that meant, because of that, he loved me too. I wish I hadn't wasted so much time pretending I felt just the opposite.

"Yes, Mom."

Her mother knew something. Mothers always knew things, though she didn't know how. But instead of questioning her further, the older woman simply walked back to the front of the café.

Sommer collected herself, washed her hands, and returned to her post. Through the open front doors, she spotted Austin's shirt fading in the distance as he walked away. It felt final, finite, and she channeled all her attention on serving ice cream to cool the hurt.

I love you, Austin.

Chapter Two

Ten Years Later

She was standing beneath a blue and white striped awning, her head bobbing to the music coming through the Farmer's Market stereo, and Austin once again found himself mesmerized by Sommer Hayes as he watched her from across the pavement.

He could only imagine how much she would loathe hearing that little piece of news—her longtime nemesis couldn't take his eyes off her at that very moment. They'd been rivals ever since the first grade when he'd accidentally puked chocolate milk on her new white blouse and had been too embarrassed to apologize. Their rivalry only increased when, in middle school, they almost came to blows when his blatant cheating on her test paper nearly landed them both Fs in science class.

However, although Sommer hadn't been very fond of him, Austin hadn't felt quite the same way about her. With skin so decadent it looked like it should have been poured over a festival apple, his teasing had only been a cover up for just how sweet he'd been on her.

The summer before they left for college, he'd come close to telling her exactly how he felt. But he'd fudged the opportunity, a slave to teenage anxiety, and two days later left North Carolina to play football at Florida State University. After four years, he was drafted in the first-round to play quarterback in Dallas.

That sweltering day downtown was the last time he'd seen Sommer up until now, but as he looked at her, it was as though no time at all had passed.

"Austin." A voice called from somewhere down near his waist. A few seconds later, a huge yellow squash was shoved into his face.

He groaned. "Ma, squash looks like a penis, so don't put it anywhere near my face."

Sixty-two year old Emma Riley snickered. "I should have done that to Jessica then, huh?"

Austin groaned again, and the familiar pang of deceit radiated throughout his ribcage. After eight months, it was still there, waiting to attack the minute anyone said Jessica's name.

"That's low, Ma."

"I'm four feet eleven inches, Austin. I have to go low."

He playfully nudged her in the side, and they continued to walk.

Jessica Costa was the Brazilian model who had stolen his heart and then, after eleven months, stamped it with a "return to sender" sticker. He'd met her at a birthday party that one of the team's wide receivers, Trent Holloway, had thrown for his fiancée, Alexandrina. Alexandrina was Jessica's cousin and had apparently been trying to introduce him to Jessica for a while. So when Jessica had finally been able to chisel some time out of her busy schedule to attend the party, Alexandrina had isolated them on a private balcony.

Much to her delight, he and Jessica had hit it off, spending most of the night talking about the places she'd traveled to during her modeling career. With her dark hair, sparkling brown eyes, and svelte, hourglass figure, Austin had made the mistake of falling in love with Jessica's beauty and completely ignored the way she never seemed interested in conversation unless she was the topic of interest. He'd turned a blind eye when she would frivolously spend her money and then borrow from him to pay her bills while his suggestion to invest fell upon deaf ears. He'd assumed the last straw was when he'd found cocaine in her purse and she'd openly admitted to using it to stay thin.

Yet, he'd remained with her for three more months, just in time for the paparazzi to snap pictures of her sailing on a yacht with an older man later identified as billionaire investor, Walter Remos.

He'd tried calling her to get an explanation, but was greeted by the message that the number was no longer in service. He'd even tried sending messages through Alexandrina, but Jessica never responded. The last he'd heard was she was pregnant and marrying the billionaire from the yacht, and the lack of closure only acted as the closed fist that further drove the knife deeper whenever someone mentioned her name.

"Austin," his mother called, "do you still eat beets, sweetie?"

He pointed to a row of vegetables. "No, but I eat eggplants. Ma, can you make some *ciambotta* while I'm home? It's not often your baby boy comes to visit."

Emma rolled her eyes...and then picked up a couple eggplants.

"Austin Riley?"

Her voice was like velvet.

Austin turned to find Sommer standing only a few feet away. Distracted, he shoved the squash into his mother's chest. Emma shook her head and grabbed it, placed it in her basket, and continued on.

"Sommer?"

"Yes, Sommer Hayes," she said. "We went to school together?"

It was crazy she thought he could forget who she was.

"Of course I remember you, Sommer." He pointed to her blouse. "Nice top."

She took a few steps backwards. "It's brand new, so let me back up here a little before I get sprayed with chocolate milk and pineapple chunks again."

"I'm surprised you remember that."

She grinned. "I could never forget that. My mother cursed you out the entire time she scrubbed that stain out of my shirt. She was upset at you for a while after. You never noticed that she always cut you an extra small slice of cake whenever you stopped by the café?"

Austin had told his mother years ago he thought Mrs. Hayes had it out for him, but she'd laughed so hard she'd ended up having to take an aspirin for a headache.

Then, one day when he was sixteen, he, his mother, and his older sister, Arielle had gone to the café. His mother had ordered three slices crème brûlée cheesecake. When Mrs. Hayes cut the slices, his mother had reached for the smallest of the three. Mrs. Hayes had then gently tapped her on the wrist and said the smallest piece actually belonged to Austin, which had made him assume that he'd finally been vindicated. But his sister and mother had remained in denial. To this day, they still teased him about what he'd referred to as the *mini-cake conspiracy*.

"I knew it," he said. "Now tell that to Ma and Arielle. How is she, by the way? Your mother?"

The smile faded from her face. "Not too good. Her cancer came back so Uncle Reese and I have been taking turns driving her to chemo. The doctor said it's more aggressive this time, so right now we're at the *wait and see* stage."

Austin started to reach out, to touch her hand, but then realized they hadn't seen each other in ten years. He had no idea if she still held the same ill feelings toward him she'd had back then.

"I'm sorry to hear that," he offered. "It must be really hard on you right now to go through something like that."

She half-smiled. "I'm managing. But, enough about me. Tell me about your exciting career as one of the top quarterbacks in the league."

He was surprised to find he was actually embarrassed. "It's really not all of that. I mean, I'm doing what I love and that's the best part of it."

"No championship this year, though?"

"Close, but no cigar. But we've made the postseason for the past three years so I feel like we have a sure shot at the championship this year. I can taste it."

Sommer's brows came together, mischievous. "I don't think I've ever tasted Championship before. What does it taste like?"

He smacked his lips a few times. "A little like blueberries with a hint of vanilla."

"But no pineapples?"

His gaze briefly dropped to the ground. "You're never going to let me live that down, are you?"

"Never. It's actually my fondest memory of you, tears streaming down your face and that shocked, slightly embarrassed look in your eyes. I mean, at that age, all I could remember was that you ruined my shirt. But as I got older, I started to remember the sadness in those freakish golden eyes of yours. You, your mother, and your sister still have the only true amber eyes I've ever seen."

Again, Austin surprised himself by blushing. It had been years since he last had a reason to be embarrassed and in a couple of minutes, Sommer had managed to turn him red in the face twice.

"You know, I never did apologize for that. So, I just want to say, 'I'm sorry I blew chunks on you.'"

She giggled, lowered her eyes. "Austin, even if your stay is just a short one, I'm glad you took some time out to come back home."

He paused before responding, waiting until she looked up at him. "You're the first person to officially welcome me, Sommer, and I'm glad it was you. We haven't seen each other in ages, and I'm glad we can finally have a conversation without getting into *fisticuffs*."

They stood in a few moments of silence. A breeze gently shook through her hair. "I hope to see you around, Austin," she said. "It was nice running into you. Tell Ms. Emma I said hello."

She spun around and walked off in the opposite direction, her stride just as lively and bouncy as her personality had once been.

Austin's gaze traveled down the curves of her hips, lingered on the way her legs filled out the black leggings she wore.

"Sommer's looking good these days." His mother walked up, handed him the basket now filled to capacity with an assortment of fresh fruits and vegetables. "You know, she's been on her own a lot, sadder than usual. Think maybe an old friend could help cheer her up?"

He looked down at his mother who winked at him and hooked her elbow through his, pulling him in the direction of a sign that read, *Home Grown Tomatoes*.

Chapter Three

"Mom, sit down."

Caroline flitted around the kitchen with a bright pink cotton bandana wrapped around her head, searching for her missing frosting bag. She spotted its metal tip sticking out from behind a breadbasket, grabbed it, and returned to finishing the coconut cake Dawn Robins had requested to celebrate Eleanor Talbot's retirement from the town's Parks and Recreation department.

"You're doing too much." Sommer followed her mother around the bakery's kitchen and backroom, reached for the frosting bag. "I can do that."

Caroline moved the bag out of Sommer's reach. "Sommer, please let me do my job."

"I am, but you're doing your job and then some. I finished the chocolate chip cookies for the kindergarten recital over at Oak Park, even the gluten-free ones, and I just put the focaccia bread in the oven. The lunch rush won't be here for another couple of hours. I can handle more than you can right now."

Caroline paused, closed her eyes, and said a small prayer underneath her breath.

"I'm upsetting you, aren't I?" Sommer asked.

"Yes, you are," Caroline said. "I don't ask you for much, Sommer, but please let me do this. You, Reese, and Marcie tripping over yourselves to make things easier on me is appreciated, but I love working. And doing what I love, it's helpful." She met her daughter's hopeful brown eyes. "Is that okay?"

Sommer let her shoulders drop. "Okay, but promise me that if you need anything, you'll ask."

Caroline reached for Sommer's hand and hooked their pinkies. "You have my word."

Defeated, Sommer walked to the front of the shop where her Uncle Reese's fiancée, Marcie, was handing a small, white pastry box to Trudy McMillan. Without opening the box, she could guess what the woman had ordered—a banana nut muffin for herself and a crème-filled vanilla cupcake for her granddaughter, Elise. It was the same thing she always ordered the first weekend of the month when Elise came to visit from Durham.

"Chin up, Sommer," Marcie teased. "Your mother's a headstrong woman, you know that."

Sommer waved and smiled as Trudy exited. "Oh, I know. I can be the same way. I just can't help feeling like I could do more for her. It's driving me crazy sitting here watching her," she lowered her voice, "waste away. She's lost close to twenty pounds, yet acts as though nothing has changed."

Marcie wrapped her arm around Sommer's waist and gave her a quick hug. "You're a good daughter, but maybe you should let your mother do things her own way. If it's one thing I know about Caroline, it's that she always asks for help when she needs it. One time, in '03, she asked me to run out and get some parchment paper. She'd really needed it."

Sommer laughed, gave her a playful shove. "She'll ask for help when *she* thinks she needs it, which isn't always when she actually does."

She moved to clean up the trash the guests had left behind on their tables. The bells on the front door chimed and she looked up, expecting to see Timothy Dugan, the elementary school's secretary dropping in to pick up the cookie order. Instead, she was staring directly into Austin's glittering, golden orbs.

He was dressed in a casual brown button-down and jeans, looking more like a Mediterranean male model than a professional football player. There was a blue gift bag in his left hand.

"Oh my word, is that Austin Riley?" Marcie hurried from behind the counter. He bent for her to reach his neck, and she planted a loud smack on his cheek before holding him at arm's length. "Sweetheart, we haven't seen you in," she turned to Sommer, "how long has it been since you all left high school?"

"Ten years." Sommer tossed out a paper carton and moved to another table.

"A whole decade? You've grown into quite the handsome man, Austin." Marcie glanced down at his bare left ring finger. "I can bet the ladies are always knocking down your door, aren't they?"

Sommer let out a sound, a mix between a snort and a laugh.

Austin sent a look her way. "I only let the special ones in."

Marcie began to poke her hand inside the gift bag. "Did you bring me something?"

"I promise I'll bring you something next time, Marcie." He tucked the bag behind his back. "This is for Sommer."

Sommer's head popped up. "For me?"

"Yes, for you."

He extended the bag. She left the wet rag on a tabletop and walked over. When she was close enough to grab it, he pulled it back.

"On one condition. Come outside with me."

Sommer's gaze went to Marcie, to the café's backroom. "The lunch rush is going to start soon and I have to help my mom and Uncle Reese in the kitchen."

Marcie, still bubbling with excitement, shook her head. "We're hours away from the lunch rush, Austin. Actually, we just finished the breakfast crowd not too long ago." She gave Sommer a gentle shove in the lower back. "Go on, girl."

Sommer followed Austin outside and they took a seat in one of the fancy metal bistro tables the café had installed for outdoor dining. He pulled out Sommer's chair before taking the seat across from her and then placed the bag on the table.

"Open it."

She eyed the bag. "What's in it?"

"There's only one way to find out."

She reached for the bag and he watched as she pushed the gift paper aside. When all the paper had been unraveled, she pulled out a stunning royal blue silk dress. Underneath the dress was a pair of gorgeous nude pumps. Gorgeous and expensive.

"I don't get it? You bought these for me?"

He nodded. "I bought them, but Ma picked them out."

She fingered the soft fabric. "Why?"

"Just because." He shrugged. "It was nice seeing you the other day and I felt like doing something nice for you."

She placed the shoes and dress back inside the bag, realization piercing her like a wayward bullet. He'd probably felt bad she was going through a "difficult time" in her life and thought a pretty dress and new shoes would make her feel better.

If he really thought that was going to work, then he'd been dating supermodels for way too long.

"I get it, Austin. Because my mom's sick. You don't have to buy me anything to cheer me up."

"It's not like that."

Embarrassed, she stood to leave the table, but he rose, wrapped his hand around her fingers, and pulled her back down to sit. "Sommer, it's not like that."

"Then why buy a gift for someone you haven't seen in ten years? Not to mention it's the same someone with which you had quite the longstanding rivalry."

When he smiled, her stomach fluttered at the way the corners of his eyes lightly wrinkled, the way the gold flecks in his eyes shimmered.

"You didn't let me finish," he said. "All the time we spent being enemies, Sommer, we could have been building a pretty tight friendship. That's what I'm trying to do now, but I don't have another twenty-eight years to try to get it right. I have seven weeks before I have to fly back to Texas, so I figured that if I want to get on your good side, I have to start now. Hence the dress, the shoes, and an invitation."

Her ears twitched. "An invitation?"

"Dinner and a wine tasting. Tonight, if you're free. Tomorrow night, if you're not."

She bit her bottom lip, eyed the bag.

"You can't say no to good food, wine, and company. And I know you like food. Remember in elementary school when everybody used to call you Sommer, spring, fall *and* winter?"

A smile peeked from the corner of her mouth. "They did not. I wasn't *that* chubby in elementary school."

Austin laughed, put his hands up in front of him. "I know, I know. I'm just kidding. You're beautiful."

Her face warmed.

"You think you're charming, don't you?"

One shoulder lifted. "A little."

She grabbed the bag, stood. "I'm free tomorrow."

He rose. "It's a date then. I'll pick you up tomorrow. Ma told me you moved back in with your Mom?"

"Yeah, to help her out. Do you remember where she lives?"

"1313 Cherry Avenue."

"Right."

He waited until she was inside the café before he moved back toward the car—the 5-series BMW she'd heard he bought as a present for his mother, but she didn't feel comfortable driving it around town.

But as he pulled on the door handle, Sommer pivoted, ran toward him.

"Everything okay?" he asked.

She stopped a few feet away from the car. "I forgot to say thank you. For the gifts. They're beautiful. I really appreciate them."

He smiled. "You're welcome, Sommer."

She walked back to the shop, turned around to wave when she reached the door. When she disappeared behind the doors, Austin pulled out of the parking lot and sped down the street.

AUSTIN WASN'T QUITE SURE WHAT HE WAS GETTING HIMSELF INTO. He'd been honest when he'd told Sommer he was interested in taking her out to work on their friendship, but in the back of his mind, there'd been something more.

She was sitting across from him underneath the diffused chandelier lighting of the old winery just outside of town, the royal blue of the dress radiating perfectly against her soft brown skin. The feelings he'd had for her, the ones he'd assumed had dissolved years ago, were still there. And they were making it difficult to get through the night without wanting to reach out and touch her in some way.

"Up next, we have our signature blackberry wine," a slender man with salt and pepper hair announced at front of the room. "As you will see, it is a favorite among many."

Austin reached across the table to touch the back of Sommer's hand, but she turned to face him before his fingers had a chance to graze her skin.

"Are you having a good time?" he asked, scanning her face to read her expression.

"I am." She sent him a slight smile. "Thanks, again. It's been a while since I've had a night out like this."

They both leaned back as the dark liquid was poured into their glasses.

"What are you usually doing on a Saturday night?" As far as his mother had told him, Sommer wasn't dating anyone around town. Of course, this information she'd volunteered without him asking.

She took a whiff of her glass. "Taking care of Mom."

"You don't go out with girlfriends? Maybe a boyfriend?"

Her brow wrinkled. "Real smooth, Riley. Who's asking if I'm dating someone? Ms. Emma? Because both our mothers went through a phase where all they did was try to play matchmaker for me."

Austin laughed. "She does that to you too? I think she believes she has a special gift because she set up Arielle and Justin."

"Yes," Sommer said, chuckling. "How are they by the way? Your sister and her husband? I heard they were on kid number three?"

"Four. They're having twins. A boy and a girl. I told them to name the boy after me, but Arielle said that only made her afraid he'd grow up to be like me."

"That was smart on her part." Sommer nodded. "The last thing that this world needs is another Austin Riley running around wreaking havoc."

Austin's mind briefly wandered to a time when he'd seriously considered having children with Jessica. Surprisingly, she'd wanted children also, but finding out about her cocaine habit had put those dreams on the back burner.

"I wasn't that bad."

"Austin," there was an incredulous hint to her voice, "did you or did you not put a dress, hat, and lipstick on Tara Hannaway's Arabian mare when we were twelve? And was this not the same dress she'd been planning to wear to the homecoming dance?"

"To be fair," he held up a finger, "she threatened to start a rumor that my sister was sleeping with Coach Kierkson all because Justin turned her down for the dance. I wasn't having it."

Their eyes followed a second, older gentleman in a three-piece suit making his way to the front of the room with his glass in tow.

"I heard about that. That's really awful that she would want to ruin both their reputations like that. You should have gone for the shoes too."

Austin grinned again. "We tried, but they were too big for the horse."

The older gentleman held up his glass and signaled for everyone in the room to do the same. Wine glasses were tipped as the liquid was drained, swirled, and then swallowed.

"Full-bodied," Austin said.

"Silky," Sommer added.

"With a hint of disgusting."

Sommer burst out laughing and frantically searched for a napkin before she sprayed wine all over the wooden tabletop. A few of the other patrons turned to stare at them, and they guiltily turned away as laughter shook their bodies.

"Do you like it?" Austin asked as she was still coughing and laughing into her napkin.

"Not at all," she managed to squeeze out. "Blackberry wine...not my thing."

Austin glanced down at his watch. "We still have time to make it out to Louie's, and I know how much you love his salmon pasta."

Surprised, she stared at him. "How'd you know that?"

He made his way around the table to help her out of her seat, her silky skin and intoxicating scent threatening to isolate blood to one region of his body. He then extended his elbow and Sommer hooked her arm through it as they exited the winery to the car.

"Your sixteenth birthday," he said. "I was there with Darrell and Kyle that same night you were there with your mother. You ordered the salmon pasta and then sent the waiter back for a take-home portion."

He opened the passenger door and she slid onto the seat, almost sliding off the edge as her silky dress made contact with the smooth leather.

"How'd you know it was my birthday?" she continued when he'd gotten in on the other side.

"In third grade, do you remember Miss Solomon had that big birthday cake poster with everyone's birthday pinned to it? I memorized yours: November eighteenth."

He started up the car. Sommer robotically slipped the seatbelt into the buckle, surprised that he could remember something so trivial from so far back. Yet, as she thought about it, she realized she'd also remembered his: August third. She could actually see it as clear as day, written on a candle made out of construction paper, attached to the poster with a thumbtack.

She touched him on the shoulder. "Why would you memorize my birthday?"

Austin hesitated before responding so he could take a moment to enjoy the feeling of her light touch. "In all the years of our rivalry, Sommer, there is one thing you never seemed to realize."

She raised both eyebrows. "What's that?"

He wrapped his fingers around her hand and slowly stroked her knuckles. It felt good to touch her and even better when she didn't pull away. He would have exploded before the night was over if the texture of her skin against his fingertips was still only in his imagination.

"You hated me. I never hated you. Matter of fact, I kind of adored you."

With the way her breath silently caught, he knew he'd caught her by surprise. But she offered no words as he pulled out onto the road, and they rode in silence on the way to Louie's Seafood Restaurant on the beach.

AS GOOD AS THE PASTA SITTING IN FRONT OF HER WAS, SOMMER

couldn't focus on the perfect combination of salmon, spinach, and tomatoes. She actually hadn't said a word since Austin's admission in the car.

He'd adored her. He'd actually said that he'd adored her.

Lies.

What kind of a man used the term "adored" anyhow? Were those the same lazy lines he'd used on supermodels and musicians to woo them out of their hundred-dollar lace panties? Was that the same line he'd used to seduce the infamous Jessica Costa?

Sommer had done her best to ignore entertainment, sports, and news channels for the past two years since they would display Austin and Jessica's relationship in at least one of their daily segments. Unfortunately, their relationship had been so ubiquitous, she couldn't avoid seeing it forever.

One day, back when she'd still lived in New York, a sudden craving for an iced latte had struck her. She'd ducked into a nearby coffee shop and as though waiting for her, it had been right there on a magazine display rack: Jessica and Austin wrapped up in a passionate lip lock on a Caribbean beach.

Although she'd seen them together before, their intimate hand-holding and flirtatious laughter had been chaste enough for her stomach not to stir whenever she saw it. At least, not that much. But the photo of them on the beach had left her uneasy for the rest of the week, and while she'd initially blamed it on the egg-white panini she'd had that morning for breakfast, she knew it had been something else.

Her lifelong hatred toward Austin had been a classic cover-up. She'd been smitten with him ever since she could remember.

She'd nearly revealed the truth when in the seventh grade, as he finished his fourth lap around the track during recess, he'd tossed a rose at her feet and incorrectly recited a few lines from Romeo and Juliet with his hands over his heart.

All the planets had aligned that day, at least until Kyle and Darrell

—the trio seemed to have been attached to each other since birth—had run up to him, looked at her, and laughed as they'd walked away.

She'd felt so foolish, swooning over Austin when he had only been making fun of her.

Then came their junior year of high school.

R. M. Loving High School's starting quarterback, Isiah Rones, had been kicked off the team after getting caught in the parking lot fast asleep with a lit joint between his fingers.

Austin had then been promoted to starter, much to both the school and Sommer's excitement since he had always been passionate about football. She'd also been insanely proud of him, but had shown it by rolling her eyes at him whenever she saw him in the hallway, which only made him grin and poke her in the side to torment her whenever they crossed paths.

During Loving High's first game, he'd shown amazing confidence and poise on the field. Eventually, he rallied the team to the school's first championship appearance, which had only left Sommer even more enamored.

After winning their last game before the state championship, as the team walked back to the locker room, everyone was shouting their congratulations—Sommer was still figuring out whether to give Austin a death stare or another one of her classic eye rolls—when he'd come right up to the chain-link fence separating the bleachers from the field and motioned for her to come closer. She'd—of course—refused, but at least had the decency to hit him with an irritated, "What?"

When he noticed that she wasn't going to agree to his request, he hopped the fence and climbed the steps until they were nearly nose to nose. Then, he bent close to her ear and said, "Third down, second-and-eight, with five minutes and forty-two seconds to go, I threw our winning touchdown pass to Darrell. As everybody was cheering, I looked over in the bleachers and for the first time in my life, I saw Sommer Hayes smiling at something I'd done. As long as I live, I'll remember that smile more than I remember that pass."

Then he'd backpedaled down the steps and back over the fence in mere seconds, leaving her speechless.

Yet, once again, Kyle and Darrell had run up behind him, looked at her in the stands, and laughed.

Sommer had vowed that night that it would be the last time Austin had taken her for a fool. But tonight, as she watched him delightedly dig into his seafood paella, she felt the swoon threatening to befall her once again. It was as if her heart literally had no recollection of ever being broken.

"It's your eyes," she suddenly said.

Austin looked up. "My eyes?"

"Yep." She speared a chunk of salmon with her fork. "They make me want to believe what you're saying, but I don't."

He folded his arms. "You're a hard one aren't you, Sommer?"

She shrugged and brought the fork to her lips. Austin looked around the room, made eye contact with their server, and flagged him down. The boy hurried over, so jubilant his feet nearly left the floor.

"Yes, Mr. Riley?"

"None of that Mr. Riley stuff, Theo." Austin waved his hand. "It's just Austin. My sister used to change your diapers, for goodness sakes. Could we have some boxes and the check please?"

Sommer frowned. "I'm not finished eating. Plus, I can pay for my own meal."

Theo's eyes darted nervously between them, unsure of whose orders to follow. In his house, the woman's word was always the final word, but this was Austin Riley. Most Valuable Player of the Year and Future Hall of Fame Quarterback, Austin Riley. Ever since Austin had walked into Louie's, he'd wanted to rush him and ask him a million questions, one of them eventually being for his autograph. However, since no one else seemed to react to him like he was a celebrity, Theo had decided to keep his cool. Even more unusual was that most of them had just referred to him as plain old Austin, Emma's boy, and Arielle's little brother.

"The boxes and the check are fine," Austin finalized. Once Theo disappeared, he turned back to Sommer. "It won't matter what that pasta tastes like once you've got your foot in your mouth."

She lay her fork down louder than she'd intended. "What's that supposed to mean?"

"It means I'm going to prove you wrong."

"And how is that?"

Austin polished off the rest of his beer, and Sommer's eyes fell to the outline of his mouth and the tempting softness of his lips. His mouth stretched into a handsome grin, and her pulse quickened.

"You'll see," he teased.

Theo soon reappeared with the boxes and offered to pack up their meal. Austin kept his gaze squared on the woman across from him he was certain he'd knocked off her cool. Though she was visibly rattled, she held his gaze and her stubbornness only made him like her even more. This was the Sommer that he knew. Belligerent. Headstrong. A fighter. When his mother told him she'd been depressed and isolated, he'd immediately known it was because of her mother's illness. She had been the same way during her mother's first bout with cancer. They'd been in the seventh grade when he first noticed the change.

Algebraic equations about x and y's relationship had started to bore him, so like he always did every few minutes, he stole a glance at her. Usually, she was already looking back at him with a waiting sneer, but she'd been distracted, looking out of the window as though captured in some sort of daze.

Kyle had purposefully dropped his textbook onto the floor, startling them both. Sommer had then wiped frantically at her eyes before turning to face the teacher, and from the sunlight coming in through the window, Austin could see the tear stains smudged against her cheek. Instantly, he'd made it his duty to make her feel better.

That afternoon before recess, he snuck into Mrs. Waters' class and stole a rose from the yearly anniversary bouquet her military husband would send from overseas. Then, after taking a few laps around the track to muster up the courage to carry out his plan, he'd tossed the rose toward Sommer's feet and yelled, *"It is my lady, it is my love, oh how I wish she knew that she was! She speaks but yet she says nothing, she eyes the courses, I will answer it. I am too bold, it is not me she is speaking to, two of the fairest stars in heaven, having some business, do they treat her eyes!"*

Even after the two hours his sister and mother had spent going over lines from Romeo and Juliet with him so he could pass English class, his nerves had still gotten the best of him and he'd fudged them.

First, Sommer had smiled with an uncontrollable bubble of laughter, but then Kyle and Darrell had run over to make fun of his affectionate display.

When the three of them looked her way, she'd shyly turned around and spent the rest of the recess period on the opposite side of the field.

"Can you ask Louie if we can keep these in the back while Sommer and I take a walk on the beach?" Austin asked, holding the cartons toward Theo.

"I'm sure that'll be fine," Theo replied with a nod. "I'll take them. It's really nice out. You guys have fun. Let me know if you need anything. I'll be right back here. My shift ends at—"

Austin's gentle touch on his shoulder ended his nervous rambling. "Thanks, Theo. I owe you one."

Sommer thought the boy would pass out from excitement right there in front of them.

Theo quietly nodded and hurried to the back to put away the food.

Austin stood and grabbed Sommer's hand, giving it a little tug to indicate he wanted her to join him. Sommer's eyes trailed over the buttons of his casual black sweater and dark rinse jeans, both which she knew hid an impeccable physique underneath. Her eyes then found his ruggedly handsome face and she gave herself quick reminder of who he was—a famous athlete that probably picked women like people picked daisies—in an effort to reign in anything that she thought that she was feeling.

When she stood, he followed her out to the restaurant's deck and down the steps. They removed their shoes and joined them with numerous other pairs on a rocky area ahead of the sand. Austin held out his hand toward her again, but she pretended not to see it and walked ahead of him. He didn't seem to notice, however, and followed her until they were standing at the water's edge. They stood side by side, Austin with his hands in his pockets and Sommer's hands cupping her elbows.

"*You're a mean one...Sommer Hayes,*" Austin sang.

She wanted to elbow him in the ribs for comparing her to Dr. Seuss' *The Grinch*. It was a big presentation every year at Christmas in Yearwood. Families would get together in the park and watch either the animated film or, more recently, the Jim Carrey version on a giant projection screen around fire pits if the weather wasn't too aggressive.

She collected herself and turned to face him. Unfortunately, his features were even more handsome in the moonlight.

"So, you adored me?"

"Everything from the hair on your head down to the birthmark on your left ankle."

She looked down at her feet.

"Bet you didn't know I knew that was there?"

"Lucky guess," she shot back. "If you so adored me, why didn't you ever, I don't know, tell me? Do something about it?"

Austin's brows lifted. "If memory serves me correctly, I've thrown roses at your feet, recited Shakespeare to you, and all but declared my feelings for you at the game before the state championships."

She turned away.

"So, you're telling me that you don't remember any of that?"

"I remember it, but you weren't being serious."

Austin tossed back his head and laughed, then gently grabbed her forearms.

"*It is my lady, O, it is my love! O, that she knew she were! She speaks, yet she says nothing: what of that? Her eye discourses; I will answer it. I am too bold, 'tis not to me she speaks: Two of the fairest stars in all the heaven, having some business, do entreat her eyes."*

His head then fell briefly before he found her gaze again. "And please, don't ask me to recite any more than that. In fifteen years, those are still the only lines from Romeo and Juliet I remember."

Sommer steadily held his gaze for a few seconds. Then, she rolled her eyes and pulled away from his grasp.

"And there it is." Austin tossed up his hands in part frustration and part amusement. "The famous Sommer Hayes eye roll. I was wondering when that would show up."

She walked until she'd put a few feet of distance between them. "Shakespeare? Really? You're going to recite the Shakespeare that we learned in *middle school* to prove that you're being honest? How many times has that actually worked for you?"

Confused, Austin moved toward her. "What are you talking about?"

She pointed a finger toward him. "No. This doesn't get to be easy for you just because…"

She let her words float and started toward her shoes on the rocks, but Austin grabbed her arm and pulled her back to him. Sommer wished that, just once, he'd let her storm out the way she'd seen it in her head.

"You're going to have to stop doing that," he warned. "I won't let you run. Trust me."

She stared at him in disbelief. "I know men like you."

Visibly intrigued, Austin folded his arms across his chest and gave her his full attention.

"You say a few kind words to get all in a woman's head, and then once things don't go the way you expected, you toss her aside like trash."

Austin continued to stare at her and realized that even when she was angry, he still found her cute as can be.

"I haven't said a thing about sex, if that's what you're referring to," he said. "And in all the years I've been dating, I've never invited a woman into my bed with the sole purpose of hurting her. I grew up with an older sister and would never want any man to do that to her, so if I don't plan on pursuing a relationship past the physical with a woman, we both have to agree on it. Oftentimes, contractually."

Sommer silently continued to listen.

"You were pretty much my only crush, Sommer. I wasn't lying to you when I said I'd adored you from elementary school up until I left for college. You're strong and selfless, especially when it comes to your family, and I admire that about you. I always have. And to be honest, I thought I'd shaken those feelings for you years ago. But when I saw you the other day at the Farmer's Market, I realized they were still there, and still as strong as though ten years hadn't passed since we'd last seen each other."

Sommer's gaze went to the water's edge. "Sure didn't look like it when you were getting all *cushy* with Jessica Costa."

She'd murmured it but he'd heard, and realization hit him when he noticed the hint of jealousy in her tone.

"Every man falls for beauty at some point and time in his life," he explained. "You're lucky you've got substance to along with yours. It's like having two beautiful red roses in your yard. The first few times you walk past them, they're stunning, but after a while, they just look ordinary. That is, until you learn that one of the roses has magical healing powers in its petals. That there's more to it than meets the eye. That extra layer is what makes it more special than all the others. That's you."

He had no idea what he was saying, but he hoped the words made some sort of sense.

"You're slipping into poetry now?" she asked with a slight smile.

He exaggeratedly threw up his hands. "I just can't stop myself."

She laughed and at that moment, it was most comforting sound in the world.

"You're not out of the woods yet though," he added. "Now, be honest. Were you jealous just a minute ago?"

Sommer felt her face flush. "What? No, I wasn't—"

"Sommer."

She looked to the sand. "A little."

It was the first time Austin noticed his pulse was racing. "Tell me why."

She inhaled a large gulp of salty air and expelled it loudly from her lungs. "I might have been lying about my hatred toward you back then. I might have hated you to hide how I truly felt."

"Which was?"

She took another deep breath. "I liked you."

Austin took a step forward. "Now, who's lying?"

"Oh, I did. I mean, writing *Sommer Hayes-Riley* all over my diary liked you."

"I wouldn't let you hyphenate."

She laughed and he pulled her closer to him.

"I wanted to ask you to prom," he admitted.

"I died a little inside when you walked in with Tammie Carter," she confessed.

They paused.

"I used to dream that we'd get married and have an amber-eyed little girl," he said.

She squeezed him, inhaled. "In Spanish class, when we were learning about Spain weddings, I daydreamed about us having one."

Austin tugged her until her body was inches from his. One of his hands went to the side of her face. He thought about her comparing herself to Jessica, and it made him wonder if she knew just how beautiful she was.

"When your Mom threw the Christmas party at the café our senior year, I tried all night to get you underneath the mistletoe. I really didn't know what I would have done if I'd actually gotten you under there, though. All I knew was that I just really, really wanted to kiss you."

Sommer boldly stepped toward him. "Really?"

His voice was thick. "Really."

"Do you still feel that way?"

To answer her question, Austin bent toward her and Sommer held her breath until she felt the soft graze of his lips against hers.

His tongue played gently against her mouth, coaxing it to open, and when her lips parted for him, he dipped his tongue inside and ladled the sweet nectar from her mouth.

Finally, he was kissing Sommer Hayes.

His other hand went to the side of her face and he deepened the kiss. Her sweet scent mixed with the salty, ocean air and filled his nostrils, increasing his thirst.

He tasted and drank from the caverns of her mouth until she had nothing left to give, but even then he couldn't stop. Whatever he'd been previously trying to deny now surged forth from his body, and all his composure dissipated when he heard the breathy moan slip from the back of her throat.

In one motion, he picked her up and she wrapped her legs around his waist.

"Austin, I—"

"Yeah, me too." He placed quick kisses against her lips, neck, and jaw.

Her voice was hot and hoarse. "Where?"

"Anywhere, baby."

"But your place, my place, we can't—"

"I can get us a suite. Anything you want. Just tell me what you want."

Sommer wanted to explode. "Okay. Okay…"

Austin paused when he picked up on the uncertainty in her voice. When he looked at her, it was clearly written all over her face. "Are you sure?"

She glanced away for a brief second before looking back at him. "I'm sure."

He placed her back on her feet and cradled her face in his palm. "Something's wrong."

"Nothing's wrong. I want to do this. I want you."

He pressed a soft kiss against her lips and resisted the urge to succumb to the overpowering hunger building inside of him again.

When he searched her eyes, he found that the uncertainty had been replaced by fear, then he recalled what she'd said before about being used up and then tossed aside like trash.

Her parents' divorced hadn't been amicable. Her father's exit had been so traumatic that he'd wiped away any good years their family had built. She could, and probably still was apprehensive about that. The most important man in her life had betrayed her. Why wouldn't he?

He could relate to where she was coming from. The most important man in his life, his father, had done the same. He'd been such filth that Austin had wiped out the years of his life he'd been his father's pawn. An embarrassment. A blemish to society.

"Sommer, I want to spend as much time as possible with you while I'm back home. All of your free time. So, go out with me tomorrow."

She closed her eyes against the feeling of his finger stroking her cheek. "I can't. I'm going to church with Mom."

"After that."

"What do you want to do?"

"It doesn't matter."

She opened her eyes. "I take it we're not making love tonight?"

"Not tonight."

"Another night, then?"

He leaned in and pressed another kiss against her lips. "You can guarantee it."

She smiled and he returned the gesture.

They stood together for a few more moments before returning for their shoes and food and making their way back to the car.

While he drove her home, Austin kept his fingers entwined with Sommer's and kissed her fingers intermittently, still in disbelief that all this time, he and Sommer had shared the same feelings.

He took brief glances at her and wondered what life would have been like if he'd known that before. Maybe Sommer would have come with him to Tallahassee and then move with him to Texas after he was drafted. If Sommer had been in his life back then, there certainly would have never been a Jessica Costa.

His entire adult life, he'd searched for a replacement for Sommer. But now that he had her, he was going to make sure nothing would ever put distance between them again.

Chapter Four

What she'd initially thought was going to be a long and difficult summer had blossomed into a time of her life that Sommer would never forget.

Austin hadn't been kidding when he'd said he wanted to spend all his free time with her, sometimes randomly showing up at the end of one of her longer shifts at the bakery. Whenever she was too exhausted to go out, they sat, had coffee and pastries, and simply talked.

To everyone around town, her change in demeanor had been the result of a friend coming back into her life. No one knew about their intimate moments—the passionate kisses behind the heavily-tinted windows of his car, the lingering gazes they shared whenever they were in the same room, or the nights they escaped to Flatwoods Park and he kissed her on the swings with so much hunger, he'd managed to slip her shirt over her head before thinking better of having their first encounter on the grass.

But the time was coming. With each encounter, their desire for one another mounted higher, and Sommer no longer had the resolve with which she'd started.

The sound of her Uncle Reese reciting his vows jolted her back to the present, and she steadied the bouquet of assorted lilies she held between her hands. She couldn't believe that her uncle had made the decision to marry again at the age of fifty. Marcie was thirteen years his junior and had spent the last eleven years working alongside Sommer, her mother, and her uncle at the bakery.

No one knew at what point either Reese or Marcie had made a move, but all of a sudden, they were flirtatiously whispering to each other in the backroom. Then, Reese was teaching Marcie how to make a rose using a piping bag with an extra, delicate touch. It wasn't until Marcie had walked into work one day with an extra bump to her already round stomach that they realized the secret was out, and finally publicly revealed they'd been seeing each other. Their son was born five months later, Josiah, and had been Marcie's first and Reese's third child.

The couple was now beaming at each other, Reese swiping at the corners of his eyes while tears rolled down Marcie's cherub-like cheeks. As their vows continued, Sommer searched the room until she'd locked eyes with Austin, and he became the only image at the end of her line of sight. Perfectly outfitted in a crisp black suit and matching silk tie, she felt grossly mismatched in the pewter, lace turtleneck bridesmaid dress that Marcie had handpicked. Marcie, already self-conscious about her weight, had wanted to make sure that she stood out as much as possible on her special day. The bridesmaids had unanimously agreed to bite their tongues and wear the putrid greenish-gray gowns, and they'd all pitched in to make sure Marcie felt as beautiful as she needed to feel. In a strapless white dress that cinched her waist and emphasized her bust, the bride looked thoroughly pleased.

An organ began to play and Reese and Marcie shared a kiss before walking back down the aisle as husband and wife. Sommer followed with the rest of the wedding party, hooking arms with one of the groomsmen. When they passed the row where Austin was seated, he pretended to be heartbroken that she was on the arm of another man, and she playfully cozied up to the groomsman even more. He then signaled for her to meet him outside, and her body tingled in anticipation of the feeling of his fingers against her skin.

The reception proceeded ahead in full speed and everyone mingled underneath the decorated white tent that had been set up on the church's expansive acreage.

Marcie and her father twirled all over the dance floor to an upbeat 1940s swing melody. She'd wanted her father-daughter dance to be nontraditional and with the split that her father had just attempted despite being a man well into his seventies, she was getting just that.

"You've been hiding from me." Austin's voice cut through the noise. He stood a few inches behind her which allowed the distance to appear friendly to those who weren't close enough to hear the mischievous things he was saying.

He was still close enough for Sommer to feel the heat pouring from his skin, and it took mountains of self-control not to turn around and tug him out of the tailored suit-jacket he wore.

"I've been looking for you, I swear," she whispered back. "I just got caught up in the festivities."

He chuckled. "Lucky you that I'm not so beautiful you could barely focus on anything but me all evening. Even in that god-awful dress, you still manage to outshine everyone here."

Mrs. Waters walked by with a glass of champagne in her hand. Austin and Sommer smiled innocently until she was out of ear shot.

"I want to peel that dress off of you. I've wanted you ever since that night on the beach."

Her nostrils filled with the scent of his cologne. "Is that so?"

"That's so."

"Well, what do you say we get out of here?"

He shook his head. "Not yet. I want you to soak with anticipation."

The father-daughter dance ended and the DJ switched to a slow, 90s love ballad. Couples flooded the dance floor. Reese navigated through the crowd to reunite with his bride and the lights underneath the tent were dimmed.

Austin touched Sommer on the small of her back. "Dance with me?"

She looked up at him. "You're serious?"

"This can make up for prom."

"I hardly think that I would have worn this get-up to prom."

Austin gently pulled her by the hand and walked backwards toward the dance floor. "What do you mean? I could definitely see you in that at prom. With some neon pink heels. You'd be the envy of all of the women in the room."

Sommer looked around the room at how the women seemed to follow Austin's every move. For no other reason, they probably envied her because of the attention he was giving her that they wished they'd had.

Squaring away a spot in the middle of the wooden dance floor, he drew her into his chest, placed one hand at her waist, and secured the other with her smaller hand, lacing their fingers together. They swayed and he kept his gaze so affixed with hers Sommer felt as though he was trying to look directly through her.

"Relax, Sommer."

"Promise you won't step on my toes?" she teased.

"I promise. And if I do, I'll kiss them and make it better later."

Eventually, Sommer allowed herself to relax and become absorbed by the music floating around them.

When Austin pulled her closer into his chest and wrapped both arms around her waist, she responded by wrapping her arms around him and laying her head against his firmness. Eyes would definitely be on them now, which was something Sommer had initially been preoccupied with. But as she felt the strength pulsating in the arms he'd secured around her, she no longer gave a damn. Even if people talked, it wouldn't matter. She was swirling, swooning, stumbling, and falling. He'd already been firmly lodged inside her heart before he'd even returned to Yearwood, and the weeks they'd spent together had only allowed the dormant feelings she'd had for him to flow freely from their chasm.

"Sommer? Are you ready?"

She didn't realize her eyes had closed when she opened them to look up at him.

He took her by the hand and led her from the tent. Several pairs of eyes followed them as they left, but Sommer still didn't care. She'd already done enough simply for the benefit of everyone around town. Now, she would shirk their judgmental stares and bask in her own enjoyment.

When they reached the car, he positioned her against the passenger door and captured her lips as though he owned them. She wrapped her arms around his neck and pulled him closer, sucking, nibbling, and tasting his every essence. When he pulled away, she immediately missed the embrace and found some satisfaction in pressing her lips along the base of his neck.

"I don't know how you do it, Sommer. It's like your lips call out to me."

"Something else is calling out to you too." She wrapped a leg around his waist and felt his need grow against her. "If you want to answer."

Austin pressed himself harder into her body, wanting to tear her clothes off and fill her right there within view of anyone from the wedding party who came walking over the hill.

"We have to go." He pressed a firm kiss against her lips, pulled her off the door, tugged it open, and quickly helped her inside.

When he hopped in on the other side, Sommer reached over and ran her hands down the front of his slacks.

"You're going to mess around and get yourself in trouble," he warned, lids lowering when she wrapped her fingers around his bulge.

"I'm counting on it." She replaced her touch with a kiss and leaned back in the seat.

Austin smiled, shook his head, and sped out of the parking lot.

He drove for a few miles before he left the road and pulled onto a paved redbrick driveway flanked by colorful rosebushes, pruned shrubs, and neatly shorn hedges. Above them, tall birch trees grew toward each other on either side of the brick to create a natural arched entrance. At the end of the driveway stood an old, white Victorian mansion now a converted bed and breakfast. Its historic elegance was preserved with its wraparound porch, dressed in spindles and posts, and wicker settee and matching rocking chairs at the front.

An elderly woman came rushing over to them before they had a chance to exit the car, and stopped when she was a few feet in front of the hood. "Mr. Riley?"

Austin stepped forward and gently shook her hand, afraid that applying any more pressure might break her. The woman looked to be in her eighties and wore a knitted cap on her head with a few wisps of white hair poking out underneath. A pair of large framed glasses obscured half of her small face, and sapphire eyes which contrasted sharply against her brown skin peered from behind the black rims.

"Yes, but please call me Austin and this is my girlfriend, Sommer. I called earlier about spending the weekend? I talked to your granddaughter and she said that even though it was short notice, she could help us out."

Sommer's stomach quivered at the word "girlfriend." In the past six weeks, they'd never mentioned having any titles or had any talk about a relationship, and she never pressed the issue. Their romance would be short-lived with him living in a different state. Once he was gone, it would end, and she'd spent more than one night preparing herself for when that would happen.

He'd probably only used the girlfriend title since many of the elderly owners of the bed-and-breakfasts in the area often did their best to deter couples looking for a place to have a one-night stand. It was even more common to find those who preferred only married couples sleeping between their high thread-count sheets.

"Yes. My granddaughter, Faye," the woman responded. "I'm Rose Westwood. My husband and I have owned this place for years, decided to turn it into a bed and breakfast when the kids moved out. Was the best decision we ever made." Rose turned around and waved for them to follow her, then stopped at the bottom of the steps leading up to the porch. "No bags?"

Austin snapped his fingers. "Yes. One minute while I—"

"No need. We have a service for that. Someone will bring them up. The two of you look tired. Let me show you where you will be staying."

Austin took Sommer's hand, a gesture she'd fallen in love with, and followed Rose into the house and up a long, carpeted stairwell.

They walked past large, ornate windows and spotted a covered pavilion out back, a secluded hot tub, and several acres of lush greenery.

"Your room," Rose announced, pushing open a set of doors at the end of the hallway.

A massive four-poster king-sized bed in the middle of the room commanded the most attention, its mahogany posts stretching nearly as high as the ceiling. A padded window seat sat along the wall furthest from the bed. The furniture was antique but well-cared for, from the checkered drapes hanging from the windows to the beaded gray wing-back chairs and matching ottoman. An open bathroom door revealed rose petals lining an oversized Jacuzzi tub, and when Rose caught Sommer's wide-eyed fascination at the romantic set-up, she chuckled.

"Young love, I tell you." Rose briefly touched Austin on the forearm before she left.

Sommer walked to the window and peered out. More greenery stretched farther than she could see, and hammocks had been set up between sturdy oak trees just off of the east corner.

Austin wrapped his arms around her from behind and placed a kiss on her cheek. "Do you like it?"

"I love it," she said. "It's more than I expected."

He placed another kiss against her cheek. "I told you that I wanted us to spend the weekend together. What did you have in mind?"

"I don't know." She shrugged. "A quickie in the lot behind the hardware store or on the swings at Flatwoods?"

Austin spun her around and pressed her back against the window. "What am I going to do with you?"

He smoothed her hair away from her face and studied her features. The way he stared, it was though nothing else mattered except her presence in front of him.

And it wasn't that she didn't think he was at least somewhat smitten with her. All the time they'd spent together had proven he was, to some degree.

However, his feelings couldn't possibly run as deep as the ones she felt. It had surprised her when she realized those years of juvenile infatuation had amounted to something.

Whenever they sat, talked, and laughed, she never noticed the hours passing by. Then, their chemistry was so apparent it was almost tangible, and she had no idea how people didn't feel the heat sizzling between them whenever they looked at each other from across a room.

He was funny and affectionate, kind and loving. She'd even envisioned him asking her to come to Texas with him, but she could never leave her mother and the bakery. Her responsibilities were much more important, no matter how far she'd fallen.

"So, beautiful, what's the first thing you want to do?" His eyes darted over to the bed.

She followed their path. "You're not giving me much of a choice."

"What do you mean? We can do whatever you want. This weekend is all about you."

His eyes gaze made another beeline for the bed.

"You want to make the bed?" She pulled him out of his blazer, tugged his shirt from his slacks, ran her hands across his stomach, and almost cried out at the perfect outline of abs hidden underneath the fabric.

"I don't know how to make a bed," he said, walking her over. "Ma will vouch for me on that one. I'll need a lot of help."

He sat along the edge of the mattress, pulled her between his legs, and touched a kiss against her chest, connecting with her warm skin through a keyhole opening beneath the turtleneck of the dress.

"Is this how I start?" he asked, lips still against her chest.

"You're moving too far ahead."

"Oh." He moved his lips to her neck. "Here?"

Sommer's lids fluttered. "Mm. Yes. That's a good place to start."

He continued his onslaught to her senses and reached around for the zipper in the back of the dress, slowly pulling it as far south as it could go. He then let the ghastly fabric fall to her feet before moving his lips back to the spot on her chest, a few inches away from the mound of flesh peeking from its lacy fabric enclosure.

"I think I remember this part. This," he fingered the fabric of her bra, "comes off. I definitely think this comes off."

Sommer reached for the buttons on his shirt and began to undo them one by one. "Not before this."

She pushed the shirt off onto the bed once the last button was freed. Just as she figured, he was beautiful. From his solid chest to his strong shoulders and sculpted arms, his physique was incredible.

"You have a Superman chest." She ran her hands over the taut surface. "I think, if I look close enough, I can even see the *S*."

"Oh yeah? Where is it?"

She bent closer. "Right here."

"Over my heart?"

"I guess so. Yes."

"Then that *S* doesn't stand for Superman. It stands for *Sommer*."

She turned away in disbelief, but her stomach still stirred. "That's a bit corny, even for you."

He laughed, pulled her back to his body, and reclaimed her lips. His tongue played with earnest. Sommer played back, the heat between her thighs rising when his hand moved to the lace overlay of her bra. Her nipples hardened in response and he flicked his thumb over the fabric, sending an aching throb directly to the center of her heat.

His thumb continued to flick, and Sommer gently bit on his bottom lip to prevent herself from crying out. It had been a long time, longer than she'd realized, and even then her body hadn't responded with this much passion.

His fingers stopped and she thought she was getting a moment's reprieve to catch her breath, but he slid his hands through the lace waistband of her panties. When his fingers found their mark, she failed to stop the cry that surged forth.

"Austin..."

Her voice was nearly foreign—low and ragged—and his fingers moved with expertise, leaving her weak, pressing her forehead into the space between his neck and shoulder.

"This weekend is all about you, baby," he reminded. "Just tell me what you want."

His fingers continued to play, gliding without effort over that throbbing nub. Parts of her body that had never before reacted to touch were crying out to him now, and he knowingly responded as though he'd been caressing her that way for ages.

She attempted an answer, but a hard knock resounded on the other side of the door. If looks could kill, Sommer was sure the person on the other end would drop dead the minute they saw Austin's face.

"Your bags?" a man's voice called.

"Can you leave them there?" Austin asked, his fingers still intimate, still stroking.

"Wouldn't want your things to get stolen," the man insisted.

Austin cursed and pressed a swift kiss against Sommer's lips before retrieving his mischievous hand. He brought his fingers to his lips and tasted her, a gesture Sommer never realized she would find so arousing.

"One minute," he called out.

He hesitated, waited for his erection to calm. After a few hard moments, he grabbed a blanket from the bed and tossed it over her body. "This thing will never go down with you standing there looking like that." He ran a hand down her thigh. "God, you're sexy."

Sommer wrapped the blanket around her body. "You're not making this any easier on yourself."

He glanced down. "I know."

When his body had finally relaxed enough to be unnoticeable, he rose and went to the door, placing himself between the man's line of vision and Sommer standing half-naked across the room.

The man at the door looked to be the same age as Rose, and Austin immediately felt guilty for not bringing up his own bags. He understood the couple's courteousness, but if they didn't hire someone else for their service soon, the man would probably die long before chivalry did.

"Good, you're getting dressed," he said to Austin. "James Westwood, Rose's husband. Dinner will be ready in five minutes."

Another curse resounded through Austin's head, but he hid any evidence of it from his face.

"Can we have ours in the room?" he asked.

"Oh no." James motioned with his hands. "We all have dinner together. It gives us a chance to get to know our guests. Plus, my wife is making lamb stew. You'll be in for a treat."

I was already getting a treat.

Austin felt his cock begin to harden, but did his best to banish the thought of Sommer standing behind him hot, ready, and covered in lace.

He took the bag from the man's hand and slipped it inside.

"The missus asleep?" James asked, trying to peer behind him.

"She's getting dressed."

"Good." He clapped his hands together. "I'll see you downstairs in five. Rose's lamb stew is truly very good. You'll be in for a treat."

Austin closed the door when James disappeared down the hallway, and turned around to find Sommer's spot vacant. He found her in the bathroom sitting along the edge of the tub.

"Is he gone?" she asked.

He nodded. "Yeah, and apparently we're expected downstairs in five minutes to meet the guests, and regale them with tales of our travels out west for the 1848 California Gold Rush over a pot of hearty, southern lamb stew."

Sommer snickered. "You sound upset."

"I am. A little bit." He smiled and crossed his arms over his chest. "I was in the middle of making you come."

Her body throbbed in response. "I hate you," she said with a sly grin.

"No, you don't. You love me."

She didn't offer a response.

Rising from the edge of the tub, she walked past him to the suitcase and threw back its cover to search for a dry pair of underwear, not that it would stay that way for long.

She found a pair, along with a white tank top and long, striped navy blue and white skirt and returned to the bathroom. Austin was still standing in the doorway with his arms folded, his eyes following her every move.

"I guess I should change for dinner too?" he groused.

"Unless you plan on wearing that suit to eat lamb stew," she said.

Suddenly feeling self-conscious, she stood with the clothes in her hands.

"You can't be serious," Austin said, realizing she was hesitant about undressing in front of him.

"'I'm not comfortable being naked in front of you right now. It's not your fault."

"But you *will* be naked in front of me."

Another throbbing response.

"I know, but not while I'm standing here exposed in this unnaturally well-lit bathroom."

His arms fell to his sides. "Well, what if I told you that I love your body?"

"Austin..."

"You'd still be self-conscious?"

She nodded.

"We'll work on that," he promised. "I want you to get the most out of this relationship, and I don't think you can do that if you close off any part of yourself from me."

And there it was again. Another reference to a relationship.

She tried to ignore his remarks, but they hung in the air like a low lying fog. When they'd first began their affair, he'd mentioned wanting to build a friendship with her, so the last thing she wanted to do was ruin the perfect atmosphere by making the awkward assumption he wanted anything everlasting with her.

Also, she was determined to finally make love to him that weekend, maybe even more so than he realized, so she would do nothing to ruin the chances of that happening—which included asking him any intimate questions about their status.

"Later," she partially conceded.

He reluctantly closed the door and she turned the lock.

Sommer slipped into the new underwear, maxi skirt, and tank top and quickly checked her appearance in the mirror before leaving the bathroom. Austin was sitting on the bed already changed into a polo and beige shorts, and she wondered what it was about men that made them more efficient at getting dressed than women.

"Ready, beautiful?" Her hand already extended by the time he reached to grab it.

They made their way down the steps and entered the dining room to a table full of waiting guests.

Austin was surprised to find dinner had managed to *somewhat* take his mind off of making love to Sommer, and that the lamb stew had truly been delicious.

The stew was served with homemade buttered rolls so rich his trainer would have had a fit if he knew how many he'd gobbled down in a short span of time. But the best part of his night had been Sommer's transformation.

His mother's words about her change in demeanor echoed throughout his head at random moments, but he watched her light up beneath the dining room's crystal chandelier and saw even more of the Sommer he'd known come out.

He'd felt like a voyeur, as though watching her natural self reemerge was akin to spying on her in one of her private moments. But it had been impossible to turn away.

Sommer loved people. Whether it was listening to them, talking to, or offering advice, being around people had always brought her joy.

When they were younger, he'd always assumed she would go on to be some sort of counselor or public relations specialist, any profession where she had a lot of contact with others. He'd initially been surprised to find out that she'd gone back to Yearwood to work at the bakery, but it had made sense once he found out her mother was ill.

Sommer reached across the table to ladle another helping of stew into her bowl, and Austin wondered when would be the right time to tell her he was in love with her.

The hours before her uncle's wedding, he'd paced along his mother's front porch and pored over ways to tell her how he felt. To his surprise, he hadn't been at all worried that she might not feel the same way, especially since he hadn't directly asked her to be exclusive.

He'd tried the subtle approach—introducing her as his girlfriend or referring to their affair as a relationship. Sommer had refused the bait and it left him disappointed that he couldn't just come out and talk about it directly.

He'd no doubt she was probably wondering what would happen

between them once he returned to Texas in a few days, but he had every intention of continuing the relationship, even if it meant flying out to see her and sending for her whenever she was free.

The eruption of lively laughter broke through his thoughts, reeling him back to the dinner table. At dinner, they'd had the pleasure of meeting the Browns, a professor and her retired businessman husband, the Califfs, a firefighter and kindergarten teacher, and the Hardings, a former Navy SEAL and his very pregnant attorney wife.

Dinner conversation flowed freely as though the five couples had known each other previously, and cheers went around the room when Rose brought out buttermilk pie and vanilla ice cream for dessert.

After dinner, before they could be invited to a game of charades, Austin whisked Sommer away from the group.

He grabbed two beers from the kitchen, led her outside to the covered pavilion, and took a seat on a rustic, wooden bench. Sommer tried to sit next to him, but he pulled her onto his lap.

"This way, if I have some difficult questions to ask you, you can't run away," he justified.

She leaned into his chest. "I didn't know I came out here to be questioned."

"I have many surprises up my sleeve." He kissed her bare shoulder. "You never know what you're going to get when dealing with me."

He popped the top on the beers and offered her one. She took a quick sip then let the condensation run down the amber bottle while it sat between her hands.

The flavors swirled around in her mouth and she glanced down at the bottle. "Yummy. This is a major step up from the blackberry wine."

He laughed and took a swig from his bottle. "If that's a compliment, then I appreciate it. But you're right, this is pretty good." He read the label. "*Infused with citrus.*"

"Mine has cherry and honey in it."

"Upscale beer." He took another sip. "Didn't realize that we were staying at the 'Pavilion de la Reine.'"

She tilted her head to look at him. "What's that?"

"This really ritzy hotel in Paris."

"Oh." She toyed with the bottle. "You go to Paris a lot?"

He quickly found a way to answer the question without hinting that he'd been there with Jessica. "I've been once or twice."

Evidently, it didn't matter.

"With Jessica?"

Austin didn't respond, mostly because he wasn't sure how to proceed. If he said no, it would be a lie, but if he said yes, it would thrust Jessica into the center of their conversation...and he wanted her nowhere near their conversation.

"With Jessica," Sommer said, answering her own question.

"A couple of times when she was shooting in France, we were invited to stay there. I mean it's nice, don't get me wrong, but it was just a little fancy for my taste."

This time, it was Sommer who fell silent, switching her attention to a group of lightning bugs sparking up near a three-tiered stone fountain.

"How did the two of you meet?" She was determined to remain on the subject of Jessica.

Austin tamed a frustrated groan. "I don't want to talk about her, Sommer, and I don't think that you want to either."

"Maybe I do."

"Why would you?"

"Why didn't the two of you work out?"

"Because she wasn't you."

He anticipated the eye roll before it danced across her face. As frustrated as he was, it still made him smile. If he hadn't known her better, he would have guessed she had no other facial expressions.

"What?" he asked.

"Don't play with me, Austin. What's the real reason?"

He sighed when he realized there was no getting out of the conversation. "She and I were just incompatible."

"How long did you date?"

"I don't know, around a year or so."

Eleven months, ten days.

It surprised him to find he'd remembered the duration of their relationship with so much precision.

"So, it took you a year to realize you two were incompatible?"

"No, it took me a year to realize I was fooling myself by thinking that I," he bit his tongue before the L-word slipped out, "had feelings for her. Don't women always say that men have one-track minds? Well, all I focused on was her looks, not that she was selfish, irresponsible and dishonest."

She spun the bottle around in her hands. "So, you broke up with her once you found out that she was?"

"Sommer, let's talk about something else. Anything else."

She didn't reply.

"Let's talk about us."

He searched his mind for a way to reveal his feelings for her that would still matter even after having Jessica rule the majority of their conversation.

"I need to stand," she said. "My leg's falling asleep."

He knew she was lying, but he let her go and she walked to one of the pavilion posts and leaned back against it.

"Sommer," he said, pulse quickening.

Suddenly, a flash of Jessica's face cut across his thoughts.

"Yes?"

Sommer, none of that matters because I'm in love with you.

He tried for the words but Jessica's face appeared, brows contorted, her hands wrapped around his throat.

Sommer was standing across from him. He was certain that he loved her. It made no sense that he couldn't just come out and say it.

"I'm sorry," she suddenly apologized. "I'm ruining the evening."

He walked over. "Yes, you are."

"Austin!"

"Well, you were the one who said it. I was just agreeing."

Finally, she smiled. "I guess I walked directly into that one."

He placed a finger underneath her chin and tipped her face up to his. There was absolutely no doubt in his mind how he felt about this woman, but just like he'd done ten years ago, he'd clammed up. Something was preventing him from saying what he needed to say, and it irked him that he didn't quite know what that something was.

He leaned down, expecting an apologetic brush of the lips, but she wrapped an arm around his neck and deepened the kiss.

The beer in his hand became obsolete, and he blindly rested the glass bottle on the nearest structure he could find.

He lifted her into the air, pressed her back against the post, and removed the bottle from her hands.

"I want to go upstairs," she whispered against his lips.

"You still upset with me?" His lips grazed her neck and her back reflexively arched.

"Yes, a little."

He carried her across the lawn and entered the house through the back door, stealing up the back stairs to avoid interrupting the riveting game he heard carrying on in the main room.

He pushed the door to their room open, tossed Sommer onto the bed, climbed over her, and sought her lips again, his passion intensifying with each quiet moan that floated from the back of her throat.

He slipped his hands beneath her top, found her breasts, and unhooked the clasp at the front of her bra. His groin tightened when he filled his hands with the creamy mounds, fingers flittering over her eager nipples.

The sensation rippled between Sommer's legs. Her body arched in response to his touch. He pulled her top over her head and tossed it aside, then bent and took a nipple between his lips.

"*Still* mad at me?" he asked, his tongue swirling.

"Yes," Sommer managed, barely above a whisper.

The ripple between her legs grew to an aching throb.

While Austin's tongue continued to tease the hardened nub, he used a single hand to slip her skirt and panties down over her hips and slide his fingers between her thighs.

He didn't think it was possible for his cock to grow any firmer, but his erection pulsed when his fingers slipped along the slickness of her arousal. It took nearly all of his restraint not to submerge himself into her body right then and there, but he'd already promised that the weekend would be all about her.

He slipped out of his shirt and found her eyes, now seductive slits, staring back at him. His eyes traveled down the length of her curvy, naked body, and as he reached to remove his belt, she stopped him, eyes beckoning him to take over. He let his arms fall and granted her full control.

Once the belt was undone, he slid out of his shorts and boxers, freeing his erection. Sommer moved forward and wrapped a hand around his shaft. Austin closed his eyes and tilted his head back while she stroked him from base to tip. When he felt the warmth of her tongue encircle the swollen head, his eyes flung open.

"I knew you were a bad girl," he said. "But this weekend is about you, baby."

"But, I want to." She looked up at him with false innocence, flicking her tongue over the tip.

And oh, how I want you to.

But he knew that if she did, it would be the end of his control. He'd only be able to tolerate so much of the hot caressing of her mouth before he found himself waist deep inside of her.

He brought his lips down to hers and moved her backwards until he had her hips right where he wanted them. He then used his fingers to part her legs once more, teasing the throbbing organ. When her eyes closed, he moved down her body and replaced his touch with his tongue.

Her pleasure-filled curse sliced through the air and her moans matched the intensity with which his tongue played. He licked and gently tugged on her sweet, feminine nub, and she gripped the sheets with so much force it sent a few pillows toppling off the side.

Austin slipped a finger inside her and matched a gentle stroke to the rhythm of his tongue. Sommer moved her hips in response, feeling weightless. Uncontrolled. His tongue flicked right where she wanted it, *needed it,* and her pleasure mounted as he gently pushed her legs farther apart to grant himself more access.

She began to climb toward climax, her breaths shallow and deep. She felt it coming hard, fast, strong. No other words came to her except his name, which she cried out several times, letting him know she was close. That she was there.

She caught her breath, grabbed his head, and screamed his name. The orgasm erupted throughout her body, shattering her senses, spreading warmth and sheer satisfaction.

Austin's tongue slowed as she shuddered. He rose, situated himself between her legs, and waited until the waves of her orgasm had fully washed over her. Then, he placed the tip of his cock against the place that ached for his entry.

"Are you *still* mad at me, baby?" He slid in an inch, holding her steady, her hips instinctively rising to meet him. "Sommer?"

"Hmm?"

"Answer the question."

He slid in further and groaned, jaw tight, when her body tighten around him.

"No," she whispered.

"I can't hear you, baby."

"*No!* I'll never be mad at you again."

"Good."

He took hold of her hips, sank into her sex. Her body clenched along his firm length, and he realized he was not completely prepared for the raw need that coursed through him.

Sex with her was unlike anything he'd ever experienced and he tempered his rhythm, trying to extend his time in the wonderful cavern that tightened around him with each hard stroke.

Sommer wrapped her legs around his waist and urged him deeper. She wanted more of him, as much as her body could handle. His girth. His thickness. She wanted every inch of his stroke.

"Deeper."

In one movement, Austin flipped her over and entered her from behind, never losing momentum. She cried out again, driving him mad with lust. Everything about this woman, every single damn thing he encountered, was wonderful. Even as he firmly took hold of her soft hips, his body surged and he hissed, sucking in a breath to avoid releasing inside her too soon. It wasn't time yet. He wanted her to make her come again.

He ran his hands down her spine and over the curve of her bottom, pulled her up so that she was pressed back against his chest. He placed kisses against her shoulder and neck and again found the place between her thighs. When his fingers brushed the organ designed only for her pleasure, he felt a flood of heat swell along his shaft, threatening to bring him to climax.

"Austin, baby—" Her hands went to her breasts, her fingers against her nipples, teasing him. Daring him closer to the edge.

He flicked his tongue against her neck. "Come for me, Sommer."

Sommer didn't know exactly how he did it, turned every single spot on her body into an erogenous zone, but when his tongue found its mark, she did as she was told.

Her body arched and her hips rocked. Sated breaths were expelled from her lungs. The feeling of her orgasmic tugs on Austin's shaft caused his climax to slam into him, and he surrendered his ecstasy into her beautiful body.

They spent a few moments in breathlessness, suspended in disbelief. It had happened, and it was better than either imagined it ever could have been.

Austin raised her hand to his lips, kissed her fingers, and fell back onto one of the few pillows left on the bed, pulling her down with him.

"I'm going to miss that," she said, her body splayed across his chest.

"What do you mean?"

"When you leave. I'll miss it. That was amazing."

"It's not going anywhere."

"I've never had a summer fling before." She ignored his protest. "It was more than I expected and I enjoyed every moment of it."

The word *fling* stung like a knife, but Austin didn't believe for one second she actually considered their time together to be a fling.

"It doesn't have to end this weekend," he said.

She was already shaking her head. "Austin, we were infatuated with each other when we were younger and used this opportunity to see what that could have led to."

"Right."

"But your life is in Texas and mine is in North Carolina."

"And?"

She eased up. "Don't do that. You never mentioned that you wanted our affair to go past this summer, so don't do it now just because you're still basking in the afterglow of sex."

He wanted to argue, but she was right. He'd spent the entire time being evasive and had never mentioned what his intentions were. He could only imagine how she felt now that, after he'd had her, he was trying to make the claim he wanted them to continue past the summer. He wasn't even sure how to now dig himself out of a hole he hadn't even been aware he was digging.

She kissed his chest. "I don't regret anything we've done, so don't feel guilty or think you've used me. I'm happy."

"That's all I wanted, Sommer." He stroked her arm. "To make you happy."

And to make you mine.

"And you succeeded. I don't think I'll ever be happier in my life than I've been in these past few weeks spent with you."

The genuineness in her admission warmed his heart.

He pulled her in for another kiss, which she deepened. He hardened against her stomach and she eased up and slid down onto his erection. Still wet and hot, she rode him, controlled him, threatened his toes to curl.

His eyes rolled back into his lids, and her muscles squeezed his shaft while she alternated between up and down, and back and forth motions.

This was the woman he loved. Whatever it was that was preventing him from telling her he wanted her in his life way past this summer, he had to find it and get rid of it, bury it. Forever.

Austin opened his eyes and smiled. "You don't know what you've started," he warned, effortlessly flipping her onto her back and sliding into her as deep as he could go.

Sommer cried out, dug her fingernails into his shoulders, and readily took in every pulsing inch of him.

~

Sommer and Austin had emerged from their room only during meal times, or at the insistence of the other couples. At the end of the weekend, they said their goodbyes, drove back into town, and talked about everything under the sun, except for what would happen the day he had to fly back to Texas.

Unfortunately, as they sat on the front steps of Caroline Hayes' two-story bungalow, the day had finally arrived. Austin's flight was taking off in a few hours, and Sommer had chosen not to go with him to the airport, knowing that she would never be able to restrain her tears as she watched him walk through the gate.

"Preseason is a lot more nerve-wracking than you'd think," he said, looking down the street. "Even though the starters only play for the first couple of quarters, one misstep can take you out of the season before it even starts."

Sommer rested her chin in the crook of her elbow. "Yeah, that does sound nerve-wracking."

They sat in silence for a few minutes.

"So, what will you be doing? Working with your mother at the bakery?" he asked.

"Pretty much." She chewed on her bottom lip. "Me, Mom, Marcie, and Uncle Reese. That and monitoring Mom's progress."

He met her eyes. "This couldn't be more awkward, Sommer."

"I know, but there's nothing we can do about it."

"You know that's not true."

"Austin, I'm sure there's enough sex in Texas." She stood. "You won't have to come back here for it."

He reached for her hand. "You know better than to think sex was the only thing I wanted from you, Sommer. Sit down."

She remained standing.

Since she wouldn't sit, he stood. "Look me in the eyes and tell me that's what you want. For me to leave and for us never to speak to each other again."

She sighed and held his gaze until a yellow Porsche pulling up into her mother's driveway caught her attention.

The person emerged from the car, and Sommer failed to hide the annoyance that washed across her face. Austin turned to see what she was looking at, then smiled broadly as the person came closer.

"Kyle Stallworth," he greeted. "How is it that you don't show up until the very last day that I'm in town?"

Kyle lowered his sunglasses and flashed Sommer a pearly white smile before giving his old friend a quick pat. After high school, Kyle had remained in North Carolina to play football for NC State and was eventually drafted by Miami where he currently held the team's single-season record for most interceptions by a safety. The third member of the group, Darrell Morton, had made the switch to basketball and now played in Toronto.

"I didn't even know you were here," Kyle said. "I was just passing through to check on Sommer and her mother." His eyes darted to Sommer. "How's Mama Hayes doing?"

"She's fine," Sommer responded, terse.

He flashed her another smile and gave her body a quick scan. Then, he turned his attention back to Austin.

"It's good to see you, Riley. You heading out today?"

"I am," Austin said.

"Same here. I'm leaving this afternoon." Kyle's eyes landed on Sommer again. "What are you doing out here anyway, Austin? The last I remembered, you and Sommer weren't exactly the best of friends."

Austin stepped closer to Sommer. "We've made amends. Sommer and I are good now."

"Really?" He clicked his tongue. "That's interesting. That's...good."

Kyle slipped his glasses into the pocket of his tan blazer, reached across, and removed an imaginary eyelash from Sommer's cheek. Then he let his finger fall slowly, deliberately stroking her jawline in the process. Sommer jerked her head away and he grinned delightfully at her reaction.

"Hold on, Austin," Sommer said, moving toward the front door. "I'll grab my keys. We can take my car to the airport after all."

Kyle gestured to his Porsche. "No, it's okay. I can take him."

"I said I'll do it. Austin and I spent a lot of time together these past few weeks so the least I can do is see him off."

Austin eyed Kyle suspiciously. Even though they played in the same league, it was a rare event for them to run into each other with the exception of when they were opponents on the same field. They would probably rarely run into each other even if they'd lived in the same city.

Kyle was a frequent face in popular nightclubs, and Austin was more of a homebody. Before his relationship with Jessica, he was usually out with the guys from the team—mainly Trent and another wide receiver, Cason Allen—at restaurants and volunteer charity events. Now that Trent had married Alexandrina and Cason was engaged, it was mostly just him.

Sommer reappeared with her purse, tossed her keys to Austin, and didn't give Kyle a second glance as she charged toward to the car.

They pulled out of the driveway, and Kyle watched until the car disappeared around the corner before he made his way back to the Porsche.

∽

"So, what's the deal with you and Kyle?" Austin asked once they'd left Yearwood city limits and hit the interstate to head into Wilmington.

"What do you mean?"

"There was nothing on your face. He just wanted to touch you."

Sommer stretched the muscles in her neck. "I don't know what his deal is."

"His deal is that he likes you," Austin clarified. "I think he has for a long time, but that's his problem. You're *mine*. What I want to know is if he's bothering you because if he is, we can turn this car around and I'll handle it."

She smiled at his defensiveness, even the way he'd possessively claimed her with words. "It's fine, Austin. He just stopped by to see Mom. Everyone's been worried sick about her since word spread about her cancer."

"So, why'd you decide that you could come with me all of a sudden?"

Sadness washed over her face. He knew the answer before she even said it. He would miss her too, immensely, and although he wasn't too fond of a long-distance arrangement, for her, he was willing to try anything.

"I want to be the last face you see," she said. "To make sure you don't forget me."

He wanted to laugh. If ten years apart hadn't erased her from his memory, what did she think would happen now? Especially, now that he'd tasted her?

"Do you really think I could?"

She smiled. "Of course not."

They engaged in light conversation for the rest of the ride, skirting around the issue of Kyle. Austin still wasn't satisfied, but he made Sommer promise she would call him right away if Kyle gave her any trouble. She'd waved away his request at first, but then after realizing he was serious, she'd promised.

Austin held her hand while they walked toward his gate, and he took a moment to revel in the fact that no one was trying to take his picture or get his autograph. The minute he landed in Texas, that would change. He'd be thrust back into the public eye and celebrity lifestyle, and it would only make him miss the small town privacy even more.

It was one of the good things about being a professional football player; he was hidden behind a helmet for much of the game, so there were still parts of the world he could escape to where his celebrity wouldn't follow. He was grateful for those moments of reprieve and knew he wouldn't stay away from home for another ten years. It felt good to be around people who simply knew him as Emma's once badger-toothed, autumn-eyed boy that a solid pair of braces and fitness trainer had done a world of good.

"I think this the furthest that I can go," Sommer said, looking around. Her grip on his hand tightened. "Austin, I have to say goodbye now."

At that moment, those were the seven most dreaded words he'd ever heard in his life.

There were tears on her cheeks and as she tried to wipe them away, more fell in their place. "Thank you, Austin, for this bit of happiness in one of the most difficult times of my life."

Her voice was laden with heartache. Austin felt his chest swell.

There was no way she'd seen them as just a fling and the evidence of that was tumbling down her cheeks. So, why was she being so stubborn? Even if every odd in the world was stacked against them, he was still willing to try.

This wasn't fate. Fate said there would be a way for them to be together, regardless of their fears or circumstances.

"This isn't goodbye, Sommer," he vowed. "And even though I'll miss your laugh, your smile, and even the way you roll your eyes," she laughed and lowered her eyes, "I won't say goodbye."

He cradled her face and pressed their lips together for what he hoped wouldn't be the last time, picked up his carry-on, and made his way through the gate. As he entered the tunnel, he turned and gave her a final wave, dropping his hand only when she disappeared from sight.

Chapter Five

※❀※

Two months later

There it was, frozen on the screen. Sommer had managed to remain in denial even after the several mornings she'd woken up feeling as if bricks were falling onto her head. Even when she'd missed her second period, she'd calmly gone to an out of town drugstore, picked up a test, and did not pass out when the display showed a hard plus sign. But there was no denying it now.

A few minutes ago, before she left the office to grab some paperwork, Dr. Stella Anim had shown her the baby. *Her* baby. Well, it wasn't much of a baby as the doctor had told her that she was only about nine weeks along. It was more of a bundle of little blips on the screen whose bumps would soon turn into a head, arms, legs, and a tummy. Yet there, growing inside of her, was the life she'd made a little over two months ago.

Then there was the issue of the father.

Nine weeks ago, she'd been writhing underneath Austin's meticulous lovemaking at the historic bed-and-breakfast. There was also no point between him throwing her onto the bed and filling her ever so slowly that she remembered inserting her diaphragm. So that, coupled with the fact that she hadn't been with anyone else since then, made it clear who the father was.

The issue, of course, hadn't been the "who." It was the "what" she would do now that she had this piece of information. She and Austin had spoken nearly every day since that day at the terminal. Although it was never about the issue of *them*—she curved the conversation every chance she got—she was pretty sure a baby didn't fit into his cushy lifestyle in Dallas.

"I'm sorry, Stella. I forgot my jacket," a woman's voice at the door said.

When the woman spotted Sommer lying on the table, she quickly apologized and backed out of the room. Then, a few seconds later, she came back in.

"Is that you, Sommer?"

Sommer looked up into the matching amber eyes of Arielle Riley-Wells, Austin's older sister.

"Arielle. Hi," she greeted with a nervous hug. She then grabbed a few tissues off of the desk, wiped the remaining ultrasound goo from her stomach, and pushed up into a sitting position.

"Sommer, are you pregnant?" Arielle asked, her eyes darting to the screen.

"Something like that. But you can't tell anybody, Arielle. Not yet."

Arielle smiled and gave her a tight squeeze. "Of course not, honey. But, I hadn't heard that you were dating anyone. Actually, correction, Ma hasn't told me that you were dating anyone."

Sommer smiled. As her mother and Emma Riley's friendship had grown over the years, the pair had eventually shifted their focus to playing matchmaker for their children. Emma was currently in the lead with her success pairing up her biomedical engineer daughter with her husband, Justin Wells, a successful attorney.

"It's a guy that I've been seeing for a little while," Sommer lied.

Arielle eased down into a nearby chair. "Is he from here?"

"New York. I met him on a day trip to Raleigh. He was in North Carolina on business."

Arielle wiggled her eyebrows. "Is he gorgeous?"

Sommer thought of Austin's face. "Very."

"What does Ms. Caroline think of him?"

"She hasn't met him yet. She doesn't know."

That information didn't surprised Arielle. The more she got to know Sommer, the more she realized how private and secretive she could be.

"Are you planning to tell her?"

"I will," Sommer reassured. There was no way she could hide her pregnancy living under the same roof with her mother. "It's just that, because she hasn't been doing well, I've been trying to keep the focus on her."

Arielle nodded, understanding.

Dr. Anim reentered the room with a folder in her hands. "Arielle, what are you doing back here so soon?" she asked. "Are you in any pain?"

Arielle looked at Sommer and then pointed to her stomach. "One of these little guys is breech. The boy. Stubborn already, just like his uncle."

Sommer's thoughts ran to Austin once more.

"But no, Stella," Arielle answered. "I thought I'd left my jacket in here and bumped into Sommer. We were just catching up."

She pushed herself up to stand and Stella came around to help her.

"Not too long now, thank goodness." Arielle sighed heavily once she was on her feet. "I'll go ahead and leave you two. I'm sure my husband's wondering where I ran off to, unless he's found the cafeteria. In that case, I could be back here in labor and he would have to make sure he finished his burger before he came over. And thanks for seeing me on such short notice. You'd think I'd know the difference between Braxton Hicks and true labor by my fourth child."

She gave Stella a hug, left, and Stella reclaimed her seat.

"Here's your paperwork, Sommer," Stella said. "You can leave the forms with Toya and she'll set up your next appointment." Her eyebrows came together. "How are you doing by the way?"

Sommer knew she was referring to her mother's situation. "I'm fine. Me and Mom will be thankful for this bit of happy news. Is the baby okay?"

Stella smiled. "For the millionth time, the baby is fine. Will the father be coming the next time we meet?"

"I'll see if he can get away." Her heart fluttered. "I'm really more concerned about him being there when we find out the baby's gender. Which, by the way, will be?"

"Around twenty weeks. Now go before you ask me to do the ultrasound again to make sure there's a baby in there."

Not a bad idea.

With a warm hug, Sommer left the office and dropped her paperwork off at the desk. She then ran across the medical center to the wing where her mother was being treated, hoping that her absence hadn't aroused any suspicion.

Caroline was already waiting for her by the time she arrived, exhaustion lines worn into her forehead.

"You're done, already?" Sommer asked.

"I'm done, baby. Only two more rounds to go. Where did you run off to?"

Sommer searched her mind for another lie. "I ran into Arielle Riley."

"Emma told me that Arielle should be having those babies any day now. She's so excited, you'd never guess she has two grandkids already." Caroline nudged Sommer in the side. "Be nice to have a grandbaby."

Sommer shot her mother a teasing look, then gave her a quick kiss on the cheek as they walked to the car.

∼

THAT NIGHT, SOMMER WAS VIOLENTLY TOSSED BACK INTO REALITY.

She kneaded the space between her mother's shoulder blades while the older woman retched over the toilet, and it left her feeling nearly physically impaired watching her mother wither away into a frail and weak vestige of herself.

She'd been spared the first time around. She'd been so young that the last thing her mother had wanted was for her to get a glimpse of the agony the illness had truly caused.

Back then, Caroline had also been able to rely upon Sommer's father. However, the man's attempts to pick up the slack and take care of the household had lost all value the minute he'd walked out the door with another woman.

Now, it was just the two of them, and Sommer knew that as she grew rounder, it would be even more difficult to be what her mother needed.

Sighing, Caroline flushed the toilet and retreated to the floor. "I raised a good daughter," she said, leaning her back against the bathtub.

"That's what good mothers do." Sommer retrieved a washcloth from the linen closet in the hallway.

"As a good daughter then, you'll understand."

"Understand what?" Sommer held the cloth underneath the faucet, dampened it, and handed it to her mother.

Caroline dabbed the cool cloth over her forehead. "That I'm moving in with Reese and Marcie."

Sommer turned off the faucet. "What are you talking about, Mom?"

"You're pregnant, Sommer."

She nearly passed out where she stood. "How did you know?"

"Mothers know."

"So, you're leaving because I'm pregnant?"

"I'm leaving because you and the baby will need the space."

Sommer gestured around the house. "Mom, this is more than enough space for me, you, and a baby."

As her strength slowly returned, Caroline pushed herself up to sit on the edge of the tub and touched the cloth to her cheeks. "Then, move in with the father."

Sommer didn't respond.

"I know you know who he is."

"I do."

"Is it Austin?"

Shock rattled Sommer's body once more, and her eyes widened at her mother.

"Don't look at me all surprised like that," Caroline warned. "You spent every waking moment with that boy when he was here and you two were still looking at each other all googly-eyed like you did when you were in high school."

As surprised as she was, Sommer found herself laughing. "You witch of a woman. The things that you know."

Caroline smiled. "Does Austin know?"

Sommer's gaze went to something in the room other than her mother's face. "No."

"When are you going to tell him?"

When she didn't answer, it was Caroline's turned to be surprised.

"You don't think I'm going to stand around and let you not tell that boy about his child, do you?"

"No." That, her mother would definitely not do. "But, if it's okay, I'd like to tell him on my own time."

"Which is?"

"The end of the first trimester."

Caroline opened her mouth to protest, but then realization sunk in. "You think you're going to lose that baby?"

"I might."

"Any reason you think that might happen?"

Sommer shrugged. "Because it happens. I wouldn't want to get Austin all upset over a baby that might not even grow to term."

Caroline tossed the damp cloth back over to her daughter and pushed herself up. Standing in front of her was a twenty-eight year old woman who wasn't sure if she was going to tell the father of her child, a man she obviously loved more than life itself, about their baby. And while she understood Sommer's reservations about miscarrying, it concerned her that her child was still living her life with too many reservations.

Sommer had always been afraid of making decisions, even the ones that were obviously good for her, because of the consequences that might ensue. Half the time, however, the consequences were what Sommer had made up in her head. It was that fear that kept her daughter at the bakery where she obviously wasn't her happiest. Unfortunately, Sommer had inherited her bullheadedness, so telling her that would change nothing.

"You don't think he'd be happy?" Caroline asked.

"He's a bachelor, Mom. I'm sure the last thing he wants is a baby."

Although Caroline didn't agree, she didn't comment. Instead, she planted a kiss on her daughter's forehead, touched her shoulder, and then made her way back to her bedroom. She'd give Sommer until the end of her first trimester as promised, but if she still didn't tell Austin by then, she would take matters into her own hands.

∽

AS MUCH AS AUSTIN LOVED HANGING OUT WITH TRENT AND CASON, this party was proving itself to be too much for him to handle. It was Trent and Alexandrina's daughter, Chloe's first birthday, and they'd celebrated by throwing a pool party at Trent's house in his sprawling backyard.

However, the spirited family atmosphere only left Austin feeling even more depressed. Two months had passed and he still thought about Sommer daily without any end in sight. He wanted her. She wanted to be stubborn.

"You're scaring my daughter," Trent told him, walking over with a beer in his hand. "I swear, every time she looks over here and sees how depressed you look, she bursts into tears."

Austin popped the top on his beer and took a swig. When the light citrus taste hit his palate, he glanced at the label. "I didn't know you were into fancy beers, Trent."

Trent lifted the bottle to his lips. "This beer isn't that fancy, Austin. You just need to expand your horizons."

Austin laughed. "I do. At times. It's just that I had this beer for the first time this past summer."

"With *Sommer*?"

"Yeah."

Trent took another swig. "Your summer with Sommer. Is that why you're over here looking so depressed?"

Austin motioned to the guests. "Can you blame me? You have Cason over there hugged up on Amelia, and then there's your little family. Even Tank brought a woman and do you know what the odds are of a woman saying yes to that face?"

Tank heard the jab, looked up, and pointed accusatorially at Austin who tipped his beer in response.

"Austin, you have your pick of the women in Texas," Trent reminded. "You just don't want them."

Austin rubbed away some of the condensation on the bottle. "Not yet. Maybe soon. I don't know."

Trent looked over to his wife and daughter. "It'll take some time. I get where you're coming from because I can't imagine what my life would be like without Drina and Chloe, but it's like this song Drina sings to Chloe at night. *Que sera, sera.*"

"What will be, will be," Austin translated. "I know it."

"So then you know that there'll be other Sommers. Who knows, maybe you'll meet a Spring. Or an Autumn."

Austin laughed and downed more of his beer.

Suddenly, the lively chatter ceased and even the sound of children's laughter died as the kids tuned-in that something was amiss. When

Austin looked up, Jessica was standing at the bifold patio doors with an arm wrapped around Alexandrina.

"Dree, what is this?" Trent asked his wife. "Why's she here?"

"She's my family, Trenton," Alexandrina argued. "She wanted to be here for Chloe's first birthday. I couldn't just say no."

Trent shot an apologetic look toward Austin. "This is still my house," he said. "I can ask her to leave."

"It's fine," Austin reassured. "Doesn't bother me."

Naturally, he scanned Jessica from head to toe and unfortunately, she still looked as good as the last time he saw her. She was wearing an olive green dress, strappy heels, and her long hair was piled on top of her head in an elegant bun. As his eyes traveled to her middle, he realized that her pregnancy must have been a rumor because her hips were just as slim as he'd remembered them. They were almost too slim, at least compared to Sommer's curvy, feminine figure.

When their eyes collided, she smiled and waved as though they'd been old friends.

She gave her cousin a kiss on the cheek, brushed a wave toward Trent, and made her way over to where he was sitting. "Austin, *bonjour*," she greeted. "You look good."

"So do you, Jessica." He decided to be cordial. "Just getting back from France?"

"And Spain. And Italy. You know me. Busy, busy, busy." She took a seat in the space Trent had vacated and Austin wondered who'd invited her to join him. "So, what have you been up to? Preparing for the new season?"

"Yep." He took another taste of his beer.

"Austin," she whined. "Don't be this way. I want us to be able to talk. Be friends."

Taken aback, Austin started to argue that it was hard to be friends with an ex-girlfriend that had absconded with another man and subsequently fell off the face of the earth, but he decided not to rehash old wounds at a one-year-old's birthday party.

"Well, if you won't talk to me, I will talk to you." She placed her purse next to her feet. "Walter Remos and I have split up."

The sound of Austin's phone chiming from his pocket came through almost like the heavenly bells. He set down his beer and retreated to a quiet corner inside the house without offering an apology about his sudden departure.

"Hey honey," Emma greeted on the line. "How are you?"

"I'm doing okay, Ma." He walked up the stairs to Trent's study. "What's up? Is something wrong?"

When he heard the baby's cry in the background, he realized why she was calling.

"Nothing's wrong, my love. Arielle had her babies. The boy was four pounds flat and the girl was four pounds, two ounces. They're beautiful, tiny little things."

Austin smiled when he heard more cries come through the line. "Yeah, that's tiny," he said. "But I guess that's the most they could grow with the small amount of room Arielle's body probably left for them."

Emma whispered something to someone in the room and then let out a hearty laugh. "Hold on, Austin. She wants to talk to you."

The phone shuffled as it was handed over, and then his sister's tired, yet elated voice appeared on the line.

"Hey Piglet," he endearingly greeted.

"Please, don't call me that after I just finished pushing out two babies," she pleaded.

"Pushing? I thought you were having a C-section."

Arielle eased onto her elbows. "I thought so too, but they came early and decided they wanted to do it their own way. By the way, we gave the boy Grandpa's name so sorry, no second Austin in the family."

Austin laughed. "What about your third little princess? What'd you name her?"

"Arabella. Ma said she looks like you when you were a baby. You looked like a baby girl when you were born."

"At least I had hair."

"I eventually caught up." She ran a hand down her long ponytail. "A couple days ago, Justin and I were visiting Mom when I thought I was going into labor. So, we decided on the name Arabella literally as I was walking into Stella's office. Actually, I forgot to tell you, but I ran into Sommer."

Austin's heart thudded in his chest. "You saw Sommer?"

"Yeah, she was in Stella's office. I was so surprised, I sat down and we talked a while. It made me realize how much I missed her."

So did he.

Arielle suddenly went silent and with the way her voice was lowered when she came back to the phone, Austin knew she was fishing for information.

"Austin, when you were staying with Ma, did you happen to run into Sommer at all?"

Run, plow, slide...

He cleared his throat. "A few times."

"Did she say anything about dating anybody or mention a name of a guy she might be seeing?"

Although Austin knew that there was a period of time where Sommer and his sister had gotten very close, there was no way Sommer had told Arielle about their affair. If she did, Arielle would have blabbed that she knew about it to him ages ago.

"No. Why?"

Arielle asked their mother to get her something to eat, no doubt trying to get her to leave the room. He assumed the coast was clear when she continued, "Well, I ran into Sommer at Stella's office."

She paused, waiting for him to piece the rest of the information together.

"And?"

"Stella's office, Austin. Stella's an ob/gyn."

"Okay?"

"She was getting an ultrasound."

"An ultrasound? Like women get when they're—"

"Yes, Austin. Look, don't tell anyone I told you, but Sommer's pregnant."

His heart slammed into his chest so hard, he was certain he'd broken a rib. Sommer was pregnant? Already? She'd gotten over him that quickly? Why the hell had he been holding on like a seventeen-year-old fool?

"I don't know anything about her seeing anybody," he robotically restated.

"Damn." Arielle huffed. "I don't want to ask Ma because if I tell her Sommer's pregnant, everyone will know. But, according to the monitor, that baby is around nine weeks along which meant that the guy would have been there at the same time you were in town. You didn't notice any new faces?"

For the second time, Austin's heart slammed into his chest. He did a quick calculation in his head and then fell into the nearest chair that he could find. Nine weeks ago, he'd been unsheathed and waist deep inside of Sommer's lovely body. However, she'd been using a diaphragm since she didn't like hormones. He distinctly remembered her telling him that.

But, he didn't have any recollection of her actually leaving to insert it. Actually, with the way things went that weekend, it was highly likely that she could've gotten pregnant. That *he'd* gotten her pregnant.

His heart slammed again. If Sommer was nine weeks along, then that was his baby. Sommer was pregnant with his baby.

"No, no new faces," he finally answered, hiding the excitement from his voice. "Actually, Arielle, I have a little bit of free time coming up. I think I'll fly out to see Mom first, then stop by you and Justin's to see the twins."

"No need." She was munching, which meant that their mother was back in the room. "I'm staying at Mom's for the six weeks. Justin will stay for a couple of weeks, then he's heading back out to Charlotte with Aria and Isabela."

Austin's head was still reeling, but he realized that the feeling bubbling inside of his chest wasn't anxiety. It wasn't even fear. He was happy, happy as hell, and he couldn't wait to see Sommer for her to tell him herself what he already knew.

"Well Piglet, get some rest," he told his sister. "I'll see you in a couple of days. Congratulations, and I love you."

She giggled. "Thank you and I love you too. You'd think that with newborn twins, Ma would be satisfied, but she's over here rambling about how all she needs now is for you to give her some grandbabies."

Austin smiled. Her wish was going to be granted even sooner than she thought.

Chapter Six

Austin lingered before walking up to the three-bedroom, Cape Cod house in which he'd spent the first eighteen years of his life. To pass time during his seven week stay, at least the time when he wasn't with Sommer, he'd repainted the shuttered exterior and replaced the damaged wooden posts on the front porch, then updated living room and entryway by laying down solid oak hardwood floors.

As he'd worked on the house, he couldn't believe he'd spent ten years away. At one point, he had even tried to convince his mother to move to Texas, enticing her with a promise to buy her a massive, six-bedroom home in University Park.

She'd firmly refused and back then, he couldn't understand why since Arielle lived hours away in Charlotte, and her friends were all busy with their jobs, businesses, husbands, and grandchildren.

Understanding had come to him when he'd taken the family's old fishing boat out onto the lake behind the house.

It was the memories she'd wanted to hold onto, which just happened to be some of the same memories he'd been trying to avoid. Even now, as he stood there staring at the house, he could see his father sitting on the porch with his ankles crossed and a mason jar of peach lemonade in his hand. He could see, in the man's eyes, the man he'd wanted him to be. The boy Austin was ashamed he'd been once upon a time.

"You think it's going to fly away?" Emma emerged from the side of the house holding a miniature shovel between two soiled gardening gloves. She was wearing her usual straw sunhat that had seen better days, garnished with a pink ribbon tied into a bow.

She climbed the steps and lovingly wrapped her arms around her son. Then, he opened the front door to follow her inside.

Another wave of nostalgia hit him when the aroma of sausage and peppers filled his nostrils, and he spotted a cooling loaf of zucchini bread on the kitchen countertop.

In the living room just off of the kitchen, Justin and Arielle were sitting on the sofa each holding a twin, and their two older daughters were sprawled on their stomachs hovering over a large picture book. The minute the girls saw Austin enter the room, they sprang up and crashed into his legs.

"I'm glad to see you too," Austin said, kneeling so he could wrap them both up in a hug. "Izzie, what's that on your head?"

Isabela, his two-year old niece, reached up and touched the ladybug plush that was attached to the end of her headband.

"Bug," she replied, patting her head.

"It's a lady bug. It's her favorite," six-year old, Aria explained. "We got it from the store. She has the dress to go with it, but Daddy forgot to pack it."

Austin shook Justin's hand.

"Daddy gets the blame for everything," Justin said.

"But you did forget the most important thing," Arielle teased. "Can you imagine how much easier our trip out here would have been if you'd brought the dress? It probably wouldn't have even rained. I might not have gone into labor."

She smiled as she received a kiss on the cheek from Austin.

"Next time," Justin resigned. "I didn't realize it before, but that dress was everything."

Justin made a funny face at Aria which sent her into a fit of giggles.

Arielle glanced down at their sleeping son. "Yes, babe, it apparently was."

Austin eased down onto the loveseat. Isabela reached her arms toward him and he pulled her onto his lap while Aria sank into his side. With the love he felt for his nieces, he couldn't imagine how he would feel about his own son or daughter.

"We didn't expect you back so soon," Arielle said. "We knew you'd come see the babies because you did the same thing with Ari and Izzie, but not in the middle of training camp."

"I didn't want to wait too long to see them." Austin pretended that Isabela was on a motorcycle by bouncing her on his knee, and she giggled in sheer delight. "Plus, you finally had your boy. I figured you'd be throwing a party to celebrate."

Justin looked to his wife. "You'd think it would be me hell-bent on having a son, but this one just wanted to keep on trying."

Arielle took a moment to stare at her brother as he played with his nieces. Something about him was different.

"I liked the little brother thing," she said.

"You didn't always." Emma appeared with a pitcher of lemonade and plate of pumpkin muffins which she sat atop the coffee table. "There were years where Austin made you want to pull your hair out."

"There were years when he did pull my hair out, Ma," she reminded. "But I liked how close we were. I'm not saying that sisters couldn't have been just as close, but the dynamic between me and Austin, it was unique. At least, to me. I wanted the girls to have that."

Emma sat and Isabela scrambled from Austin's lap over to her grandmother.

"What's it like?" Austin found himself asking. "Being a parent? I was just thinking about how I feel about Ari and Izzie and I can't imagine anything greater than that."

Arielle and Emma exchanged looks.

"You can't explain it," Emma said. "It's love, protection, pride—a mix of emotions wrapped into a ball to make one feeling they don't have a word for yet."

Arielle nodded. "Then take that feeling and magnify it by about a hundred percent." She took another glance at her son. "You'll know the feeling one day."

Austin did his best to suppress his grin. "Maybe."

"You will," she insisted. "But until then," she rose and walked over to where he was sitting, "hold your nephew."

Even more cautiously than usual, Austin held the nearly weightless baby in his arms. Silky black curls poked from beneath his blue cotton cap, and Austin ran a finger down the boy's small, soft cheek. As if responding to his touch, a corner of his mouth turned up into a smile that revealed a crater of a dimple.

"Did something happen?" Arielle suddenly asked. Austin had always been a good uncle and Aria and Isabela adored him, but with the way he studied his nephew, she saw something different. She saw a man who wished he was holding a child of his own.

"What?"

"Did you and Jessica get back together?"

He looked up. "No. Why?"

"Is your biological clock ticking again?" she teased.

"No, Sommer," he answered and, as the room fell silent, he immediately realized his tongue slip and searched for a way to explain himself out of it.

Although he wanted to tell his family the truth, he didn't want to say anything without talking to Sommer first.

"I meant, *Arielle*," he corrected, turning toward his mother. "And I was going to ask you, Ma, if Sommer worked early at the bakery today."

Emma paused, her suspicion piqued. "No. She told me today that she'd be closing."

The clock on the wall was pushing toward six-thirty, which meant he only had a half hour to drive out to the café and try to catch Sommer there alone.

He rose and gently handed his nephew back to Arielle. "I'll be right back, then. I have to go ask her something."

Arielle's curiosity was doing everything except spurting from her face. The move to a more densely populated city like Charlotte had done nothing to curb her small-town nosiness.

"Ma, can you hold—"

"I've got him." Emma was already scooping her grandson from Arielle's arms.

Austin knew that protesting was futile, so he let Arielle follow him out the door, stopping only when he got to the car and felt the weight of her stare on his back.

"You're going to ask Sommer about her baby, aren't you?" she accused.

"Maybe." He shrugged. "But it's not like you don't want to know about it."

Arielle rubbed her arms as a cool breeze off the lake brushed by. "You two must have gotten pretty close when you were here."

"You could say that." He tugged the car door open.

Arielle narrowed her eyes. "Austin, you know something."

"Arielle—"

"Did you already know she was pregnant?"

"No." He slid onto the seat and pushed the key into the ignition. "But my sole reason for going over there is because she's pregnant and taking care of her sick mother. Doesn't that sound like someone who needs a friend?"

Arielle pushed the door closed. "Hell, even pregnant and married sounds like someone who needs a friend. I sure did. But promise me that you won't ride in there like a knight in shining armor, say you'll be there for her, and then fall back on that promise. If you do, I'll fly all the way out to Texas and kick your ass."

He grinned. "You'll upset millions of Texans counting on a championship ring this year."

She motioned with her hands. "Bring 'em on."

He pulled out of the yard, and Arielle couldn't help but wonder what it was that her little brother was up to. She'd heard from their mother that he and Sommer had spent a considerable amount of time together when he was home, but even though everyone had kept their fingers crossed, it didn't appear a romance had blossomed. They'd only evened out their rivalry, one that dated back to even before they both could remember, and had built a solid friendship.

Arielle, however, refused give up on the hope that Austin would find someone to suit him just like she'd found Justin, regardless of what kinds of myths their father had tried to embed into their heads. She hoped that her marriage to Justin had shown him, if even in the slightest, what love truly looked like.

∽

SOMMER WAS LUGGING A BLACK TRASH BAG TO THE DUMPSTER behind the café when Austin pulled into an empty spot at the entrance. All the lights had been turned off and the doors locked, so tossing out the trash was the last thing she would do before hopping into her car and heading home. Although he knew he could have just met her there, he wanted to catch her when she was completely alone.

He scanned her body as she walked, zeroing in on her stomach. So far, what he knew about her pregnancy had come from Arielle's mouth. There was still a small voice in the back of his head telling him that Arielle had been mistaken and that Sommer truly wasn't pregnant.

But when she tossed the bag into the receptacle, turned around, lifted her shirt, and looked down at her stomach, all of his doubts disappeared.

Her lips moved as she said a few smiling words to her belly, and seeing her in such a tender moment only made him love her more.

He emerged from the car and, taking a deep breath, prepared himself for her to ask what he was doing back so soon, or stubbornly ignore him because he'd stopped by to see her without her knowing.

Instead, she raced toward him.

He moved forward and lifted her into his arms. She tightly wrapped her arms around his neck. They held onto each other for several heartbeats until Austin's brain finally accepted that she was really in his arms, then he let her back down to her feet.

"You're back," she said, nearly breathless. "I didn't expect you to come back. Not this soon."

He tugged her into his body. "I missed you, Sommer. Of course, I'd come back."

"I missed you too. Did you come back to see Arielle's twins?"

He pressed a kiss against her lips and then led her toward the car. "Partly. I want to talk to you. Do you have time to go out to Flatwoods?"

She nodded, and they hopped in the car, reaching the park less than two miles away from the café in under five minutes.

Walking to a picnic bench in the middle of the grassy clearing, Austin pulled Sommer into his lap and for a moment, they sat in silence, both realizing that life, at that moment, couldn't have been any more perfect.

"The twins are beautiful," he finally said. "And so small. It's been such a long time since I've held a newborn that I forgot how weightless they can be."

He felt her stiffen at the word "newborn."

"It's been a while since I've even been around a baby, too," she added. "They'll come popping out next spring though. Stella's always busy in March and April."

A pair of headlights filtered through the leaves of a massive willow oak the town had fought to preserve years ago when developers had come in to redesign the park. At first, the mayor had been on board with tearing it down, claiming that a more open space would be a better attraction for town residents. But nearly everyone in the town signed a petition stating otherwise. In the end, the tree stayed and he was ousted from office the next election season.

"You can stop by Ma's and see the twins," Austin suggested. "I talked to Arielle when she was in the hospital and she told me that she missed you."

She found his eyes. "How did my name come up?"

"She told me that she ran into you."

"Did she say where?"

"Yes."

She stood and put a few feet of distance between them, biting her nails as she paced in the grass. "What else did she tell you?"

"She told me something else that she thinks, but isn't sure about. That's the other reason I'm here."

Instinctively, her hands went to her stomach. Just as quickly, she dropped them to her sides.

"Sommer," he began, "Arielle told me that you're pregnant."

She clenched her fists, held them tight for a second, and then released them with a breath. Tears filled her eyes.

Austin walked toward her. "Is it true?"

She released another breath. "Yes. It's true. I'm nine-weeks pregnant."

He took a step closer and she backed away.

"Is that why you're here?" she asked. "To find out who the father is?"

Austin narrowed his brows. "No. I know who the father is. I just wanted to hear it from you that you're pregnant with *our* child."

Her surprise brought on the tears, and she let him get close enough to thumb the moisture away from her cheeks.

"I was so afraid you'd be upset," she confessed. "That you would think I was trying to trap you for your money."

He bellowed out a laugh. "Sommer, if you were trying to trap me, I gave you all the *ammunition* you needed that weekend. But no, I'm not upset. I'm...there are no words to describe how I feel, so happy will have to do."

More tears streamed down her cheeks, and he could tell that these were tears of happiness. He he had no tears of his own, but his heart swelled with elation.

Years ago, when Sommer was just an unrequited crush, he'd never expected that they would be standing in the middle of a park discussing the child they were going to have together.

Even when he used to envision them together back then, the real world would always infiltrate and dismantle their happiness. He would feel like a piece of the person his father had tried to create was still in him, and nothing he would try to build with her would be real.

But that had just been in his imagination. His father was gone, and he had the world at his fingertips. Everything would be perfect for Sommer and their baby. He was going to make sure of it.

He placed a hand against her stomach. "This is so crazy, Sommer. We're having a baby."

"I know." She grinned. "I can't believe it either."

"Does your mother know?"

"Before I even told her. I don't know how she knew. She even knows that it's your baby."

His eyes widened. "How do old folk know these things?"

"I don't know." She shrugged. "Does Ms. Emma know?"

He spun her around and pulled her back into his chest before returning his hand to her stomach. "Not yet, but we'll tell her on our own time. Now, you come to Texas with me."

Sommer tried to release herself from his grasp, just like he knew she would, but he held her firmly against his chest. One day, she would realize how serious he'd been when he told her that he would never let her run. Not from him.

"Mom somewhat suggested the same thing," she revealed. "She said she's moving in with Uncle Reese and Marcie, but I can't leave her here like this. Not when she's so sick. If I left now, I wouldn't be any different than my Dad."

Austin turned her to face him. "Your father left with another woman without ever intending to come back. That's not the case here. We're starting a family, and I want to be there for the entire pregnancy. From the morning sickness, to the crankiness and foot massages. I want to see you swell up."

She playfully elbowed him in the stomach.

"Okay, then. Let me rephrase. I want to see how your body changes as he grows inside of you."

"Much better," she replied. "He?"

"Yes, we're having a boy."

She burst out laughing. "I love how serious your face was when you said that."

"It's because I know. Fathers know."

He'd assumed calling himself a "father" would feel unusual, but the word fit right into place.

"Uh huh, fathers know," she teased, looping an arm behind his neck and bringing him in for a kiss.

"So, yes to Texas?"

"Let me think about it. I'll need to talk to Mom about it too. I don't think she was thinking straight when she suggested that I move in with you."

He nodded, scooped her up into his arms, and headed for the rental car. "Well, we only have the weekend, so how about we go talk to Ms. Caroline right now?"

"Austin…"

"That sounds like a yes to me." He set her back on her feet when they reached the passenger door. "I really meant what I said back there about missing you. Even if you weren't pregnant, I wasn't sure how much longer it would be before I said *eff her plans* and came right back to see this face."

He waited for the eye roll but she caught him off-guard by smiling.

"You and those corny lines, Austin Riley."

He stole a quick peck. "Austin Riley Sr."

He pulled open the door and Sommer slid inside the car.

"Austin Riley Sr.?"

"Yep. You have a problem with that?"

When he took the seat across from her, she reached over and ran her fingers over his scruffy cheek.

"I have lots of problems with that. First of all, I liked the name Solomon Grundy Riley if it's a boy, and Blanche Rose Dorothy Sophia Riley if it's a girl."

He tossed his head back and laughed so delightedly that Sommer couldn't help but break out into laughter herself.

"Damn, I've missed you," he told her. "I don't care what your mother says, your beautiful butt is flying back to Texas with me. And, as soon as we get there, I'm going to do things to you."

Sommer clapped her hands in delight. "Oh, what kinds of things?"

"Filthy things. Dastardly things. And I'm just letting you know now that some of them might be illegal in some states."

She laughed again and he sped off in the direction of Cherry Avenue, ready to use whatever charm he had left to persuade Sommer's mother to convince her to come to Texas with him. Even if she agreed to a short stay, he'd try his damndest to get her to fall in love with him and eventually agree to stay forever.

∽

As they drove up to the house, Sommer spotted a silver, luxury convertible in the driveway and immediately knew who was inside.

"Who does your mother know that drives a Bentley convertible?" Austin asked, parking on the curb.

Although he also had a few expensive models of his own back in

85

Texas, anyone who drove a Bentley into Yearwood was only trying to be a big fish in a small pond.

"It's Kyle," she replied. "I've never seen this car before, but whenever you see six-figure cars rolling around Yearwood, it's usually him."

Sommer led the way to the front door and sucked in a breath before walking inside. Kyle was sitting in the loveseat across from her mother, and when he looked up and saw her, he flashed her a grin.

When Austin appeared, the grin was replaced by a scowl.

"My goodness, Austin, I didn't expect to see you again so soon," Caroline greeted.

She attempted to stand, but Austin took a seat next to her on the sofa instead, wrapped an arm around her shoulders, and placed a kiss against her cheek at which she blushed.

"It's like every time you leave and come back, you're even more handsome." Caroline gave him a squeeze. "Kyle and I were just talking about that."

Austin's eyes fell on Kyle. "You were talking about how handsome I am?"

"You know what she meant," Kyle snapped. "We were talking about you finally coming home after a decade and how, all of a sudden, you and Sommer are the best of friends."

Sommer sat on the sofa arm. "Kyle, I was hoping that I could have some time to talk to my mother in private."

"You're not going to get rid of me just yet. Where are the two of you coming from?"

Austin began to respond, but Sommer cut him off.

"Austin brought me home after work."

Kyle glanced at his watch. "Didn't you close up at seven? It's over an hour later. What were you doing all that time? The café's barely ten minutes from here."

Austin's jaw clenched. "You're asking an awful lot of questions."

"They're valid questions," Kyle shot back.

"Valid for who?"

"I'm just asking about what Sommer was doing, for an entire hour, with *you*."

Caroline felt the muscle flex in Austin's forearm. "Kyle brought me some herbal tea," she intervened before the tension got any higher.

"It's green tea," Kyle clarified. "It's got antioxidants and a whole other host of compounds in it that's supposed to be good for the immune system." He touched the space next to him. "Sommer, you look uncomfortable. Come over here and sit next to me."

Caroline felt another muscle constrict in Austin's arm and found it surprising he was able to restrain himself with the amount of power she felt coursing through his body.

"Actually, take my seat, baby," Caroline suggested, moving to the empty space next to Kyle.

Sommer slid next to Austin, their thighs grazing, and although Kyle's expression remained stale, he seethed inside at their closeness.

"It's a good thing you two aren't in Texas," he spoke up. "With the way Dallas loves them some Austin Riley, if they saw you together like this, the media would be all over it."

Sommer froze. "The media?"

"Yep." His expression changed from stale to smug. "I mean, it's different out here because this is Yearwood, population-five. But if you two were back in Dallas spending all of this time together like you're doing now, you'd be front page news."

He squared his gaze on Sommer's face with a sly smirk.

"Even if Sommer and I were dating in Dallas, I don't think that would be a problem," Austin argued.

Kyle's eyes darted between the two of them. "Dating?"

"Hypothetically," Sommer clarified.

Kyle still looked less than pleased. He'd already guessed that something was going on between them, but had assumed it was just sex. Sex, he could handle. But, if he found out that Sommer had actually been dumb enough to start catching feelings for Austin Riley, then there

87

would be a problem. She was a Queen; she didn't have to stoop to dating her oppressor.

"Don't lie to her, Austin," he accused. "I mean, in Texas, I'm sure people even want to know what color your piss is."

Caroline cleared her throat. "Language, Kyle."

"I'm sorry, Mama Hayes, but it's true." He leaned closer to Sommer. "He's got his face on billboards, he's in commercials, and he's got some of the biggest endorsement deals in the league. You two in Dallas? The media would crucify you."

Sommer tapped her fingers on the sofa. "Why do you think that? You don't think that they would like us together?"

Kyle leaned back, feeling triumphant. He'd managed to instill doubt in her mind about a future with Austin, which was all he'd really need. "No, I don't think so. With guys like Austin, people expect supermodels and actresses to be on his arm. People they know. People that have been in the public eye. And you know I'd never lie to you, baby girl—"

"Yeah, Kyle, go ahead and leave now," Austin's voice sliced in.

Kyle sneered. "This isn't your house, Riley."

Caroline gently touched Kyle on the shoulder. "Sweetie, why don't you come see me again tomorrow?"

Kyle's eyes darted around the room before they settled on Caroline. "Okay, Mama Hayes. I'll stop by to see you before I head back out."

He squeezed her hand and then leaned toward Sommer for a hug, but she moved out of his reach.

"Really, Sommer? It's like that?"

When Sommer didn't respond, he shook his head in disgust and left through the front door.

The room remained silent until the sound of his engine disappeared down the street.

Austin turned toward Sommer and wondered if it was too late to undo whatever damage Kyle had already caused.

"What did you want to talk to me about, Sommer?" Caroline asked. "Did you tell Austin about the baby?"

Sommer's head shot up. "I did, but I know you did that on purpose to try to force my hand, just in case I didn't."

Caroline smiled as Austin wrapped an arm around her daughter's waist. She only hoped Sommer could see, as clear as day, how much the man sitting next to her loved her.

"But what I wanted to talk to you about is your moving in with Marcie and Uncle Reese. You can't."

Surprised, Austin met Sommer's eyes.

"So, you've decided that you're not coming back to Texas with me, after all? All because of what Kyle said?"

She felt tears stinging the back of her eyelids. So far, hormones were her least favorite part of her new pregnancy.

"That's a lot to take in, Austin. Was he wrong?"

"I'm not saying he was wrong about the media circus that's my life," Austin explained, "but he was definitely wrong about them having a problem with me dating you."

"We're not dating."

Austin groaned and ran a hand over his face. He refused to fight with her over this again.

"Honey," Caroline began, "you need to be with Austin right now."

"I need to be with you, Mom. In case you haven't noticed, you have cancer."

"But I'm not dead," Caroline shot back, louder than intended. She closed her eyes and touched a hand to the base of her throat. "Yes, I have cancer, but it's not a death sentence. You need to be focused on what's best for you and the baby."

"I can't leave you," Sommer stubbornly declared.

Caroline studied her hardheaded daughter's face. "Sommer, what have you done for your own good, lately? You left having your own place and a job you loved in New York to come here and take care of me."

"Which wasn't a problem."

"I'm not saying that it was."

"How is moving to Texas any different? It's the same thing, my making a decision for someone other than myself. Especially now, when you need me here."

Austin and Caroline exchanged exasperated looks.

"Sommer, do you *want* to come with me?" Austin asked. "If we considered nothing else, do you actually want to come with me? Because if you don't, I will stop asking right now. We can make arrangements for me to fly out for appointments, pay for any and everything you might want or need, and schedule times for me to be with you and the baby."

Sommer bit her bottom lip. At the end of the day, going with Austin was exactly what she wanted. The truth was screaming inside of her so loudly that she had to lie out loud just to deny it. But, her mother's prognosis was still uncertain and with this battle being her second time around, the oncologist had stressed that it was possible it could be more difficult for remission.

"Yes," she answered.

"Then go," Caroline urged. "How about this? Go for a few weeks so you two can get your heads wrapped around the fact that you're going to be parents. At least, figure that part out and go from there."

Austin pressed a kiss against Sommer's temple and her heart fluttered at the hopefulness in his eyes.

He leaned in and pressed a kiss against her lips, and her lids lowered in embarrassment. Caroline, on the other hand, was grinning from ear to ear. The last thing she wanted was for her daughter to make the same mistake she had and settle for a man who didn't offer her true, passionate, and shared love.

"Fine," Sommer conceded with a small smile. "But I'm still worried about the media thing, Austin. And Mom, you have to promise me you'll go to Marcie and Uncle Reese if you need *anything* while I'm gone."

Caroline nodded.

"I get your fear about the media circus," Austin said, "but what do you want to do about it?"

"Why don't you take separate cars?" Caroline suggested. "You can be on the same flight, but drive to Austin's in separate cars."

Austin resisted the urge to slip his hand into Sommer's shirt. Something about her agreeing to come with him had set him off, and he tried to think about something other than laying her on his bed and peeling her clothes away from her body.

"You won't have to drive anywhere," he reassured. "I'll have a car pick you up, drop you off at my building, and take your stuff upstairs. I'll have to make a stop before I go home so," he reached into his back pocket, "I made you a key."

Sommer's mouth fell open. "You had this the entire time?"

"Pretty much."

"You were that sure I'd say yes?"

"Not even in the slightest."

Caroline pushed herself up out of the chair. "Well, that settles it. I'm going to turn in and tomorrow, we'll spend the morning packing, Sommer."

"And I'll set up your ticket," Austin added.

Sommer touched the side of his face. "Then we fly to Dallas together?"

Caroline smiled before leaving the two alone on the sofa. When her bedroom door closed, Austin dove in for a kiss which Sommer heartily reciprocated. He smiled when he realized it would have probably been just like this, them stealing kisses in her mother's living room if they'd gotten together when they were younger.

"Then we fly to Dallas together," he said, his chest once again swollen with happiness.

Sommer grinned and walked with him out to the car where they ended up wrapped up in another passionate embrace. She wanted to tell him that she loved him, and exactly how much she loved him, but there was still an odd fear hanging over her head that she wouldn't get the response she was hoping for. Even with his child growing inside of her, she still wasn't sure just how deep Austin's feelings ran.

"I'll see you tomorrow," he said against her lips.

"Yes, you will."

Austin realized that standing there with her, with her eyes sparkling at him the way they were, would have been the perfect time to tell her that he was in love with her. But he didn't want to try again only to find out that Jessica's face still haunted him. He also didn't want to make the mistake of telling her when she wasn't ready to hear it, only for her to end up changing her mind about flying out with him.

Instead, he held her face between his hands and pressed a kiss against her eyelids and nose, before returning to her lips. Then, when they were both completely expended of air, he let her fingers slip from his grasp one by one and watched her until he heard the lock click on the front door.

He jumped into the car and his mind switched to his next task: finding the right way and time to tell his sister and his mother that a new Riley was on his way to the household.

∽

KYLE'S FACE CONTORTED WITH REVULSION WATCHING AUSTIN AND Sommer in his rearview mirror. Just as he'd expected, they were fooling around, and he was disappointed that Sommer hadn't been bright enough to see through Austin's façade.

He knew Austin much better than she did, and the truth was that Austin didn't care about her. He never did. Austin could never care about someone like Sommer, and he would never be able to appreciate everything that she had to offer. However, she was never going to be able to see that for herself. Her heart was too big and she'd always had a thing for Austin so, to her, anything Austin said was law.

He was going to have to push her, and while he didn't want her to be hurt in the process, finding out the truth was never an easy thing.

He pressed the call button on his console and waited for the voice on the other line to pick up. If he remembered correctly, it was only an hour later in Rio.

"Hello, this is Marcus speaking," a voice answered.

"Marcus, this is Stallworth. I need to speak to Jessica."

"One moment."

After a few seconds, she appeared on the line. "Kyle?"

"Miss Costa, how is Brazil treating you these days?"

She giggled. "Very nice. I am going to Sao Paulo in a few days to see my family. I am surprised to hear from you. Is everything okay?"

He drummed his fingers on the steering wheel. "Everything is marvelous. Your shoot in Miami was fantastic, by the way. Thank you for inviting me."

Her nails clinked against a wine glass. "It is never a problem, Kyle. You are welcome any time."

"Good. Good." He traced the car's emblem on the wheel. "I was just calling to find out if you and Austin are a thing again yet."

She sighed. "He wants nothing to do with me, it seems. I messed up. I made a mistake. I had a good man and I messed it up."

Kyle faked surprise. "Really? Because I just talked to him not too long ago and your name literally came up in every sentence."

He heard glass being set down on a surface.

"You are lying to me, Kyle."

"Never, Jessica. I mean, understandably, the man is hurt because you did embarrass him. Nationally. But that doesn't mean he doesn't still love you. Matter of fact, he's flying back to Dallas tomorrow evening. You should go meet him there."

He felt almost guilty at the amount of excitement in her voice.

"You think?" she asked.

"Yeah. The season's starting soon so you know there'll be lots of cameras. Imagine how that will look, you on Austin's arm again like old times."

She clapped her hands together. "Yes, that sounds wonderful. Thank you, Kyle. You are really a good friend to me and to Austin."

The corner of his mouth turned up. "It's the least I can do. I hate to see my good friend walking around all depressed like he is."

He wrapped up the conversation and when she hung up, any guilt he'd previously had was no nowhere to be found.

He knew just the guy to send to the airport to make sure that he snapped the photo of Austin and Jessica. Then, once their reignited romance was front page tabloid news, he'd personally deliver the edition to Sommer.

Even if she wouldn't have him, he refused to leave her to be free game for a man like Austin Riley. She would probably be upset at first, but over time, she'd understand. Then maybe, now that he was a changed man, he would be able to give her the life she truly deserved.

Chapter Seven

The last thing Austin said to Sommer before they exited the plane was that there was a car waiting for her, and all she had to do was find the driver who was holding up her name.

Then, he followed her off the plane and they branched off into two separate directions—she in search of the car he'd sent, and him into a swarm of people that seemed to have already been waiting for him at the terminal.

She stopped for a moment to watch him handle the crowd like a pro, flashing smiles, posing for pictures with fans, and signing autographs. She'd assumed that seeing him like this, in his second element, would have been a turn-off. That it would be too far removed from the Austin she'd grown up with. But, in the middle of him signing a little boy's jersey before returning the excited hug the boy gave him, he met her eyes across the terminal and she realized that he was still there. Mischievous, sometimes exasperating, yet hopelessly lovable, funny, and warmhearted Austin Riley. And that same wonderful man was going to be the father of her child.

She glanced down, touched her stomach, and cursed the tears that threatened behind her lids.

"Excuse me? Miss Hayes?"

In front of her was a short, elderly man holding a sign with her name on it in front of his chest, adorably dressed in a black suit and red bow tie.

"Yes, that's me, but you can call me Sommer."

He extended his hand. "Oh good. My name is Walter Jackson, but you can call me Walt. We have your bags already." He gestured toward a black Town Car that was waiting at the curb. "Are you all ready to go?"

Sommer started after him, but an excited scream across the terminal stopped them both in their tracks. Walking with a crowd flanking her on each side in a pair of high-heeled fashion sandals and a yellow dress that showed off her tanned shoulders, was the infamous Jessica Costa. With her svelte silhouette and long, shiny hair, she was everything Sommer hoped she wouldn't be.

Jessica glided across the waxed airport floors in Austin's direction, and an emotion Sommer couldn't quite place flashed across his face. He glanced over at her standing next to Walt and his expression briefly turned apologetic before it was replaced by a dazzling smile as he wrapped his arms around Jessica, and accepted a kiss on the cheek.

"I'm ready to go Walt," Sommer said.

He extended an elbow. "Of course. And it's nice to finally meet you, Sommer."

Jessica place an immaculately manicured hand on Austin's shoulder before curling it around his bicep, and he searched the terminal once more, finding Sommer's gaze again. This time, she turned away, hoping that the distress in her stomach was merely a bout of pregnancy-related nausea.

"Can I ask you a question, Walt?" she asked as they exited the terminal.

"Of course."

"What exactly did Austin tell you about me?"

"Well," he cleared his throat, "he told me that you two grew up together in North Carolina and that you'd be staying with him for a little while. And, he also told me about the little one you've got cooking in there."

Sommer placed a hand over her stomach. "I didn't expect him to tell you that."

Walter took one last glance at Jessica and Austin. "Sommer, I've known Austin for a good amount of time. I've been by his side since the first day he stepped foot in this league. He trusts me and any secret that he tells me, I will carry to my grave. So yes, I know that's his baby baking in there."

Sommer's heart slammed into her chest. Hopefully, Walter was a man of his word because she didn't want to imagine what would happen if it was discovered that Austin had a baby on the way, and especially a baby with her...a small town nobody. Although she despised Kyle, there was some truth to his words.

"I also know that you're worried about his relationship with Jessica," Walter added. "But like I said, I know that boy in there. That man parted a sea of people with his gaze to find you across the room. Only one other man I know of that ever parted a sea of anything."

He helped her into the car before easing in next to her. "Don't worry, honey. Everything will be okay. And if he does anything that you don't like, you just come to old Uncle Walt and I'll sock him good for you."

Sommer burst out laughing. "I'm keeping you to that, Walt."

He smiled. "By all means, do. And once again, it's lovely to finally meet you, Sommer Hayes. Welcome to Texas."

~

NO MATTER HOW MANY TIMES HE LOOKED AT IT, AUSTIN STILL marveled at the Dallas skyline as the elevator made its way up to the penthouse level of his building. Soon, the city's brimming nightlife would filter its own unique weekend light show into the downtown scape. This time, however, he wasn't going to be watching it from his balcony alone. At least, he *hoped* he wouldn't be.

Sommer hadn't looked too pleased when Jessica blindsided him at the airport. But instead of trying to assault her with an explanation the minute he walked through the door, he decided to wait to get a sense of how she felt. That way, he could better explain that even though he hadn't welcomed Jessica's advances, he still had to smile and pretend they were cordial for the cameras.

He didn't even know why there were so many cameras there in the first place, as well as tabloid reporters, as though they'd been expecting for he and Jessica to run into each other. Camera phones and requests for autographs he was used to, but the fact that there was even one major tabloid reporter there stunk of a preplanned Jessica Costa photo op.

He stepped across the entryway and onto the polished, walnut-colored wood floors. Everything looked oddly undisturbed, and a knot tightened in his stomach as he walked through the space and found no evidence that Sommer had even been there. Running was Sommer's thing, which was why he was determined never to let her do it. If she got too close to anyone, she risked letting them in enough to be hurt by them. Her father had been one person with her and a completely different man otherwise. There were several layers of trust that had to be scraped through to get to Sommer's heart, but he had the time and patience.

"Austin, is that you?"

She appeared at the top of the stairs and the fact that she'd showered and changed into a top and silky pajama bottoms put him at ease.

He moved to the bottom of the stairs. "Did you miss me?"

"Not really." She bit back a grin. "It's just that Walt's been up to check on me several times in the last few hours, and apparently, he doesn't even live in the area. I just wanted to make sure it wasn't him. By the way, I never pegged you as a man who needed a personal assistant."

He climbed two steps. "Walt's more like a friend."

"He seems more like a father figure to me."

He climbed the rest of the way to the bottom platform and faced her standing at the top level. "I can give you that. Walt acts more like a father than mine ever did."

Austin placed his foot on the first step and she backed up an inch. Where are you going?" he asked.

Sommer shrugged. "Nowhere."

He climbed another step and again she backed away, biting her bottom lip to hide another smile. Lifting his foot, he hovered over the next step and she watched it intently, her body slightly turned down the hallway.

"I'm faster than you are," he warned.

"I beg to differ."

"Oh, really? I can take these steps three at a time and be on you before you even make it to the bedroom door."

When she opened her mouth to respond, he charged up the stairs and she screamed in delight, stumbling a bit before catching her footing and running toward the bedroom door. Austin caught her around the waist before she made it into the room, carried her like a package against his side, and then placed her on top of the plush mattress. He looked down at her expecting to find amusement, but the smile had faded, her lids were half-closed, her chest was heaving, and her nipples were now visible through the soft cotton top she was wearing. Immediately, he felt his cock stiffen.

"Come here," she invited, and he joined her on the bed.

"Settling in okay?" he asked.

She reached for his belt and tugged it off, then pulled his shirt over his head and ran her hands along his chest, her eyes intently focused on her task.

"Yes, but your shower's weird."

"You have to turn the handle to the left first."

She moved her hands over his shoulders and her lips went his to chest. "You tell me that *now*. I damn near gave myself hypothermia."

He laughed and tried to wrap an arm around her waist, but she pushed his hand back onto the bed and straddled his middle. Sighing, she held his gaze.

"What's wrong, beautiful?" He attempted again to wrap his arms around her.

She pushed them back toward the bed another time, then began to grind her hips in a circular motion on top of him. "It's gorgeous here, Austin," she answered, pulling her shirt over her head. Her areolas were visible through the sheer, black lace bra she'd had hidden underneath, and Austin tried a third time to reach up and run his thumbs over her firming nipples.

She caught his arm, pushed it back toward the mattress, and held it there. Leaning forward, she touched the softness of her breasts to his chest, thickening his erection.

"The skyline, the city...I never thought buildings could be beautiful." She went on as though she didn't know she was torturing him by denying every attempt he made to touch her. She was trying to take control, but he didn't know how long he'd make it before he flipped her onto her back and tore off the bottoms she was wearing.

"I thought the same thing when I first moved in," he said, groaning as her hips switched to a rocking motion. "I didn't think things other than nature could be relaxing."

"*Mhm.*" Her hands now at his waistband. She tugged him out of the rest of his clothes and tossed them off the side of the bed.

She removed her pajama bottoms and knelt over him, trailing her eyes over his nude body. Austin flexed his fingers to stop himself from snatching off the bra and panties she *still* wore.

"You knew that this would happen, didn't you?" She met his eyes. "That I would fall in love with being in the city and start to question going back home?"

He cautiously reached toward her and this time, she didn't stop him as he ran his fingers along the moisture that had soaked through her panties.

"That's not the best part," he said. "After the airport, I stopped in to see a realtor."

She closed her eyes and moved her hips to match the rhythm of his stroking. "You're moving?"

"Not me. Us. We'll need a house. This place is nice, but I think a house would be better for when the baby gets here."

He pushed the panties aside and slipped a finger into her wetness, but she grabbed his hand and coerced it back to the bed. He brought the finger to his lips and her eyes pooled even darker.

Moving further down his body, she wrapped her hands around his shaft, kissed the tip of his cock, and then swiftly took him into her mouth.

The softness and heat of her mouth threatened to send Austin over the edge. She flicked her tongue over and gently sucked on his sensitive tip, and he groaned as the waves of pleasure extended to his toes. There was no way that he was going to let this woman leave. *Ever.*

And now, he was ready to regain control.

Slipping his arms from her grasp, he tipped a finger underneath her chin and brought her lips to his. He captured her mouth, hungry as he unclasped the hooks of her bra with one hand before flipping her over onto her back. Then, he tugged at her panties. When Sommer heard the sound of tearing fabric, her eyes widened.

"Austin—" She stopped mid-sentence when she felt his cock slowly fill her body.

"I'm sorry," he said, his voice hoarse.

"You tore my panties."

Just as slowly, he pulled out. "I'll buy you another pair."

"No, no. I like it.

He entered her again, deeper this time, and his name crept quietly from her lips. She dug her nails into his back. It was time to repay her for the torture that her curious mouth had put him through, and when he reached between her legs, she whispered his name a second time.

"There's nobody here but us, Sommer," he told her. "Scream."

Her cries echoed around the room. He swelled inside of her, shaft languishing every aching curve and crevice. As wonderful as she felt, and as hard as it was for him to retain his self-control, he tempered his pace, not wanting the moment to end a minute too soon.

He almost came undone when her hands went to her breasts and she teased him by running a delicate finger over her throbbing nipples. She smiled at him and his body threatened to erupt again, but he wanted her writhing in pleasure before he allowed himself his own conclusion.

He reached for her hands, clasped their fingers above her head, and pushed even deeper, leaning down to press their lips together again.

Their tongues played. Her moans became more frenzied. Her body rocked against his, and her legs tightened around his waist until she was screaming his name, much louder this time, and he the familiar tugs of her orgasm rippling along his shaft. Satisfied, he moved inside of her until ecstasy washed over him, and he released his climax into her trembling body.

They waited a few moments for their breaths to steady, then he pulled her onto his chest and kissed the top of her head.

"We're really going to do this, aren't we?" she asked, making a circle against his chest.

"Yeah, we are."

A beat passed.

"Honestly, I'm a little scared, Austin."

"I am too, but we'll figure it out."

She looked up at him. "Were you really serious? About buying a house?"

He brought her fingers to his lips. "As a heart-attack."

She felt the urge again to say, "I love you, Austin," but still couldn't bring herself to do it. It was a bit ridiculous when she thought about it since they'd just finished making love and were bringing a child into the world together, but there was still something about the way he'd looked at Jessica at the terminal. It was as though he was still holding onto something, and she hoped that whatever he was holding onto didn't have anything to do with an undying love for his ex-girlfriend.

"Think it'll be a boy?" he asked, pulling her from her thoughts.

"Mom says it'll be a girl."

"That would be nice. To have a little princess."

She laughed. "I can see you now, as big as you are, in one of those toddler chairs in a tutu drinking from a play teacup and saucer."

"Hell, yes." He kissed her fingers again. "Tea and crumpets with my little princess."

"Or football with your little man."

They fell silent for a few moments.

"God, Sommer, we're really going to be parents." He extended his hand. "Good luck, Mommy."

She laughed again and firmly shook his hand. "Good luck, Daddy."

She reached up and touched their lips together before slipping her tongue into his mouth. Blood rumbled to his cock. He wrapped his arms around her before positioning himself over her. With a wicked grin, she turned over.

"Oh my, all this ass? Just for me?" Austin ran his hands along her back and hips. Her laugh was cut short when she felt him enter her, and they spent the rest of the night riding the waves of bliss, several times over.

∾

KYLE CLIMBED THE STEPS LEADING UP TO CAROLINE'S FRONT DOOR with an extra pep in his step. He tapped his back pocket to make sure the magazine was still there. On the front cover, in large print, it read:

REKINDLED ROMANCE FOR STAR QB AND SUPERMODEL??

But that hadn't been Kyle's favorite part. What he'd most enjoyed was the picture of Jessica with her hands wrapped around Austin's bicep, and her head on his shoulder. Then, at that same moment, Austin had looked down at her and to anyone who didn't know how he truly felt about Jessica, they would think he was falling for the Brazilian beauty all over again. At least, that's what Sommer would think.

Switching from a look of joy to one of concern, Kyle knocked on the door. Caroline appeared with a warm smile. In his heart, he knew that Mrs. Hayes probably preferred him over Austin anyway.

"Mama Hayes, how are you feeling?" he asked with a quick hug.

"I'm good, Kyle. I'm still standing."

He peered behind her into the house. "Is Sommer home?"

"No, Sommer's not here."

"Will she be back soon? I can wait arou—"

"Sommer's not in Yearwood."

He took a step back. "Is she out of town picking up supplies for the café?"

Caroline eyed him, carefully deciding whether or not to tell him the truth. She'd assumed that all of Kyle's visits had been innocent up until the last time he was at her house.

It was obvious he had something for her daughter. Knowing Kyle, that something was probably sex and heartbreak, but Sommer was one of the few women in Yearwood who didn't fawn over him like he expected. And now, Sommer was with Austin.

She'd never understood Kyle's and Austin's relationship, a veil of friendship shrouding fiery animosity. At least, from Kyle's perspective. It was like the man would do anything to try to destroy Austin, even becoming his friend, a keeper of secrets he could one day use to his advantage.

"No." Caroline shook her head. "Sommer went on vacation."

"Vacation where?"

"Not in Yearwood."

Kyle closed his eyes, clenched his fists, and took a deep breath. "I know *that,* but where did she go? When will she be back? I have to talk to her."

"I don't know when she will be back. Can't you call her?"

"You know I can't call her," he growled, but lowered his tone when Caroline's smile disappeared and her expression turned stern. "I'm sorry, Mama Hayes, but you know Sommer doesn't return my calls."

Caroline folded her arms across her chest. "And if she doesn't return your phone calls, why do you think I would tell you where she is? Obviously, she doesn't want to talk to you."

He took another breath, glanced down the street, and then settled his gaze back on her. "So, you don't know where she is and how long she'll be gone? That doesn't worry you as her mother?"

"Not at all." She shook her head. "And I never said I didn't know where she is. I just won't be telling you."

He had the strongest urge to grab the frail, middle-aged woman's arm and twist it behind her back until she talked. But, he refrained. He was, after all, a changed man.

"Then tell me this. Wherever she is, is she with Austin?"

"Why would she be with Austin?"

"Because she's always with him these days."

She sighed and leaned against the door frame. "Sommer has given up a lot for me over the years, Kyle, and I granted her an extended leave so she could take time for herself. I suggest you grant her the same leave, as in *leave her alone.*"

With that, she stepped inside and closed the door.

Kyle felt his anger rise as he trudged back to his new baby, a beautiful cobalt blue Maserati he'd admittedly bought only after hearing of Austin's similar purchase in a deep garnet color.

He hopped inside and took a deep breath, tried to quell his anger again, but ended up spending the next sixty-seconds in a boxing match with the steering wheel. Sommer would never leave her mother alone in Yearwood without good reason, and an impromptu vacation wasn't a good enough reason. Plus, he'd seen the doubt all over her face when he'd told her about Austin's life in Texas, so it wasn't likely she'd gone there.

He was left high and dry. He had no idea where she was.

He threw two more punches into the steering wheel before backing out of the driveway. She couldn't lay low for very long and he'd be back when she reappeared. But if she didn't reappear when he was ready, then he'd just have to call up a buddy of his to track her down.

In the meantime, he'd work on Jessica. Wherever Sommer was, there was bound to be a TV and it wouldn't take long before she caught her new boy-toy with his tongue down Jessica's throat.

As he drove away, Kyle ignored the little voice in his head that tried to convince him Austin truly had feelings for Sommer. Because if Austin did, then it would be extremely difficult to catch him in any compromising position with Jessica. Virtually impossible. Austin just wasn't that type of man. He wasn't the sleaze his father was, and probably still is.

However, if that were the case, he wasn't above stooping to some pretty dirty lows to break them apart. Sommer had always been meant for him. Year after year, he'd have to listen to Austin, puny, pale, and with a mouth full of metal, pretend he wasn't interested in Sommer. Then, all of a sudden, he's *in love* with her? All of a sudden, she's all he can talk about in high school? And it just happened to be *right* after Kyle pointed out how hot she'd become?

Bullshit.

Kyle gave the steering wheel one more punch, sending the horn blaring into the night. If push really came to shove, he had no qualms about taking his gloves off.

Chapter Eight

Sommer's pregnancy was moving along even better than she could imagine. The weeks flew by without effort or interruption, and with them, they brought along major changes and surprises to her life.

In just a few months, she'd gone from living with her mother in her old bedroom, to owning a home with Austin—a beautiful, French-style home in Highland Park. At first, the house's size and opulence were intimidating. Several of her mother's houses could fit in its main room alone, but with just a few personal touches, paint colors, and furniture they'd both handpicked, it became the warm and cozy family home she'd always dreamed of.

Then came the big news at her twentieth-week appointment.

Austin had flown in on a red-eye from New York. To tease them, the doctor, a woman named Maria Renault that Sommer had grown to love, had frozen the image of the ultrasound up on the screen while she left the room to grab some paperwork. The five minutes she was gone felt more like hours, and Sommer and Austin spent the time betting on what they thought the baby's gender was going to be. Sommer won the twenty dollars when Dr. Renault returned to reveal the news: they were expecting a baby girl. It was finally time to tell the family. *Everyone* in the family.

It was a secret they could hold no longer. Little Sommer and Little Austin from Yearwood were not only dating, but they had a baby girl on the way. All the things the townspeople of Yearwood, NC had hoped to come to pass had come true.

While Sommer had dabbed happy tears away from the corners of her eyes, Austin had remained still and speechless, gaze fixed on the screen. Even as they'd pulled into the driveway later that morning, he still hadn't said a word. Worried, Sommer had touched him on the shoulder and asked him what was bothering him.

"I'm going to have a little girl," he'd replied, his voice barely above a whisper. The, he'd turned to her, took her hand, touched a kiss in the middle of her palm, and stretched his hand across her stomach.

"I'm going to be the father of a little girl," he'd repeated. Then, he met her eyes. "Will I be a good father?"

The uncertainty and fear in his eyes had tugged at Sommer's heart. Although she'd also had reservations about being a mother, she was confident in the example her own mother had set. But, even though she didn't know much, she knew that Austin's relationship with his father hadn't been ideal. She could only imagine the amount of doubt something like that could place in his head about his own parenting capabilities.

"Austin, you'll be a wonderful father," she'd told him.

He'd simply smiled and kissed her on the forehead before they went inside to start planning for the nursery.

Now, eight weeks away from her due date, she was sitting in the back of a luxury SUV at the airport while Walter combed the sea of arriving passengers for her mother. The day before, Austin had picked up Arielle, the twins, his nieces, and his mother, but had booked them a suite at a hotel not too far from the house. His mother had protested because she *desperately* needed proof that her son had actually bought a house, but he'd quieted her by saying that there was still paint drying in the living room whose fumes he didn't want to twins to breathe in.

Sommer glanced at the clock on the console. It was a little past three, which meant he was already on his way to the hotel to pick up his family. Then, they would meet at the house to announce her pregnancy and prepare for a small gathering with a few of Austin's closest, and most trusted friends.

Although there were a few times he'd brought up the idea of breaking the news of the baby to the *world*, by the end of the day, she'd swayed his train of thought. The world that adored him wasn't ready for the baby he'd be having with her, and the last thing she needed was to see anyone saying negative things about their baby online. Already, felt the fierce, motherly protectiveness.

The SUV's back door opened and Caroline peered in, squealing in delight when she saw her beautiful, glowing daughter. Walter helped her onto the backseat and she wrapped her arms around Sommer, squeezing her tight.

"Baby, it's so good to see you," she said, kissing her daughter on the forehead. "You look absolutely beautiful."

Sommer smiled and took in her mother's familiar scent. "My hips have spread, my face itches, and I feel like my nose is taking up half of my face, but thank you, Mom. It's good to see you too."

Caroline held her daughter at arm's length. "Your nose is fine, baby. You don't have the pregnancy nose. Now me, I got it when I was pregnant with you. It grew twice its size. I kept bumping into things, couldn't walk into a room sideways."

Laughing, Sommer playfully swatted her on the arm.

"I've missed you, Mommy." She pulled her in for another hug. "And you look so good. So much healthier since the last time I saw you."

Caroline touched the top of her head. "It's because I've got my good wig on."

Sommer held her stomach as her body erupted with more laughter.

Walter pulled out of the terminal and Caroline leaned back into the seat, her hand still clasped with Sommer's. "You don't know how hard it's been keeping this news from Emma," she said. "I feel like such a bad friend. I don't know why you guys wanted to wait, but I did my best to respect your wishes."

Sommer stroked her knuckles. "Well, tonight everyone will know so you won't have to deal with the guilt anymore."

Caroline placed a hand on Sommer's stomach. "My little grandbaby. Grammie is going to spoil you rotten."

Sommer's brows narrowed. "Mom?"

"Hmm?"

"You brought stuff, didn't you?"

Caroline exaggerated a touch of her hand to her chest. "I have no idea what you're talking about."

"For the baby," Sommer prodded. "You just couldn't resist, could you?"

Caroline pointed to the trunk. "You didn't see that I brought three bags for just a few days? Two of those bags are packed to capacity with baby things. I've got bibs, bottles, one-sies, socks, hats, booties, the cutest little dresses…"

Sommer stared at her mother's face as her list continued. The tired lines in the woman's face were gone, her dark circles had faded, and her sunken cheeks were beginning to fill in. She couldn't believe life was working out the way it was. Her baby was healthy, she was in love, and her mother was getting better.

"Then I bought this absolutely adorable pink polka-dot blanket with an owl on it, a gift basket with powder, ointment, things you'll need, this cute little infant toothbrush, you know, to get her used to brushing her teeth…"

Sommer leaned into her mother's side and sighed. Somehow, the entire thing no longer seemed daunting now that her mother was here. As long as she had her mother, everything would be alright.

"AUSTIN, I SWEAR IF I HAVE TO SING BACKUP FOR THAT DIVA ONE more time," Arielle complained, taking a bite out of her burger.

"What diva?"

"Aria."

Austin burst out laughing, nearly choking on his burger. "I really thought you were talking about someone other than your *six-year old* daughter."

Arielle smiled before popping a french fry into her mouth. "But she never lets me sing lead on the Disney songs. She always has to be Ariel, Jasmine..." She touched a hand to her chest. "Just once, can it by my *Whole New World?*"

Austin continued to laugh, shaking his head.

"But, thank you for taking me out for burgers," Arielle added. "I hope Ma doesn't go crazy alone at the house with both girls and the twins. They're mobile now and I swear, even though they can't talk, they collaborate. Just a couple weeks ago, Arabella crawled up to me and started blabbing up a storm while behind me, Antonio was pulling a cookie from Izzie's plate off the kid's table. What I think is, Arabella was the diversion. They planned it. He even shared the cookie with her afterwards."

He shook his head with a chuckle, took another bite of his burger, and glanced at the clock on the wall. He couldn't wait to see the look on his sister's face when he and Sommer revealed their news.

"Ma will be fine," he reassured. "She's in her element when she's with her grandkids."

Arielle dipped a french fry into Austin's ketchup, took a bite, and then scrunched her nose. "*Ick.* I still prefer my french fries plain."

He grabbed a few fries, doused them in ketchup, and tossed them into his mouth. Closing his eyes, he moaned in delight while Arielle continued to scrunch her nose.

"Austin?"

They both looked up when they heard his name, and Arielle groaned when she saw Jessica's face.

"Hi, yet again, Jessica," Austin greeted.

"Funny running into you here." Jessica's eyes flicked over to Arielle. She bent her wrist. "Jessica Costa."

Arielle glanced at her hand. "Are you expecting me to kiss it or something?"

Austin grinned. "Arielle..."

"I mean, with the way she's got it bent back and everything..."

"I'm sorry," Jessica apologized. "It's a habit." She turned to Austin. "Did you say Arielle? As in your sister, Arielle?"

"We look nearly exactly alike," Arielle pointed out. "Who else would I be?"

Austin shook his head again at his sister's sharp tongue. It might have been something that had embarrassed him on numerous occasions when they were younger, but as he got older, he grew to appreciate it. He even grew to admire it.

"I don't mean to intrude—" Jessica began.

"Too late for that," Arielle cut in.

Jessica pursed her lips. "Do you have a problem with me?"

Arielle glanced over at Austin in disbelief and clasped her hands on the table. "Let me get this straight," she prefaced. "You dated my brother for what, almost a year, only to end up spreading your legs for some old geezer because he had even more money. Then, you left without ever offering an explanation as to why. You do know that Austin being my brother means he's my family, right? So, you hurt my family, someone I love, and now have the nerve to ask me if I have a problem with you?"

Jessica stared at Austin.

"What?" he asked.

"You are just going to let her talk to me like that?"

"Jessica," he massaged his temple, "for somebody that had nothing to say to me when she was sailing on a yacht in the middle of the Atlantic, and didn't want to even talk to me afterwards, I've been seeing you a lot lately. What are you even doing here? You don't come to places like this."

She cradled the base of her throat. "I came here because I missed you, Austin. I remembered that you took me here for one of our dates, so I stopped in because it makes me think of you."

Suddenly, he gestured to the seat next to Arielle. "Sit."

"What?"

"Sit. I want to hear what you have to say."

Arielle shot him a look, but he ignored it.

Jessica slid onto the padded leather seat and placed her oversized purse on the table.

"Here's your chance, Jessica, and this will be the only chance I'll give you. Talk."

She glanced nervously between him and Arielle. "I don't know what—"

"Why'd you run off with Remos?" Austin interrupted.

"I think we all know the answer to that one," Arielle argued.

"You're right," Austin agreed. "Why did you leave me, then? Is that a better question?"

Surprised, Arielle glanced at her brother. The hurt Jessica had caused by walking out on him was still evident on his face. People who pretended to care about him and then turned out to be exactly the opposite had always been his Achilles heel. It also didn't take a psychiatrist to figure out that it had everything to do with who their father was. He'd tried to change them both, mold them into tiny, monstrous versions of himself. She'd resisted because of their mother. Austin had resisted because he'd been infatuated with Sommer longer than even he knew.

"I don't know, Austin," Jessica said, and some of the driest tears Arielle had ever seen began to form at the corners of her eyes.

"How long were you involved with Remos before the tabloids spilled your little secret?" he pressed.

Jessica bit her lip. "Four months."

"So you were sleeping with me at the same time you were screwing him?" He didn't wait for an answer. "Why didn't you return any of my messages after I found out?"

Arielle folded her arms, also waiting for an answer.

"I was ashamed, Austin," Jessica cried. "I didn't know how to face you knowing what I did, so I just avoided it and hoped for the best."

"And what was the best?"

"For you to forget." She fished a tissue from her purse and dabbed gently at her eyes. "I just hoped that with time, you would forget about me. Forget about what I did. I know I'd hurt you because you're a good man, Austin. You treated me like a queen and I didn't even want to meet your family. I refused to cancel minor engagements to come to your games. I lied to you. I kept things from you. All I could hope was that you would forget about me and move on."

Austin smiled as an image of Sommer skated across his mind. "Well, you got your wish."

Jessica's tears instantly dried up.

"I've moved on. I got over you."

Both Arielle and Jessica stared at him.

"She's perfect for me, and I love her," he added.

"Who is she?" Jessica demanded.

Standing, he tossed a few bills onto the table and nodded toward the door. "Ready to go, Arielle?"

A wicked grin took up most of Arielle's face, glad Jessica had been put in her place. Now, she was curious about who it was Austin claimed he was in love with. She would be disappointed that it wasn't Sommer since she'd always dreamt the two would end up together, but Sommer had been away on vacation for the past few months and was most likely with the father of her baby. Either way, she was happy for him. She was happy for them both.

"Right behind you," she said, taking one last look at Jessica. Wrapping an arm around his waist, they continued to chat as they left the burger joint.

When they got to the house, Austin spotted the SUV parked in the garage, which meant Sommer and her mother had made it back and were hiding upstairs like they'd planned.

Inside, his mother was on the floor playing with the twins while Aria and Isabela danced to music coming through the stereo. Arielle rushed over and jumped right in, eliciting giggles from both daughters. Austin watched them for a moment, even more excited than he'd been before, then ran upstairs to get Sommer. It was as if he hadn't seen her in ages.

He wrapped her up in a hug before pulling her in for a kiss so deep, it robbed him of his breath. When the kiss finally broke, Sommer blushed and glanced at her mother.

"No need to be embarrassed, baby," Caroline reassured. "You're already pregnant. There's not much more damage he can do."

Austin laughed, brushed a kiss across Caroline's cheek, then led them both by the hand down the stairs.

When they reached the main room, Arielle was the first to spot them and let out a shriek he was sure had cracked a few of the glasses in the cabinets. Emma eased up off the floor and her mouth fell open when she spotted a pregnant Sommer with her son's arms lovingly wrapped around her from behind.

Arielle sprinted over and grabbed Sommer up in a hug.

"I saw you," she accused, tears in her eyes. "I saw you at Stella's office. Are you trying to tell me that you were actually sitting there pregnant with my first niece or nephew?"

She paused.

"Niece," both Austin and Sommer answered, and Arielle looked like she would pass out.

Emma was now beside them, still in shock. From the very first time they met in preschool when Austin had asked Sommer to play race cars with him, and she'd tossed the cars clear across the room, she and Caroline had joked that they were destined for one another. Then, with the way she would always catch Austin staring at Sommer with that little smile on his face when he thought no one was paying attention, completely hypnotized by her, both women began to realize how real the possibility of their children ending up together could be.

Her eyes darted to Caroline. "You knew all this time and kept it from me?"

Caroline chuckled. "And it was so hard, Em. I wanted to show you all the things I'd bought for my granddaughter and gush over what she might be like."

Emma pulled Sommer in for a hug and kissed her on the cheek. Then, she pinched Austin on the forearm.

"*Ow...Ma!*"

"For keeping secrets from your mother." She smiled and he bent to also receive a kiss on the cheek.

"When's the baby due?" Arielle asked.

"In eight weeks," Sommer answered.

Arielle quickly calculated in her head. "That's close to the championship game, isn't it?"

"She's due the week after," Austin explained. "But I'm not worried. I'll be there for both."

Sommer leaned into his chest. "Austin's been putting up the best numbers of his career, so I know they're going to the big game. And, once they do, Dallas is going to shut the house down. I'm actually hoping she arrives before it so she can be here to see her Daddy's victory."

He kissed the top of her head and received a chorus of "awws" from the three women.

"So freakin' cute," Arielle screamed.

"What are you going to name her?" Emma asked.

"They won't say," Caroline answered.

"We want it to be a surprise," Austin explained.

"More surprises?" Emma placed a hand over her heart. "I'm still reeling from this one. I can't even begin to tell you how happy I am about the baby, about the two of you."

The doorbell chimed.

"I've also invited some of the guys from the team over," Austin added, walking toward the door. "Then, because I know you two want to buy gifts, you can throw Sommer a baby shower later."

"But *you* can't buy any more gifts." Sommer turned to Caroline. "You probably cleaned out the entire state of North Carolina."

Caroline shrugged, a picture of innocence.

Austin opened the door and started to greet Trent, but then his eyes moved to Alexandrina standing next to him.

"I made her swear to keep quiet about Sommer," Trent reassured.

"No offense, Drina, but you're Jessica's cousin." Austin wasn't convinced that Alexandrina's word meant anything. Her loyalty historically always lay with her family.

"I really won't," she promised. "I just wanted to be a part of this celebration with you."

It was a lie, but he didn't press the issue. The main reason she'd tagged along was because Alexandrina never let Trent out of her sight. A few years ago, she'd found out about a woman he'd been sleeping with in Denver and went ballistic, almost taking his head clean off with a ceramic cleaver. Ever since, Trent buckled down on his fidelity and she'd ramped up her surveillance.

The next reason she'd probably tagged along was simply because she was nosy. She wanted to check Sommer out so she could compare her to Jessica, and there was no guarantee she wouldn't blab to her cousin once she did. If she did blab that Sommer was pregnant, it wouldn't be long before reporters would be knocking down their door to interview her. The last thing he wanted was for Sommer to feel pressured, uncomfortable, or unwelcome.

It might not have mattered to him, but diving headfirst into this life wasn't something a girl from a small town could do. He'd had trouble adjusting himself, at first. And this was nothing like the time she'd spent in New York. This would be like holding a magnifying glass over an ant in the sun.

However, they were already on his doorstep so there wasn't much else he could do.

Austin ushered them in. Eventually, Cason and his girlfriend, Amelia arrived, both who he trusted completely because they'd also kept their relationship out of the public eye for some time. Sommer and Amelia had also built a friendship that Austin had enjoyed watching develop because it helped Sommer feel more rooted in Texas. Then, it was Walter and his wife, Tank, the head coach, and a few other people in his life that he kept close.

The event carried on without a hitch. Sommer blushed as she opened gifts, each one more unique than the other as if everyone had been in competition to have the most memorable present. Afterwards, everyone enjoyed cake, ice cream, punch, and mingled.

At the end of the evening, after the last guest had left, Emma pushed Austin and Sommer upstairs and urged them to shower and go to bed while she, Caroline, Walter, and Arielle stayed downstairs to clean up.

After taking a shower and saying goodnight to his nieces and nephew, Austin stood in the bedroom doorway and watched Sommer as she sat cross-legged on the mattress with a baby book perched on her stomach. As her body had changed over the past several months, she'd grown even more beautiful than he could ever imagine. The smile that had twisted his stomach into knots several times over the years had grown more radiant, the arms whose smooth skin he loved to caress had turned into the true meaning of home, and the voice he'd always searched for in classrooms, crowds, and even other women, was the sound that centered him whenever his world tilted even slightly off its axis. He used to believe that it was impossible to love someone eternally, but the thought that he could ever stop loving Sommer, for any reason at all, was the most absurd thing he'd ever come across in his life.

"I love you," he said from the doorway.

Her head popped up. "Huh?"

Walking toward her, he sat along the edge of the bed near her legs. "I'm in love with you, Sommer, and I've fallen so far that you'd have to go all the way to hell just to pull me back."

She closed the book and set it on the nightstand. "Really?"

He laughed. "Really."

"For how long?"

It was the perfect question.

"That I've loved you? It might be a better question to ask when was it that I didn't."

Her head fell and she nervously twiddled with her fingers. Then, when she looked up, her eyes were sparkling with tears.

"I love you too, Austin," she said, biting on her bottom lip.

With a sigh, he pulled her into his arms and wiped the moisture away from her cheeks with his thumb before pressing a kiss against her eyelids.

"Why didn't you say it before if it's been all this time?" she asked.

He shrugged. "Honestly, Sommer, I don't know."

"Were you afraid I didn't feel the same way about you?"

He tilted her head and brushed a kiss across her lips. "Even if you'd told me you couldn't stand my guts, I'd probably keep telling you that I love you until you got sick of hearing it."

She shook her head. "I don't think I could ever get sick of hearing that."

"Good." He kissed her again. "Because I love you."

"I love you too."

They climbed into bed and she contentedly nestled deep into his body. While she drifted to sleep, Austin stared at the ceiling with a small smile on his face. All this time, Jessica's face had been infiltrating his thoughts because he'd lacked closure. It wasn't that he didn't love Sommer or that it was never going to be the right time to tell her. Intuitively, he'd known that telling her before completely addressing his anger toward Jessica would have been unfair to her. He needed to be assured that he was all in. And, he *was* all the way in. For the long haul.

Now that they had the house, the baby, the life together, the love, and the support of their families, there was only one thing missing. One thing that was still needed to make their little family complete.

∼

"That was nice, wasn't it?"

Trent spread a layer of toothpaste onto his brush and peeked out the bathroom door at his unusually silent wife. He found her sitting at the edge of the bed staring at the nightstand, her hands moving mindlessly together, coaxing a coat of lotion to absorb.

"Dree?"

She stirred. "Oh, I'm sorry, Trent. What were you saying?"

"That it was a nice party."

She scooped another dollop into the palm of her hand. "Yes, it really was."

He turned to the bathroom mirror. "Austin loves that woman. I can tell. I thought he was crazy at first, getting all depressed over one woman when women all over Texas were practically handing him their panties, but I get it now. They're good together. Plus, and don't get mad Dree, Sommer's pretty damn easy on the eyes."

When she didn't respond a second time, he spat into the sink and peered out again. "Something bothering you, baby?"

Alexandrina replaced the cap on the jar of lotion, walked across the room, and placed the jar on the dresser. She shook her head and tightened the ties of her silk robe.

"Nothing's wrong. I'm going to go check on Chloe."

The tail of her robe swished behind her as she padded across the hall to their daughter's room.

She slipped inside and peeked into the crib to make sure that Chloe was sound asleep, then took a seat in the nearby rocking chair and pulled out her cell phone where the screen displayed a third missed call from Jessica. Glancing at the door to make sure that Trent hadn't followed, she pressed the button to return Jessica's call.

"Where have you been?" Jessica answered, her voice teetering between anger and panic. "I have been trying to reach you for hours."

Alexandrina glanced at the door again. "I'm sorry, Jessica. I was out with Trent. Is everything okay?"

She heard Jessica slam a door shut. "I saw Austin today," she revealed. "He told me he is in love with another woman."

Alexandria cringed. "Oh, I am so sorry to hear that. Are you okay?"

"Of course I'm okay." After a moment of silence, she added, "I am *not* okay. How can he claim to already love another woman when not that long ago, he said that he loved me?"

Alexandrina sighed and leaned back into the rocking chair. "Men, that's how they operate. You know of the problems I had with Trent."

"But that's different," Jessica countered. "Trent didn't love those women. He only slept with them. Austin, he says he loves this woman, but if that's the case, why have I not heard of her?"

Don't say a word, Alexandrina's mind urged. Biting her lip, she listened as her cousin continued.

"I know that, after we broke up, he went to some charity event with that green-eyed violinist woman. What was her name, again?"

"Victoria Ellington," Alexandrina replied. "And it's not her."

Immediately, she put her hand over her mouth and prayed Jessica hadn't picked up on her slip. Unfortunately, it was already too late.

"It's not her? What does that mean?"

Alexandrina pressed her lips together.

"Tell me what you know," Jessica demanded.

Chloe stirred in the crib and Alexandrina rose to check to make sure she hadn't woken up. "I might know something," she admitted, stroking Chloe's back. "Tonight, I went with Trent over to Austin's. It was for a party. The girl was there."

A sound broke through the phone, a loud crash as if Jessica had dropped her cell. A few seconds later, she reappeared on the line. "So, she is real?"

"Yes, very real." Alexandrina refastened a button that had come loose on her daughter's pajamas.

"Do I know her?"

"No."

"Should I know her?"

"No. They grew up together. She is from his hometown in North Carolina."

Jessica paused and Alexandrina already knew what question was going to follow.

"Is she hideous?"

Alexandrina took a moment to mull over her answer. On one hand, she could tell the truth about Sommer's flawless, radiant skin, charming smile, and captivating brown eyes, but that would only make Jessica feel worse. However, if she lied, Jessica would know. She always seemed to know.

"You're taking too long to answer," Jessica resigned. "That means she is gorgeous."

"And she wasn't even wearing makeup when I saw her," Alexandrina added. "She even has a pretty name too. Sommer."

"*Ay dios*." Jessica touched a hand to her forehead. "So, what was the party for? Are they getting married? Was he announcing his engagement?"

"Dree?" Trent's voice resonated throughout the hallway, startling Alexandrina to the point where she almost dropped her phone into Chloe's crib.

"No," Alexandrina whispered. "It wasn't an engagement party."

"So what was it?"

"Dree?" Trent called again. "Are you still in Chloe's room? Did she wake up?"

Her heart thrashed against her chest as she heard his footsteps draw nearer. "Jessica, I promised Trent that I wouldn't tell you about the party and even what you now know is too much."

"*What was the party for?*" Jessica demanded.

Trent pushed open the door. "What are you up to in here?"

Alexandrina placed a finger over her mouth. "Shh, you're too loud. You might wake Chloe."

He entered the room, looked into the crib, and took a moment to run his hands over his daughter's curly head.

"Who are you talking to?" he asked.

"Jessica."

His head shot up. "Dree…"

"We're talking about this rocking horse that my grandfather made when were little," she quickly explained. "How he spent days making sure that it was the perfect gift for our Aunt Beatriz."

Still doubtful, Trent narrowed his brows. "And how'd that just pop up into the conversation?"

On the other side, Jessica listened intently.

"Chloe's next birthday," Alexandrina added. "Jessica was asking me what she could possibly get for the little girl who has everything."

Trent eyed the phone and then his wife, but said nothing. However, he didn't leave the room and Alexandrina knew he wasn't going to until she was off the phone.

"So about the rocking horse," she said to Jessica. "Do you remember the one I'm talking about?"

Jessica closed her eyes and tried to figure out why her cousin was hinting at the wooden rocking horses their grandfather used to hand carve.

"Drina, that rocking horse wasn't a gift for Aunt Beatriz," she said. "Aunt Beatriz doesn't have any children. *Avô* only makes rocking horses for new babies."

She gasped as realization struck her.

"Yes, the rocking horse," Alexandrina added. "You remember it?"

Jessica's eyes stung with tears. "They're going to have a baby together?"

"Yes, that's right," Alexandrina confirmed. "I just know that Chloe would love a little wooden rocking horse, just like *Avô* used to make."

Trent motioned with his hands that he wanted her to wrap up the call.

"But I have to go now, Jessica," she finished. "Call me if you need me."

There was no answer, so she ended the call and Trent ushered her back to the bedroom. She wasn't sure why Austin had wanted to keep the mother of his child a secret in the first place, but she hoped that whatever the reason, what she just told Jessica wouldn't do too much damage.

~

JESSICA TOSSED THE PHONE TO THE FLOOR AND LET HER HEAD FALL into her hands. How could she have let this happen? Austin had been the perfect man: considerate, kind, loving, and faithful. He'd doted on her without so much as a complaint when she'd fractured her ankle trying out a short-lived "jogging in heels" fad she'd heard about in Los Angeles.

Even when he'd found out about her occasional cocaine habit, all he'd done was make her promise that she'd stop using and had worked on a meal plan with her chef as an alternative way for her to keep her slim figure. But greedily, she'd wanted more. Walter Remos, with his seven-figure diamond-encrusted watch collection, luxury yacht, Gulfstream jet, and private island had dazzled her, and she let the dollar signs drag her into the arms of a man too odd and peculiar for her tastes. His oddities she might have even been able to put up with if he'd at least been interested in marriage, but what good was an old billionaire if there was no promise of his money?

Then, as if the world was going to remain on hold just for her, she'd waltzed back in expecting to fall right back into Austin's good graces. She'd noticed that there was something different about him at Chloe's birthday party, but she would have never guessed it was another woman. And one he grew up with? That made it even worse! It was like a fairy tale. Friends turned lovers. And she'd been the impetus. The force that had put their entire romance into motion.

Rising, she strode across the floor toward the balcony and ignored Marcus holding up his hand indicating yet another person she needed to speak to. Now just wasn't the right time.

"*Mizz* Costa?"

He poked his head through the glass balcony doors, and she realized that he obviously wasn't well-versed in reading body language.

"Not now, Marcus."

"But it's Kyle Stallworth." He jutted the phone toward her. "You told me to make sure to give you the phone if he called."

Kyle Stallworth was the last person she wanted to hear from. He was just another product of the small town in North Carolina where Austin was born, but she took the phone anyhow.

"Kyle."

"Jessica."

He couldn't see her, but Kyle could sense that she was frowning.

"Something wrong, Jess? You sound upset. You and Austin had a fight?"

She cackled a laugh. "Austin and I will never ever be again, Kyle."

"And why do you say that?"

She dabbed at her eyes. "Because, he's having a baby."

All of a sudden, Kyle got a sinking feeling in the depths of his stomach. "What? With who?"

"I don't know her. Maybe you might. Apparently, they grew up together."

He hesitated. "She's from Yearwood?"

"Apparently. Drina and Trent went to their little baby shower get-together thing tonight. You didn't go?"

He ignored the question. "Did she tell you how far along the woman was?"

"No."

"Well, what does she look like? Did she say anything about that?"

"No." Marcus reappeared and before he had a chance to relay his message, she waved him away. "All I know is that she is some gorgeous woman from his hometown who is so beautiful that she doesn't need makeup." She forced back more tears that threatened. "Oh, and that her name is Sommer."

She felt Kyle's change in emotion all the way through the phone.

"Sommer?" he asked. "Are you sure?"

"Positive. It's a pretty name. I would remember."

A deep, guttural noise escaped from the back of his throat. "Jess, can I call you back?"

His abrupt need to end the call was suspicious, but Jessica wasn't in the mood to pry.

"Yes, you can. I'm flying out to Australia tomorrow for a photo shoot. I will be there for a week."

"Ok, no problem."

When she ended the call, Marcus reappeared again.

"What is it now?" she demanded.

"It's Lorenzo. He's calling with some specifics about your shoot in Sydney."

Sighing, she followed him inside. It was time to throw herself back into her work as it was the only alternative she currently had. She and Austin were no longer an option, and never in a million years would she have ever thought that knowing their relationship was officially over could hurt this much.

Picking up the phone, she inhaled to collect herself and plastered on a fake smile.

"Lorenzo. Hi."

Kyle had never understood the expression of "seeing red" until that moment as he sat in a brown leather club chair in the middle of his den. So, Sommer had gone to Texas after all. And even worse, she'd been stupid enough to let Austin knock her up.

The dark head of hair down near his thighs stopped moving.

"Something wrong?" the woman asked, looking up.

He scowled down at her, stood, tucked his dick back in his pants, and trudged to his study. Jerking open a drawer, he rummaged through an assortment of papers before pulling out a business card. The woman reappeared in the doorway.

"Kyle?"

While he would normally be instantly aroused by a naked silhouette in his doorframe, he was so upset he could barely see straight. Austin Riley *always won*. The man had lived the life of Midas but without the repercussions. It made him sick to his stomach the way people fawned over him, like he was some sort of king. Even the way they'd protected him from not only his father's history, but his father's influence. His father's mark on Yearwood.

There was no way that man's blood didn't run through Austin's. Now, he was having a baby with Sommer and keeping it under wraps. Why? If he loved her so much, why wouldn't he tell the world?

Kyle knew he could bring it to an end. Even if *he* couldn't have Sommer, that fake bastard wouldn't either. Soon, the world would know the truth behind their golden boy QB. The roots that had created him.

"I'm fine, Gina—"

"Tina," the woman corrected.

"Dammit, you know your name." He pointed to the ceiling. "Go upstairs and wait for me. I have business to take care of."

It took all of his patience not to run over and shove her into motion with the slowness it took her to exit.

Once she was gone, he went back to the den to grab his phone. After several tries, he finally got the number punched in.

"Luke Maisley," the person answered.

"Luke, it's Kyle Stallworth."

Luke stretched his foot onto his desk. "Kyle, I haven't heard from you in a while."

"That's because I haven't needed you to write any pieces about me for a while."

Luke angled his head. "True. I'm assuming you have one now?"

Kyle took a series of deep breaths as his anger threatened to send him into a fit of dizziness. He couldn't believe Sommer would do this. *His* Sommer. The same Sommer that, in high school after lunch, would go outside to sit and read a book while the other girls giggled incessantly and flipped through gossip magazines.

The same Sommer who had a beauty only him, or a man like him, could appreciate. He'd changed for her. Gone to countless anger therapy sessions to quell his ravaging beast, the desire to climb through her bedroom window and fuck her before she even realized she wanted him. And that had been when they were sixteen. He was completely different now.

"I do," Kyle answered. "Four words: Montgomery, Alabama. William Riley."

Chapter Nine

It was 8:41am on the most perfect Tuesday morning either Austin or Sommer had ever witnessed. Outside the hospital window, the bay glittered as the sun's rays reflected off of its glass-like surface. For a millisecond, the hospital room fell completely still...until a shrill cry broke through the silence and resonated throughout the entire ward.

As the cry resounded, time slowed. Leaning forward, Austin peered into her eyes for the first time. *His daughter.* His little girl. So perfect with her ten toes, ten fingers, and pouty mouth, she made her grand entrance by screaming at the top of her lungs to let everyone know that she was here, and that she was well.

Sommer's eyes locked with his. Tired and breathtakingly beautiful, her face flushed before she mouthed, "Is she okay?"

All he could do was nod and take a step back to create a pathway for the nurse to place their perfect little girl in her mother's arms. Immediately, he was at Sommer's side pressing kisses to her temple, telling her how happy he was to have her, how much he loved her, and fumbling to find the right words to explain the complete elation he felt whenever he looked at their daughter.

Olivia.

He placed his finger in the small hand jutting out from the pink blanket, amazed at how tiny the grasp was on his finger, but how strong it felt wrapped around his heart. Even six weeks early, she weighed in at a solid six pounds and was eighteen-inches long.

"Austin."

He looked at the woman who undoubtedly was going to be his wife one day. Soon.

"Hold her."

Just as he'd done with his nephew, he cradled the blanket between his arms, but his sister and mother had been right. There were absolutely no words to describe the mixture of pride, protection, and love pumping through his veins. The feeling magnified when Olivia opened her eyes and looked up at him, her golden-amber orbs glimmering as if they were his own reflection.

"Wow," rushed from his mouth.

Sommer touched his arm. "Yeah. Wow."

The door opened and Emma walked in with Caroline following behind. Austin swallowed a lump down the back of his throat at the sight of tears rushing from his mother's eyes. She walked over and gently pulled the blanket away from Olivia's face.

"*Sei bellissima*," she said between tears. "Austin, Sommer, she is magnificent."

Caroline, grasping a tissue in her hand, was speechless.

The first time she was diagnosed with cancer, one of her biggest fears had been that she would never see her only child grow up, graduate from college, get married, or have children. She'd gone into remission, but then the second wave hit, and she'd been convinced she would never get the chance she was now granted. The chance to meet her grand-baby.

More tears surged forth.

"Sommer. My baby." Caroline tried a smile, but her face contorted as more tears formed rivulets down her cheeks.

Maneuvering around the bed, she opened her arms and Sommer

squeezed herself into them. Both women cried as they silently reflected on all the past year had brought, and that they couldn't think of a better culmination to what had been the most trying period of both their lives.

"Ms. Caroline?" Austin called. "Ready to hold your granddaughter?"

Caroline nodded and he placed the adorable little girl into her arms. It was just like holding Sommer again, from the tiny body and small face, and to the outpouring of love she felt just looking at her.

"What did you two name her?" Emma asked, dabbing at the corners of his eyes.

"Olivia," Sommer answered.

"Olivia Camden Riley," Austin added.

Emma chuckled. "First Arielle names Antonio after my father, and now you two give Olivia my mother's name."

Emma wrapped an arm around Austin's waist, and he leaned down as she touched a kiss to his cheek. Then, she turned him to face her. Although he'd done a good job of keeping his composure up until that point, she knew what she was about to tell him might unravel him completely. As if he sensed it, he reluctantly met her eyes.

"Don't doubt yourself," she told him.

"Ma—"

"I'm serious, Austin."

His gaze finally settled on hers, the brilliant orbs shining even brighter than before.

"Don't doubt yourself, Austin," she repeated. "You know who you are and who you've always been, despite the things he tried to put in your head. You will never be to your little girl what he was to you. You'll never do to your little girl what he did to you. Regardless of what happened in the past, the man I see standing here today has surpassed all of that."

He closed his eyes and tilted his head back.

"Honey, I need you to look at me," she urged.

He took a deep breath and pulled back his lids to reveal the mist coating his whites.

"Ma," he cleared his throat, "I never thought that I could know this. That I *would* know this. When I think about the fact that he tried to keep me from it, from her..."

He cleared his throat again.

"Ma, I love Sommer. I mean, I *love* Sommer. It's like nothing I've ever experienced before. And Ma, she loves me. I don't even have to think twice about it. And now, we have Olivia..."

His voice broke. He hung his head and squeezed the space between his eyes. Emma nodded, understanding exactly what he meant. She'd watched from the sidelines as Austin had tried, countless times, to hide who he truly was from a father who'd wanted him to be different. Who'd wanted him to be ugly.

Contemptuous.

But, regardless of what had occurred in the past, this was Austin's time. As long as he stayed true to the woman he loved, and the child they'd brought into the world together, he would be perfectly fine.

Emma pulled her son into her arms and held him close. It had been years since she'd last held him like this and just like back then, he'd fought the tears that wanted to flow as if their existence threatened his manhood. But even without them streaming down his cheeks as they'd done when he was a little boy, she saw the emotion glittering across his face.

They continued to swoon and gush over Olivia whose cries were replaced by curious, contemplative stares. Eventually, both Emma and Caroline filtered out and on the phone, Austin listened to the excited banter of his nieces and nephew as Arielle told him she couldn't wait to see Olivia when she visited the next day.

"It's funny," Sommer said, yawning. "I would have never thought that this would be us. At least, not us together. I'd resigned myself to the fact that I'd go on to marry an accountant named Barry whose favorite pastime involved discussing his stamp collection."

Austin laughed. "Never. But can you imagine what would have happened if I didn't go back home this summer?"

"No, and I don't want to think about it."

He kissed her forehead. "You need to get some sleep, beautiful."

She reached for his hand and twined their fingers together. She was tired, but she wanted to feel his lips pressed against her skin for a little while longer.

"I will. In a minute." She yawned again. "I want to stay up and talk to you a bit."

He stroked a finger across her cheek. "It's not like I'm going anywhere. I'll be here when you wake up." He looked across at Olivia. "I can't promise that she'll be here, though. I still feel like I'm in a dream."

She glanced at their daughter. "Me too. Overall, I think we did good."

"Yeah, I think we did too." He pressed another kiss against her forehead. "Sleep, Sommer."

She tilted her head and he pressed a kiss against her lips. Then, she settled into the bed and dozed while he took a few more moments to watch Olivia's chest rise and fall as she slept.

A nurse entered the room, saw him standing over her, and smiled.

"Is everything okay?" he asked.

Austin looked over at Sommer, then back down at their sleeping daughter.

"Yeah," he said. "Everything is perfect."

Chapter Ten

"We didn't come this far to go home empty-handed."

Trent stood in the middle of his huddled team members and looked into their faces. Most of them looked determined, but a few were nervous, which he understood. It was their first trip to the big game. Virtually, the entire world would be watching.

He was one of the few who'd already been, back in his second year when he'd played in Arizona, so the adrenaline was familiar. The rush was welcomed. The only difference was, this time, he'd be going home with a ring.

He looked toward Austin who, as usual, was focused.

"Fourteen and two, best record in the league and in franchise history," he continued. "Three players lost to injury. Personal struggles," his eyes flicked over to Cason who'd lost both parents in a car accident that year, designating him sole caregiver of his seventeen-year old sister, "and tribulations. People saying that we weren't going to make it..."

His gaze bore into the offensive line.

"What's O-line's job today?"

"Keep our QB's jersey looking like he just came from soaking it in some Tide detergent," came Tank's southern drawl.

The men chuckled.

"Damn straight," Trent added. "We plan to use the hell out of that rifle tonight."

Austin "Rifle" Riley was the nickname the media had given Austin after he'd barreled a forty-yard pass to Cason for a game-winning touchdown in overtime against Washington.

"We're going up against one of the greatest teams in the league," Trent went on. "They didn't get here by chance, they got here by skill. We know we got the talent. We know we have the determination. What separates us from the team that did, the team that's out there waiting for us right now, is our heart. Our drive. No one got us here but ourselves. We won as a team, we lost as a team. We busted our asses in practice to get better, and we rallied around our brother when his world flipped inside out. We've grown and we've changed. This game is the pinnacle. This game is the top. It's the peak of Mount Everest and I can see the summit."

His eyes traveled around the circle.

"Everything you got, everything you can possibly give, you go out there and give it. Today, the only number that matters, is one-hundred."

When the huddle broke, the men made their way out of the tunnel and were greeted by raucous cheer. Austin looked up into the massive crowd as people waved signs cheering on the team, as well as signs designed specifically for him. The outpouring of support left him with an overwhelming feeling of gratitude.

When he finally reached the sideline, his mind went to Sommer. A few days after Olivia's birth, Arielle, his nieces, and his nephew had flown back to Yearwood. Caroline had followed, and though Sommer had pleaded for her mother to stay a while longer, Caroline had reminded her daughter that she had to go back to run the café and oversee the hiring process of the person that would replace Sommer's position. After she was done with that, she'd hand business operations over to Reese and fly out to spend a couple of months with her daughter and grandbaby. Emma had made the decision to stay for a few weeks to help him and Sommer transition into parenthood.

Austin's first five weeks as a father had been shaky. He learned about all the things babies did that he hadn't even known existed, Trent laughing at him along the way, and he'd learned that it was even possible to find the straining face Olivia made when she was pooping in her diaper absolutely adorable. His new role had even transferred over to the field since he wasn't just playing for himself anymore. Realizing that had made him more focused, poised, and confident.

Once Dallas' spot in the final game was secured, he'd made arrangements for his mother, Sommer, and Olivia to fly out to Glendale to be with him on that day. Sommer had been hesitant because she was still comfortable being in the shadows and adjusting to her post-baby body, but this was the woman he'd planned to ask to marry him if Dallas won the game. He didn't want to hide her any longer as if he was ashamed of the woman he loved, and the beautiful little girl they'd made together.

That morning, he'd assumed he'd risen first since excitement had kept him restless for most of the night, but he'd found Sommer sitting on the balcony looking out toward the stadium. He'd moved to the doorway and, sensing his presence, Sommer had suddenly said, "You've got this, Riley," before turning around to look at him.

"I've got this?" he'd asked.

"Pittsburgh doesn't know who they're messing with. *My* Austin Riley. My baby. I have nothing but faith in you, and I'm so proud of the work that you've put in not only to be a great player, but also an excellent father."

The compliment had made him grin as sheepishly as a sixteen-year old boy.

"Thank you, beautiful," he'd replied. "I love you. I love you so much."

Leaning down, he'd kissed her soft, delectable mouth. This was a woman, *his* woman, and he was never going to let her run away from him. Tonight, the world was going to meet his little Olivia, and the future Mrs. Austin Riley.

"It's heads. Dallas will receive," the referee said after Trent made the call. Austin slipped on his helmet, adjusted the chin strap, and looked over at Cason. Cason winked, and after Dallas' special teams' twenty-yard return, the offense took the field.

~

SOMMER SHOOK ALL THE WAY DOWN TO HER FINGERTIPS. SHE WAS thankful that it was Emma holding Olivia. She'd initially been concerned that the noise and crowd would be too much for Olivia to take, but her daughter loved it. From above in the luxury box, she'd studied the field, the people around them, and had even cried briefly when Cason's fiancée, Amelia, had to hand her back to Emma to go grab a bite.

The game had been intense and tied virtually every step of the way. Now, there were seven seconds left on the clock and Dallas was down by four points. It was fourth down and long at the goal line, and though Austin appeared collected as the coach relayed the final play to him, Sommer knew his heart was pounding in his ears. If he didn't make a touchdown on this last drive, that was it. Pittsburgh would get the title.

Sommer's phone vibrated in her pocket and startled her out of her seat. Seeing her uncle's name across the screen, she eased into the slightly quieter hallway, but kept an eye on the field.

"Uncle Reese?"

"Hi baby girl." From the tone of his voice, she immediately knew that something was wrong.

She walked down the hallway and ducked into an alcove.

"Uncle Reese, what is it?"

He didn't respond.

"Reese Williams..."

"How soon can you get home?"

"Why? What's wrong?"

"It's your mother, Sommer."

When the crowd roared, Sommer looked up just in time to see Austin and Cason connect for a touchdown in the end zone.

∽

THE MOMENT THE CLOCK WENT TO ZERO, AUSTIN LOOKED UP AT THE scoreboard to make sure he truly understood what was going on around him. With only seven seconds to go, he and Cason had pulled off nothing short of a miracle play. They'd needed four points. A field goal wouldn't have cut it. Somehow, the pass had landed.

They'd won. They'd really won.

He nearly fell over as players crushed into his back, squeezing him into the air. It was the first time in his life he'd seen so many grown men in tears, but they'd fought hard to get where they were. It was an overwhelming feeling to see that their hard work had ultimately paid off.

Cason was in the middle of the field on one knee with his forehead against the back of his palm, the coaching staff and the rest of the team surrounding him. In week six, when Cason's parents were killed, he'd assumed that he'd lost everything. But, the team had rallied around him. He'd fought for himself and his sister, and Amelia had been his rock.

Austin walked over, knelt with him, and soon the crowd also lulled to give Cason his moment of silence. After a couple of minutes, his head went to the sky and he recited a silent prayer before standing. He received congratulatory hugs and pats from the team, then smiled at someone standing behind Austin. Amelia pushed her way through the crowd and rushed into his arms.

Austin turned around to find his mother standing there with Olivia, but Sommer was nowhere to be found.

He gently touched Amelia on the back of her arm. "Where's Sommer?"

"We couldn't find her," she replied. "She got a phone call, stepped out, and when I went to get her so she could come down with us, she'd just disappeared."

A man came running up to Austin. "They're naming you MVP, Riley. Did you want to do your special announcement before or after your speech?"

Austin scanned the sea of faces for the one he wanted to see the most. "We'll do it after."

A championship T-shirt was handed to him and he tossed it over his shoulder, lifted Olivia from his mother's arms, and parted the crowed as he walked up to the podium to give the customary MVP speech. Looking around one last time, he hoped Sommer showed soon.

"Before I actually begin my speech," he began, "I would like to introduce everyone to a special lady in my life."

A cameraman zoomed in on Olivia's face.

"This is Olivia Camden Riley, my little princess."

～

IN THE LUXURY BOX, SOMMER LOST TRACK OF TIME.

She sank to the floor. Her uncle was still on the phone, but his words were coming through in short bursts—metastasized, surgery, collapse. Somewhere between the words, the dizziness, and the chaos swirling in her head that impeded any ability for coherent thought, the only thing she'd been able to make out was that her mother needed her.

"Olivia Camden Riley."

Her head popped up when she heard Austin's voice. There, on a flat screen TV, was their daughter's little light brown face.

THE GAME OF LOVE

She raced back the luxury box and searched for Amelia and Emma, both who were nowhere to be found. Grabbing her purse, she dashed to the elevator. She loved Austin with every fiber of her being, so she completely understood why he continuously fought her on the issue of keeping their relationship a secret. But, there was still something bigger that she was concerned about. Something she was pretty sure that neither she nor Olivia would be able to handle.

"Austin Riley has a baby?" She overheard a woman say as she waited for the elevator.

"Seems so," the friend standing next to her answered. Then both women exchanged a look as the camera zoomed even closer to Olivia's face and Austin's finger stroking her cheek. His much lighter finger compared to Olivia's slightly darker, cappuccino complexion. Lighter than her mother's, but darker than her father's, a perfect blend of the two.

"Hmm," the first woman spoke up.

"My thoughts exactly," the friend chimed. "Where did Irish-Italian Austin Riley get a little mocha baby?"

∽

LUKE MAISLEY CURSED AS HE PUSHED HIS RENTAL CAR OVER A bumpy, unlined road down the back street of an eerie Alabama neighborhood. Moving the lever to park, he switched on the cabin light and double-checked the directions that the man at the gas station had given him, secretly wishing he'd written them down wrong for an excuse to hightail it out of the creepy suburb that looked straight out of the 1950s. But, he'd gotten it right: four miles down Lee Street, left onto Naples, the last house on the right—the one with the purple wisteria clinging to the windows.

He parked along the curb at the front of the house and immediately began to question his judgment. Generally, the only news Kyle Stallworth ever brought to the table had to do with Kyle himself. Luke never complained because both their careers had been bolstered by Kyle's high-profile relationships, public controversial statements, and brushes with law enforcement. However, he was admittedly doubtful when Kyle had told him that this man, William Riley, was supposedly Dallas quarterback Austin Riley's estranged father.

If Luke remembered clearly, when Austin had spoken about his father on draft day, he'd alluded to the press that his father was dead. Because no one was the wiser, everyone had accepted it and moved on to asking him about how different he thought life in Dallas would be compared to what he'd been used to in Tallahassee for the past four years. But if Kyle was correct—and Luke had a hunch that he was—then finding out that Austin's father was alive and living in abject poverty was already the start to a pretty solid story that would rattle the millionaire QB's wholesome, pretty-boy image.

A faint spot of light in one of the windows indicated that there was the possibility that someone actually lived there. Cutting the engine, Luke hopped out of the vehicle and made his way up the concrete walkway. He tightened the straps on his leather satchel and walked through a wooden gate attached to the front porch, but as he prepared to knock on the door, emerging from the far end of the porch was a snarling, brown and black Doberman pinscher.

"Easy now," Luke tried to coax while he tried to decide what would antagonize the dog least, taking a step backwards or remaining firmly in place. The dog bared its teeth in response and Luke's eyes darted to the car. If he ran now, there was still a chance he could make it inside the car before the dog had a chance to pounce.

"Heel!"

The command came from inside the house. Luke carefully pulled his attention from the dog and placed it on the tall man standing in the doorway. If he'd had any doubt before, all of it was completely dashed. He was looking at the spitting image of Austin.

"He's all bark," the man warmly reassured, stepping onto the porch. He bent to scratch behind the dog's ear, and Luke couldn't believe the same vicious creature that had made his life flash before his eyes was now whimpering under its master's gentle massaging.

"Could've fooled me," Luke replied.

"You a reporter?" The man eyed his bag.

"Yes. Luke Maisley. I'm a journalist. Are you William Riley?"

He turned back to the dog. "Depends. Are you here about Austin?"

"Yes."

"Never thought I'd ever see one of you out here." He motioned to the front door. "You want to come in, or do you want to stay out here on the porch with Gus?"

Luke nervously chuckled, then followed the man into the dark house.

Inside, Luke half-expected to walk in and find images of Austin ranging from birth to adulthood plastered everywhere, but instead, the paneled walls were bare. The front room housed an old, patchwork recliner, a mismatched sofa, and a flat-screened TV in the middle of the hutch of an armoire. Quite fittingly, the TV was turned to the championship game. Austin appeared on the screen, standing on the sidelines with his hands tucked into his shoulder pads as his defense massacred the Pittsburgh offense.

There'd been something markedly different about the QB this past season. He'd obliterated records, putting up more yards in a single-season than any other player in football history. It was as if there'd been an invisible force right there with him on the field helping him call plays, dodge sacks, and adding wings to his feet.

"Lemonade?"

Luke carefully took a seat in the sofa. "Sure."

William reappeared with two glasses in his hand and a platter of barbecued chicken wings.

"The lemonade's not bad," he seemed to be warning, "but it's nothing compared to what my wife used to make."

He placed them on the coffee table and sank into the recliner. When Austin's face reappeared on the screen again, William looked up and smiled in such a way that Luke wondered what could have possibly caused the father and son to be so estranged.

"You said you never expected me to come out here? You mean, a reporter?" Luke asked.

William nodded and tore his gaze away from the screen. "Most people think that Austin's father's dead."

Luke reached for his glass of lemonade. "Which I did, up until a few days ago."

"What happened a few days ago?"

"A source." Luke took a sip and the overpowering tartness of the lemon bit at his tongue. Clearing his throat, he put the glass back on the table. "Someone recently informed me that you were alive and living out here in Montgomery County."

William swigged his drink as if he couldn't sense that it needed at least four teaspoons more sugar. "Had to be somebody from Yearwood. Not many people know where I went."

The crowd roared and he craned his neck just in time to see Austin throw a thirty-yard pass to Cason Allen. William pumped his fist and roared.

"Do you watch all of his games?" Luke asked.

"Every single one of them since he was with them Seminoles in college." William took another sip. "If it wasn't for football, I probably wouldn't even have cable, but I got one of those special packages to make sure I can see every game Dallas plays."

Austin handed off the ball to the running back who picked up another first-down on the carry.

"You must be really proud of him," Luke offered.

A flash of sadness moved across William's face as he reached for a wing. "I am."

"Mr. Riley, do you mind if I ask you some questions about Austin for a piece I'm doing?"

William pumped his fist again as Austin dodged a heavy lineman racing toward him to land a ten-yard pass to Trent Holloway.

"Don't think my son would like that very much," he advised. "Think he's content with having the world think that I'm dead."

Luke searched his mind for an explanation, unprepared for the fact that maybe William didn't want to remain hidden in the shadows. He'd assumed the man would have wanted the world to know he was alive in order to reap some of the benefits of Austin's celebrity.

"You might think differently if I told you my source."

William cringed as a defender crushed into Austin, but then celebrated when a penalty was called. "And who's that?"

"Emma Riley."

William's eyes flicked over to him and Luke prayed that he wouldn't call his bluff.

"She still goes by Riley?" He slapped his hand against his thigh. "I'll be damned. I would have never expected that."

Luke relaxed some and grabbed a wing. What the man lacked in beverage-making skills, he made up for with his talent on the grill.

"I'm sure she's still as beautiful as ever, even in her sixties," William said. "Got the eyes of a lynx. And the same big ol' feet."

Luke quickly wiped his fingers and reached for his laptop. "So, how did you two meet?"

Austin threw a touchdown pass to Cason and William bellowed with excitement before answering. "Met her right here in Alabama, which is where I was born and raised. She worked in a restaurant at the time with her parents. I was twenty-eight, so she had to be around sixteen or so. She was born in Italy and her family came here to open their restaurant, which made no sense to me since Italians always went to New York, but if they hadn't come here, I would've never met her."

Luke typed the notes on his computer. "So, what made you decide to move to Yearwood?"

"That was Emma." William grabbed another wing. "She hated Alabama. Em's more of the free-spirited, liberal type. A product of the sixties. Alabama was too backwoods for her. 'Antiquated' was the word she'd used. Where she really wanted to go was New York, but I couldn't take that fast-life type of stuff, so we decided on North Carolina and ended up settling in Yearwood, strangely enough. That place is so small, you probably can't even find it on a map."

Luke decided not to skirt around his real reason for visiting any longer. "So, Mr. Riley, why is it that Austin makes it seem like you're dead? Why the fallout?"

A defender crushed into Austin on the screen. Austin fell onto his back and remained still for a few seconds. William hopped up out of his seat and spewed profanities at the television. After the play was reviewed, the officials determined that the defender had led the tackle with his helmet, and called the penalty against Pittsburgh. The call didn't seem to appease William.

"You see how they're beating up my boy out there? Dirty players in Pennsylvania, I tell you. They're trying to take him out because they know that Dallas will never win without him."

William flopped back down into the chair and downed some more lemonade. "God, that's awful," said, looking over at Luke. "Why didn't you say anything?"

Luke, confused because the man had already had several sips of the beverage, wasn't quite sure how to respond.

"You asked me a question," William said, as if he suddenly realized. "Oh, that's right. What happened between me and Austin."

He grabbed another wing and Luke waited until he finished munching so that he could continue. When the man didn't, he cleared his throat.

"So, what happened?" Luke prodded.

"My past caught up to me," William replied, then abruptly got to his feet and disappeared down the dark hallway. Several minutes later he still hadn't returned, and Luke tossed a glance toward the front door to make sure Gus hadn't found his way inside.

He dared another sip of the lemonade and popped a wing into his mouth. Austin's face appeared on the screen again but this time, he was smiling and chatting with Cason since Dallas was finally up by a touchdown.

William's heavy footsteps came trudging down the hall and he reappeared with an antique, brown-leather photo album in his hands. Taking his seat again, he kept the photo album in his lap and trained his attention back on the game.

"What'd I miss?" he asked an even more confused Luke.

"Nothing. Dallas is still up by a touchdown."

William nodded. "Good game, but my boy's gonna win."

Luke's eyes fell to the album. "What's that?"

William didn't turn to look at him as he spoke. "It's an old photo album. Don't worry, I brought it out here for a reason. I'm just waiting for halftime before I show it to you."

Luke glanced at the game clock and realized that halftime was still seven minutes away, so he closed his laptop and leaned into the seat cushions.

He didn't really too much care for football, or any sport for that matter, which was why he hadn't attended the game. His type of journalism was more along the lines of the gossip magazine, so unless a football player had arrived at the stadium with his mistress while his pregnant wife tried to barter a ticket at the gate, he wouldn't be finding any stories there.

He glanced around the small house again. Austin was worth millions. Between the explosive contract he'd signed two years prior that had over fifty-five million dollars in guaranteed money, and his endorsement deals and investments, he was set for life. Therefore, it made no sense that his father would be living the way he was, unless something major had caused the family separation.

The clock slowly ticked down to zero, and Dallas jogged back into the locker room only up by four points with the field goal that Pittsburgh kicked right before the time expired. Luke anxiously tapped his foot as he waited for William to explain why he'd brought out the album.

William lifted the remote to mute the television. "I don't too much care for halftime," he declared. Then, he looked down at the album. "I'm guessing you're itching to find out what's inside here, aren't you?"

"You could say that," Luke answered.

"Before we go traveling down memory lane, I do want to say something first." William's long, thin fingers traced the grooves in the leather. "No matter what you see in these pictures, one of the hardest things that I had to come to terms with was the fact that my son is smarter than I am. Even at the age of seven, he was already a better man than I was, but I was too stubborn to see it. I was set in my ways and let my roots control me."

Luke reopened his laptop. "So, what does that mean? Your roots controlling you?"

"I had a hard time accepting change."

"Which means?"

William blew out an exasperated sigh. "My ex-wife has a best friend named Caroline Hayes. Those two women became fast friends within minutes of us settling in Yearwood. They even had babies the same year. Em had Austin and Caroline had a daughter named Sommer. Sommer Hayes. Now Sommer, she was a hotheaded little thing and even though I didn't want to admit it back then, she was as cute as a button. The first time my son laid his eyes on Sommer, he was hooked."

He paused, waiting for Luke to catch up.

"Hooked how?" Luke asked.

"Smitten," William cried out. "In love. He's been throwing ga-ga eyes at that girl ever since he could say 'ga-ga,' and I didn't like that."

Confused, Luke frowned. "Why not? Was there something wrong with Sommer?"

William opened the album and scraped his hand across the plastic covering the pictures to remove a layer of dust. Luke steadied the laptop on his palm as he walked over to the chair.

The first picture Luke saw was one of Austin as a chubby baby with bright eyes and dark hair. William smiled at the photo and ran his finger over baby Austin's cheek.

"Ask me that question years ago, and I'd tell you that Sommer was just plain born wrong," William said. "But no matter what I did, I couldn't stop Austin from staring at her. At the bakery. After school. During downtown events. All the damn time. Then, his friends Kyle and Darrell started coming around and that, well that just made me more upset."

William flipped a few more pages, showcasing pictures of Austin and Arielle at different stages of life, as well as younger versions of him and Emma. He pointed at a little girl in pink overalls sitting on a beach next to Austin.

"He's two years old here," William explained. "See this little girl sitting next to him? That's Sommer."

As Luke looked over the charming little girl, he began to understand.

The next page held a series of photos, one of which was face down. William's hand hovered over the overturned photo, and his fingers trembled.

"Before I turn this over, I want to know why you're writing about my boy," he demanded.

Luke, caught off-guard, nearly dropped the laptop. "Because Austin's a big deal right now," he partially lied. "I'm writing a piece on his family and thought that interviewing Arielle and Emma were it. Then, Emma told me that you were still alive and out here in Alabama. I figured that maybe, with all these years in the shadows, you'd want to get your voice heard. Make amends with your son so that he can stop having people think you're dead."

William swallowed to clear a lump of emotion in his throat. "I do want that. And while I don't think I can be a regular father to him, I would still like the opportunity to apologize for the hell I caused."

Luke placed a hand on William's shoulder, but then quickly removed it when William shot him a look.

William's fingers went to the edge of the photo. When he flipped it over, Luke's heart came to a screeching halt. He couldn't and didn't want to believe what he was seeing, but that one photo suddenly made everything else make sense.

"I'm not proud of it," William remorsefully expressed, "but that's who I was for a good part of my life. That's who I tried to turn Austin into."

Loud cheers signaled that the players were returning to the field. William unmuted the TV, stood, and set the album on the chair.

"This lemonade is terrible. Want a beer?" he asked.

Tearing his gaze away from the photo, Luke met his eyes. "Beer? Yeah. Sure."

William disappeared into the kitchen. Luke pulled out his phone and snapped a few quick images of the photo.

He put the phone away when William returned and graciously accepted the beer before returning to his seat. William closed the album and clapped his hands at the TV.

"Come on, son. You can do this," he cheered.

Luke sat back and watched the second half, throwing in intermittent questions which William half-heartedly answered. The photo had given him his entire story, but leaving too soon would only arouse William's suspicions about the true intent of his story about Austin. As he thought about Gus on the porch, the last thing he needed was a dog taking a bite out of his new CK slacks.

The game sprinted by. Though games usually didn't hold his interest past the first quarter, Luke found himself fully engrossed in this one. However, he couldn't tell if his excitement was because of the exclusive story he was going to print, or if it had actually just been an extremely good game.

In the last few seconds, William nearly bellowed the roof off of the house as Austin tossed a game-winning touchdown to Cason. Luke even found himself jumping up and down with him, as well as slapping their hands together in jubilant high-fives.

William had only a few minutes to calm down before he was roaring again when Austin was named MVP. Then, both men froze in surprise when Austin walked up for his speech with a baby in his arms.

"Is that his baby?" William asked. "My grandchild?"

Austin's announcement for the crowd to meet his daughter answered William's question before Luke had a chance to fumble for a response.

William crumpled into his chair. "You said your name was Luke, right?"

"Yes, sir."

"Well Luke, I know you're just a reporter, but I'd like it if you did whatever you could to get me back in my boy's life. I can't make up for what I did to him, but maybe he'll let me be in my grandbaby's life. Maybe they both will. He and Arielle."

Luke couldn't tear his eyes away from the little girl. Austin had never mentioned seeing anyone ever since Jessica Costa, which was unusual since that relationship had been highly publicized. Had Austin hidden this new woman out of shame? Even if he hadn't, would anybody believe him after this article was released?

"Of course, sir," Luke finally answered. "I'll do everything in my power to give this story the platform it deserves."

꩜

AUSTIN, STILL ON A HIGH FROM THE WIN, ENTERED THE HOTEL ROOM with a sleepy Olivia in his arms and his equally tired mother trailing behind him.

"Sweetie, I'm going to lay down for a bit," Emma said, reaching up to peck him on the cheek and blowing a few kisses against Olivia's cheek. "I'll see you two in the morning."

Then, she left the suite and dragged her feet to her room the next floor down.

Sommer hadn't shown up on the field even after he'd given his speech, but five minutes before Austin had decided he would send a SWAT team to search for her, she'd texted his mother to let her know that an emergency had come up, and that she'd gone back to the room.

He walked through the suite, never liking the feeling he got whenever everything inside looked undisturbed. Although he knew Sommer would never leave him and Olivia behind, he still couldn't shake the feeling that she would eventually declare this life too much for her and run back to Yearwood, leaving a gaping hole in the middle of his chest no one else would ever be able to fill. He'd even wondered if she'd somehow figured out he was going to propose to her on national TV and had avoided it.

Little did she know, it was still going to happen. She was still going to be his wife.

"Sommer, are you in here?"

"I'm in the room," she answered.

When she appeared in the bedroom doorway, he could immediately tell that something was wrong. Gravely wrong.

"Baby, what is it?" he asked, crossing the room to examine her face closer.

She smiled, which seemed more like a struggle than a gesture, and reached for Olivia. "Here, let me feed Livvie and put her down so you can get ready for bed. You've had quite the day."

He shook his head. "I already fed and changed her, so how about you rest while I give her a bath and put her in the crib? Then, when I get back, you'll tell me what's bothering you."

She tried another smile, this one even more pitiful than the last. "Are you sure? You look exhausted, honey."

"Positive. Order up some room service." He kissed the top of her head. "I'll be right back."

He disappeared with Olivia, and Sommer looked over the room service menu but was unable to focus on anything written on the sheet. Although her uncle hadn't said much, she'd still understood plenty—her mother needed her.

She had to go home. Unfortunately, she knew that if she told Austin she had to go, he'd want to go with her even though he had weeks of TV appearances and events planned that he'd already committed to. Plus, she wasn't sure what kind of state her mother was in and part of her wanted to witness that firsthand, alone. The people in Yearwood knew of her mother's cancer, but none of them had actually seen what it could do to her.

She finally decided on a New York strip for Austin, and salmon with beurre blanc sauce for her. When Austin returned, the food was in the process of being dropped off by a timid looking girl in her early twenties. When she looked up and saw Austin emerge, her face flushed and her gaze dashed over to Sommer.

"Congratulations, Austin," she said only a couple of decibels louder than a whisper.

"Thank you," he peered at her name tag, "Christina. I really appreciate it."

She blushed even deeper. "Olivia is your daughter?"

Sommer realized the question was being directed at her. "Oh yes, she is. She's our daughter."

"Cool. She's gorgeous."

The girl lingered for a few seconds before walking back to the door. Just before she exited, she turned around.

"One more thing," she said. "I'm mixed too. I have friends from all different backgrounds. My best friend, she's Indian, but she's from Trinidad. I just wanted to tell you that while I've always respected you, Austin, what you did tonight made me like you even more. You didn't let anyone tell you who to love, so ignore all the bad things people are saying."

Before Sommer had a chance to ask her what she was referring to, the girl was out the door and down the hall.

Her gaze landed on Austin. "What bad things are people saying?"

"You're not changing the subject."

"I really want to know, though."

"What's got you looking so down?" he asked. "Did you really want Pittsburgh to win?"

She tried another smile, but he could still see the sadness hidden behind the gesture. Frustrated, he pushed the food to the side, tugged her up out of the chair, and led her to the balcony. He flopped down into one of the padded wicker chairs and pulled her onto his lap.

"We're just going to leave the food in there like that?" she asked.

"No, we're going to go back and eat it. Don't get me wrong, I'm so hungry I can barely see straight, but I want to get to the bottom of this first. Now, talk to me."

Sommer sighed. "Something's up with Mom."

"What do you mean?"

"Uncle Reese called and said she collapsed. Her cancer metastasized and they're currently going over more aggressive treatment options."

"So, she's in the hospital?"

Sommer blinked back tears. "Uncle Reese took her to the emergency room earlier today. They were watching the game at the café when it happened."

Austin pulled her closer. "Wow, baby. I'm sorry to hear about all of this. Do you want to fly out tonight or in the morning?"

Sommer closed her eyes, enjoyed the comfort his embrace brought. "I already talked to Walt. He switched our tickets. Mine and Livvie's. We're going to North Carolina in the morning instead of Texas."

"Without me?" Austin asked, surprised.

"You're flying out with the team. You guys have appearances and a parade in Dallas tomorrow. You're obligated to do those things, Austin. Especially as MVP."

"And you don't think I'd cancel that to be with you and Ms. Caroline?"

She raised her hand to stroke his cheek. "No. I know you would."

"So, what's the problem?"

"The problem is that right now, you can't."

"I can do whatever I want."

"But think of your fans."

"And you're my family."

She nibbled on her bottom lip. "At this point, I don't know what kind of shape my mother's in and I don't want to drag you into it until I know what I'm dealing with."

Austin shifted in the chair. "Interesting choice of words. *Drag* me into it."

"You know what I mean."

And he did know what she meant, but she wasn't understanding what *he* meant. What if, when she went home, her mother was in extremely bad shape? Then, he'd have to think about her being alone to handle that as well as take care of Livvie when it was his job to be there to help her shoulder the weight.

"Sommer, when two people love each other, they share the weight," he explained. "Everybody's got some kind of burden to bear and the more they take on, the heavier it gets. But, we're not mules. So when someone tells you that they love you, and they really love you, they're telling you to give them some of that weight. Just put a little of it on their shoulders. The more people you have around that love you, the more you can evenly distribute the load so that no one is left crushed."

He sighed and brought her fingers to his lips.

"Baby, you have your mother, Livvie, and you're still recovering from having a baby a little over a month ago. That's a lot of stress you're putting on yourself. Stress takes years off of your life and I want you around for a while, even years after I'm gone, so let me be there for you."

Sommer swallowed her tears. "I understand, I really do. I'm not shutting you out. Just let me go in first. See how things are. Then, we'll go from there."

He wasn't satisfied, but he also knew that he was fighting a losing battle. She wouldn't change her mind.

"How long will you be gone?" he resigned.

"Just a couple of days. Your mom's coming with me. We're going to try to convince my mom to come back to Dallas. Uncle Reese hired a new girl, Faye, who used to run her own bakery back in Louisiana. She's picking up the ropes pretty quickly, so I can't think of any excuse Mom could give me about not coming to Texas."

He buried a kiss in her hair. "Two days, Sommer. If you're gone any longer than that—"

"You're going to come find me," she finished.

"And then, I'm going to—"

"Drag me by my ankles to the plane, even if I throw a tantrum in the middle of the terminal."

He pressed another kiss into her hair. "Promise me that if it gets overwhelming, you'll call me. Doesn't matter what I'm doing, I'll come right to you. You and Livvie, you two are my life. My family. Appearances, parades, all of this shit? None of this is more important to me than you two."

Sommer nodded, forcing back another round of tears. "I know, Austin. I know."

They quietly looked out onto the city while he lazily stroked her arm, and she nestled herself deeper into his embrace. Then, his stomach growled.

"Let's go eat." Sommer eased out of his lap and pulled him up to stand. "I also ordered some dessert since you now know what a championship tastes like."

He grinned and tried to grab her around the waist, but she stepped out of his grasp and hurried inside. He chased her all the way to the table, then trapped her body between his arms against the glossy wood.

"Two days," he reiterated.

"Boy scout's honor," Sommer promised.

"Doesn't count if you weren't a boy scout."

"Then girl scout's honor."

He kissed her nose. "You were never a girl scout."

He moved so that she could slip out of his grasp, and they sat at the table to find the food surprisingly still warm.

"I was a girl scout," Sommer attested, digging into the salmon. "For two days."

"Oh, excuse me. My mistake."

She smiled and it still didn't reach her eyes, so he did his best to keep a smile on her face. However, he'd been dead serious. If in two days she wasn't on her way back to Dallas, he would go get them. Kicking and screaming, if he had to.

～

"AUSTIN'S NOT PICKING UP," SPORTS AGENT GARY WEST SAID, tossing his phone across the room. "Do you think he's seen them? The social media responses to Olivia?"

The other two gentlemen that had been pulled out of bed for the emergency meeting exchanged quizzical looks.

"And where's Selina?' Gary yelled. "She should be on top of this!"

"She's working on it," one of the men, Eric Oldson, said. "We're hoping that it blows over. It's no big deal."

"No big deal? Blows over? We're talking about Texas for crying out loud." Gary pointed at the second man, Ryan Townsend. "Tell me, what are people saying now?"

"The same stuff as before," Ryan answered. "We have people sending in messages that revolve around adoring Olivia, but then there's the nasty ones."

"And what about the web searches?"

"People are wondering if Austin is half-black, or if Olivia is half-black, but the biggest jump of all is a search for *Austin Riley's baby mama.*"

Gary grimaced. "But nothing else right now? No one's coming forth and saying that they know who she is?"

Eric shook his head. "Not as far as we can see."

Gary took a seat at the meeting table and clasped his hands on the tabletop. "Okay, good."

"There might be one issue though," Ryan spoke up. "Some people have inquired as to why Austin has been hiding Olivia's mother as though he's ashamed to say he had a baby with an African American woman. If that point of view picks up steam, we might have an issue."

Gary rhythmically tapped his fingers together. It was why he'd encouraged Austin to simply come out and say he and Sommer were together. People were going to see what they wanted to and all they needed was a little bit of rope. All companies needed was a little bit of negative press to end endorsement contracts.

"Well, if nothing's changed for right now, let's sleep on it," he suggested. "If it ends up on the network, we'll have Selina squash it. Get the focus back on the championship win."

The men rose, shook hands, and then returned to their rooms. Gary tried Austin a fourth time, and again the phone went to voicemail.

"Damnit."

He tossed his phone again, this time onto the bed. Austin was at the pinnacle of his career and had never had any indiscretions to speak of. For years, different media outlets had tried to find ways to portray him in a negative light with all of them failing. Many of his endorsement deals also relied on that good moral character, so all it would take at this point was someone with a single shred of information, although false, to make it appear that Austin was ashamed of Sommer. If they weren't careful, this small event could become a large controversy.

He flopped onto the bed. His stomach was uneasy, but it wasn't because of indigestion. Something big was coming, and he only hoped that whatever it was, their team either had a way to deflect it, or enough ammunition to fight it.

Chapter Eleven

When Reese picked Sommer, Olivia, and Emma up from the airport, from the look on his face alone, Sommer could tell that something wasn't quite right.

He'd remained stone-faced and silent on the entire ride as though battling something inside. Then, when they passed the medical center and headed in the direction of the Cherry Avenue, Sommer knew. Her mother wasn't in the hospital, which meant that she was at home... against doctor's orders.

The two-story house seemed foreign as they pulled into the driveway. Weeds grew up through cracks in the cement, and the hedges looked as though they hadn't been pruned in weeks. That had been the second indication that something was wrong. Caroline Hayes was an avid gardener. She handled her shrubs, flowers, bushes, and herbs with as much care as one would handle a newborn baby. There was no way a healthy Caroline would have left her *babies* looking so unkempt.

"Would you like me to stay outside?" Emma asked, reaching for Sommer's hand.

"I don't know anymore, Ms. Emma," Sommer said, the muscles in her throat sore from holding down fits of emotion. "I thought I could handle this, but this wasn't what I was expecting. She's not in the hospital."

"She left against doctor's orders," Reese said, telling Sommer what she'd already figured out. "Som, you need to talk to her. She's talking crazy."

Sommer glanced at the house. "Crazy how?"

"Like quitting crazy."

"You mean, like giving up?" Emma's grip tightened around Sommer's fingers. "You're not telling us everything, are you Reese?"

He shook his head, but didn't say anything more.

"I should've let Austin come." Sommer's gaze hovered over to Emma. "I was wrong. I can't do this alone."

Emma pushed the car door open. "You don't have to. I'm coming in with you."

Sommer mechanically exited the car and reached inside to remove Olivia from the car seat. Reese gently touched her hand.

"I'll bring her inside," he offered, removing the straps. "You two go on in."

Climbing the steps felt as though she was wading through a marsh. Her legs felt thick and heavy, and her chest tightened and expanded like elastic. Emma was holding her hand but she could no longer feel the woman's fingers. She couldn't feel much of anything outside of the sheer anxiety that mounted with each sluggish step.

When she pushed the door open, there lay the third indication that something was wrong and had been wrong for quite some time. Caroline Anne Hayes never kept a messy house. In all of Sommer's years, she'd never seen more than a few specks of wayward dust on the pristine oak cabinets. However, clothes were now strewn on the sofa and spilling onto the floor, the dining table was littered with envelopes, folders, and paperwork. Pots, pans, and dishes were piled high in the sink.

"You never checked on her?" Sommer asked as Reese walked in behind them with Olivia in his arms.

"I promise you, Sommer, I didn't know it was like this until I brought her home today. She kept coming over to me and Marcie's and we figured she was just lonely, so we didn't push it."

Sommer moved to the hallway. "She's in her room?"

Reese nodded.

"How did she look when you last saw her?"

His head fell. "Just go in, Som."

Sommer's eyes darted to Emma who nodded to help bolster her courage. Then, swallowing more nervous saliva down her quivering throat, Sommer pushed through the slightly ajar bedroom door.

Two lamps by the bedside were turned on. The window blinds were drawn shut. Scattered clothing spilled out of half-opened drawers and littered the bed. She found her mother on the mattress, slightly askew as if granting more room for the clothes than her own body. The covers, a pink and beige floral quilt, were pulled up to her chest and her soft curls were low on her head. As Sommer drew nearer, she saw sunken eyes and tired, grey-tinted skin.

"Why are you walking so slow?" Caroline's once strong and youthful voice was now a pained, hoarse squeak. "Come over here, Sommer."

Sommer moved closer, stumbling slightly before her knees were touching the side of the bed. She'd been dead wrong. She needed Austin.

"Mom, why did you lie to me? We talked just a few days ago. You said you were fine, doing well. You said your results looked promising."

Caroline reached for her daughter's hand. "I'm sorry I lied to you, honey, but I didn't want you worrying over nothing."

"Nothing?" Sommer gestured to her mother's frail body. "You call this *nothing?* Mom, I'm standing here looking directly at you and I can't even find you. I can't find your eyes, your voice, your face—"

"There wasn't much we could do." A tear spilled down Caroline's sunken cheek. "The chemo didn't work. I already knew the cancer spread. Months ago."

"So, when you were in town for Olivia's birth—"

"I knew."

"What else did you know?" Sommer hoped her mother didn't say what she felt was coming.

Caroline sighed. "Baby, I'm going to—"

"Don't you dare say die," Sommer snapped. "Don't you dare tell me that you're going to die."

"I've known for some time now, Sommer."

Pulling her hand from her mother's grasp, Sommer moved across the room. She was trembling, hard. The room was spinning and there didn't seem to be enough air to draw a breath.

She plastered her body into the corner. "Why would you keep this from me?"

"Because there was nothing I could do."

"You could have come to Dallas. I could have taken to you to see a specialist. Some of the top specialists in the nation."

Caroline motioned her daughter over, but Sommer didn't budge. She couldn't. At that moment, she couldn't even *will* her feet to move.

"Look, Sommer, we both already knew that this second time around was going to be difficult," Caroline said. "When my test results came back, I decided to focus on living the best life possible. That best life included seeing my daughter fall in love and start a family. If I'd told you I was sick, you would have been on the first flight out to Yearwood. But, you needed to be in Dallas. You needed to be with Austin."

"I needed to be here," Sommer contested. "Mom, I love Austin. I truly do. But no one can replace you."

"And no one can replace you, Sommer. How you see me right now is how Olivia will see you one day. She might even already see you that way. But, you're so stubborn and scared of everything that I had to push you to start your life. You're the only woman I know who was actually reluctant to start a family with the man she loves." Caroline motioned again. "Come over here, baby."

Sommer pushed herself off of the wall and over to the bed.

"Are you happy in Texas?" Caroline asked.

"I don't know anymore, Mom."

"Are you happy in Texas?" Caroline repeated.

"Yes ma'am."

"And how is Austin treating you?"

Sommer's eyes began to burn. "He's been perfect."

"And how about Olivia?"

"Even more perfect."

Caroline nodded. "Good. You'll be well taken care of."

The tears finally broke through their restraints and plummeted down Sommer's cheeks. "Taken care of?"

"When I'm gone," Caroline answered with more nonchalance than Sommer cared to hear.

"You're not going anywhere," Sommer argued, face contorting with grief. "You can't, Mom. Caroline Hayes, you're not going anywhere."

Tears rolled down the side of Caroline's face. She was on borrowed time, she knew. She'd known months ago that she didn't have very long left. It was only days now.

"Is Livvie here?" Caroline asked. "I want to see my grand-baby."

On cue, Emma appeared, her face moist and her nose red. Olivia was in her arms, innocent and fast asleep, and Emma's legs suddenly took on extra weight as she carried Olivia across the room to the bed.

Caroline pushed up into a sitting position and swatted at Sommer's hands when she tried to help. Emma gently placed Olivia into Caroline's arms and pressed a kiss against her dear friend's temple.

"Don't you breakdown on me, Em," Caroline teased, but the two other women didn't laugh. Couldn't laugh. It was as if Caroline couldn't see or hear how ill she sounded. Or, if she could hear it, it was if she didn't remotely care.

"So beautiful," Caroline cooed, finger brushing Olivia's chin. Olivia's eyes fluttered open and her brows came together as she looked up into her grandmother's face.

"This is your face, Sommer," Caroline said. "My goodness, it's like looking down at you when you were born. That first night I held you, life seemed perfect. I remember your beautiful eyes looking up at me, so big and brown. I fell in love with you over and over again. Gosh, how easy and perfect life seemed back then. Even your *father* had stared at the two of us like he was taking a mental photograph. Like he never wanted to forget that moment."

She ran her fingers over Olivia's soft black hair.

"I felt like I had all the time in the world back then. That my life would be filled with experiencing all of your firsts—first steps, first words, first day of kindergarten, first boyfriend. I could go on. And, for the most part, I was blessed with the ability to see most of them. I even got to see my first grand-baby. I just never expected to leave you so young..."

Her voice trailed off and a sob escaped from the back of Emma's throat.

"Caroline, why didn't you say anything?" Emma pleaded.

"There was nothing anyone could do," Caroline reiterated. "But, it's okay."

"It's not okay," Sommer cried. "You're sitting here acting as though everything is fine, but you're scared, Mom. *I'm* scared. Mommy, I need you. Mommy, *I love you*."

Caroline smiled and placed Olivia back into Emma's arms. Reaching forward, she wrapped her arms around Emma in a tight hug. Then, she looked toward Sommer.

"Come give your mother a hug, Sommer."

"Mom—"

"Sommer." Caroline's voice was stern. "Come over here and give your mother a hug."

Sommer walked over and climbed into the bed into her mother's loving embrace.

"You're coming back to Dallas with me," she demanded. "We're going to see an oncologist."

"Okay," Caroline replied, stroking her daughter's back.

"Then, when you're better, I'm going to take you to this seafood place in the city. They make these grilled scallops I know you'll love. You have to try them."

"Scallops are my favorite food," Caroline answered.

"Then, I'm going to take you to this Mom and Pop bakery me and Austin found. Their chocolate cake is out of this world. It's not too sweet and it has just the right amout of frosting. Whipped, homemade frosting too. Not the thick stuff."

Caroline kissed the top of her head. "I can't wait."

Then, everyone fell silent. As though sensing the tension in the room, Olivia's cries broke through the quiet and Sommer reluctantly pulled herself from her mother's grasp.

"She might be hungry," Sommer said, her voice echoing throughout her head. "I know I just fed her, but she might be hungry. Mom, what do you—"

When she turned around, Caroline was seizing on the bed.

"Reese," Emma called out and within seconds, he was at the door. "Call an ambulance."

He pulled out his phone and began to dial. Sommer, nearly blinded by tears, climbed onto the mattress and turned her mother over onto her side.

"Help's coming, Mom," she whispered. "They're on their way. Hang on. I love you. Hang on. *I love you...*"

∼

In five, four, three, two, one...

"AND WE'RE HERE, LIVE FROM THE CHAMPIONSHIP PARADE IN Dallas, Texas. I'm your host, Wendy Carter, and with me I have three special guests, all assured Hall-of-Fame contenders. Wide-receivers Trent Holloway and Cason Allen, and MVP quarterback, Austin Riley."

"Glad to be here, Wendy," all three men answered.

"And it's good to have you. So tell, me, are you guys still on the high from that win? I mean, game-winning touchdown in the last few seconds? What a performance!"

"It was intense," Cason said.

"But you all made it look so easy," Wendy replied. Trent laughed and flirtatiously ran his tongue over his lips. Somewhere, Alexandrina was fuming.

"It might have looked easy on the outside, but I could feel my fingers tingling," Trent added. "That last play was supposed to come to me because Pittsburgh had been on Case all night, but it was as if they sniffed out the play. I had three defenders in my face."

"Yeah, that blitz came in pretty strong," Wendy chimed in. "But you read right through that, didn't you Austin?"

"I did," Austin said, succinct and ignoring the way her pupils grew whenever she looked at him. Seven years in the league, numerous interviews with Wendy, and still, she didn't seem to get the hint that he wasn't interested.

"So tell me, Cason," she redirected. "When that ball was whizzing through the air, what was on your mind?"

Cason smiled. "My parents. My sister, Jasmine. My team. Everything just started to stream through my mind. Then, there was Amelia. I don't know that I would have made it through all of this in one piece without her."

Austin patted his friend on the back.

"That's beautiful," Wendy acknowledged, nodding. Then she looked toward Austin again and tried not to lose herself in the glimmering depths of his irises.

"Austin, easily one of the greatest performances of the post-season, yet people aren't buzzing about any of that. What they're talking about is the darling little girl you introduced us to after the game. Can we get a shot of Miss Olivia Camden Riley?"

A still of Olivia's small face adorned by a pink, flower headband was displayed on the screen, followed by a chorus of "awws" from parade onlookers.

"Beautiful." Wendy smiled. "But, as you know by now, the internet and social media scene has been abuzz with knowing something else."

A man held up a five finger countdown and Wendy turned to the camera.

"After the break, we'll talk more about the mother of this charming little baby girl."

And, cut!

Austin rose from his seat to grab a quick drink of water, and Wendy grabbed his forearm before he could make it to the refreshment table.

"She's beautiful, Austin," she whispered. "Olivia. She's an absolute darling."

"Thank you," he replied.

"So, who's her mother? I mean, not too long ago you looked pretty cozy at an airport terminal with Jessica Costa, and now you appear on national TV with a baby girl that looks like you and, I don't know, Tyra Banks could have made her."

"Lay off of it, Wendy," Gary called, approaching them from the far end of the set. "We already agreed to give you everything on air. Isn't that enough?"

Wendy scoffed. "If he's going to tell the world anyhow, why not just tell me now?"

Gary flitted his fingers. "Run back to your little group of sharks while you still have some credibility left in this city as a respected journalist. My sister became an anchor for a major news network without once flopping onto her back. Maybe you could have at least tried to have done the same."

Wendy clenched her fists, but she walked away without responding. Austin watched her go and wondered what had made her think that they ever had a chance together given her reputation.

He popped the top on a bottle of water and took a swig before turning toward Gary.

"Ready for this?" Gary asked, genuine concern outlining his features.

"I am."

Austin opened his mouth to say more, but Gary's phone buzzed in his pocket. Gary smiled when he saw Emma Riley's phone number, but his smile quickly faded once he put the phone to his ear. Then, he held the phone out toward Austin.

"It's your mother," he told him.

"What happened, Ma?" Austin answered.

"She couldn't call you," Emma began, her voice quivering. "And I couldn't reach you on your phone."

"Who couldn't call me? Sommer? Is something wrong?"

In the background, he heard the familiar clamor of a hospital emergency room.

"Things were worse than we anticipated," Emma added.

Suddenly, in the background, a scream pierced through the speaker. Sommer's scream.

Austin's chest squeezed. This was exactly what he'd been trying to avoid.

"Was that Sommer?" His eyes darted around the set. Across the room, a man signaled that he had one minute left before they went back live.

"She wouldn't call you," Emma reiterated, her voice now muffled with tears. "But, she needs you, Austin."

Austin loosened the tie around his neck. "I'm on my way."

He tossed the phone to Gary.

"Everything okay?" Gary asked.

"No. I have to go. Family emergency. Wrap up here for me?"

"I'll handle it," Gary reassured with a nod.

Wendy noticed him walking toward the exit and hurried after him as fast as her four-inch Manolos could carry her.

"Austin, wait up." She grabbed his arm right before he reached the door. "Where are you going? We're back on live in a few seconds. You can't leave."

"I have a family emergency, Wendy," he answered.

"Family emergency, or are you just trying to get out of telling the world who Olivia's mother is? Are you ashamed that you had a baby with a *black* woman, Austin? You're okay with presenting your mixed child to the world, but not her brown mother?"

For one brief second, Austin wished that Wendy was a man just so he could comfortably punch her in the face.

Refusing to dignify her accusation with a response, he turned and left the set. There was only one thing he could think of that would cause Sommer to scream out in pure grief like that, and he hoped to God he was wrong about that one thing.

He disappeared down the hallway, and Wendy folded her arms across her chest.

"Where's Austin going?" one of the producers asked, tugging at his headset.

Wendy shot him a look of pure contempt, spun around, stomped a heel, and released a shrill curse into the air.

∽

IT WAS NIGHTTIME BEFORE AUSTIN FINALLY ARRIVED IN YEARWOOD. He briefly stopped at his mother's house to give Olivia a kiss before she was put down for the night, and did his best to ignore the solemn look on his mother's face. He'd even refused to ask her what was wrong when she broke down in his arms, still unready to hear the news. For some reason, he wanted it to come from Sommer.

Emma, understanding, had resigned herself to sobbing lightly into his chest. Then, she'd told him that Sommer had left her with Olivia to go off to have a few moments by herself. However, no one knew exactly where she'd gone.

After he was sure the two would be okay, he set back out to see if he could figure out where Sommer had gone. According to Reese, she hadn't gone back to Cherry Avenue as her mother's house now stood drearily on the lot as though all life had been sucked from it. So, on a whim, he headed for the bakery although it had closed about an hour before his flight had landed.

There were no cars out front, but one of the lights to the kitchen in the back was on. He walked up to the door and pulled the handle to find it unlocked, then navigated his way around the front, guided only by light coming in from one of the posts on the street. When he approached the door that led to the kitchen, he knocked.

"Go away," Sommer's voice came through, robbed of all its strength.

"It's me, Sommer," he said. "Can I come in?"

There was silence for a few seconds, then a quiet, "Yes."

When he pushed the door open, she was sitting on the floor with her back pressed against the large, wooden island that sat in the middle of the kitchen. In front of her on the floor was a large pie with a few slices cut out of it, and a half-eaten slice on a plate in her lap. Her hair was pulled back into a disheveled ponytail with a few wisps falling out of the elastic tie, and her face was stained by streaks of tears.

Austin slid onto the floor next to her. Sommer reached into one of the island's built-in cabinets, pulled out a second plate and fork, and roughly cut him a slice of what he recognized as Caroline's signature chocolate pie with whipped cream and coconut flakes. She would make a fresh batch every Friday evening right before the dinner crowd rushed in, and the pies were always cleaned out by the end of the night with people begging her to make them available more than one evening per week.

The fact that Sommer was sitting in her mother's bakery and eating the dessert that she was best known for, only meant one thing.

"When?" Austin asked, accepting the portion she offered.

"Two forty-two this afternoon," Sommer barely got out.

"What happened?"

"Brain herniation." She stuffed a piece of pie into her mouth. "Cancer spread to her brain."

Silence.

"And you?" Austin asked.

Sommer's throat quivered as she swallowed. "Devastated."

He wanted to reach out to her and pull her into his chest, drain all of her sadness into his body, but it wasn't time yet.

"Talk to me."

She leaned forward and cut another sliver of pie. "I wasn't there when she needed me. I was in Dallas, playing house. I should have been here. Being a daughter."

It stung him to hear her refer to their arrangement as "playing house" when it was clearly more than that.

"I had duties here." She cut another slice without even touching the first one. "Responsibilities. But what did I do? I shucked them and got knocked up by the first guy that came along. Then, I had the audacity to think I deserved a happily ever after."

Austin set aside his slice. "Don't do this to yourself, Sommer."

She reached to cut off a third slice to add to her other two uneaten pieces, but she cut the wedge too thin, causing it to break in half.

In a fit of anger, she tossed the knife across the room, pushed the plate aside, and finally looked over at him. When he opened his arms, she fell right into them, releasing all of the emotion she'd been keeping pent up inside. She gripped his shirt and he fastened his arms around her, pulling her into his chest. Restraining his own feelings at the sight of her devastation, he cleared his throat and pressed kisses into her hair.

"She knew she was dying," she forced between tears. "And I've been sitting here for the past two hours trying to think of the reason she would keep that from me. Why she wouldn't tell me she was dying. Then, when I can't come up with a reason, at least a reason I can accept, I get so mad, Austin. I get so pissed. She didn't give me a chance to help her, didn't even give me a chance to prepare. She waited until she was on her deathbed to call me when she *promised* she would reach out for help when she really needed it."

Sommer thought back to the day they'd hooked pinkies right there in the kitchen.

"But, no matter how much I want to be angry at her for not giving me the chance to help her, I get it. I get it, Austin. I was sitting here thinking about what if this had happened and I had no one to be there for me. No Ms. Emma, no Olivia, no you..."

Her voice trailed off.

"Baby, I'm so sorry." He struggled to find the right words. "I know how close you were with Ms. Caroline. Right now, you probably feel like there's no future to this world. I mean, how do you go on living when a part of you has died? Who can answer that for you?"

She shook her head. "I don't know, Austin."

"Well, what do you think your mother would want you to do?"

She shrugged. "I think...I think she would want me to mourn her loss and keep her close to my heart. She'd want me to think about the little girl fast asleep right now at your mother's house, the same little girl who shows me the world whenever I look into her eyes. Then, she'd want me to think about you. The way you're always there for me regardless of whatever else it is you have going on, and the way you sat here on the floor with me instead of trying to pull me up. How you got down to my level and let me grieve instead of trying to pull me out of my misery."

Austin pressed his lips into her hair.

"Austin, I want to be pissed at her for not giving me the chance to try to have her around for a few more years, but every time I try, all I do is miss the way she smells, the way we joked together, the way she looked at me like I was a priceless treasure—"

"Which you are," Austin cut in. "She looked at you that way because you are. To her, to me, and to Livvie."

"Which...I am," she echoed, her voice low. "As much as I try to be mad at her, I realize that I can only be thankful for the way she pushed me, the opportunity she gave me to see a new place and to fall in love with you and Livvie. And, I know that I'll be this way for a while, sad and heartbroken over the fact that I'll never be able to hold my mother again. But there's this weird calm that comes over me whenever I think about her."

She placed a hand on her chest.

"She's still here, Austin. My mother has always lived in my heart. And, because of that, she'll never be gone. She lives on through me, through Livvie, and the lives she's touched. God, Austin, I miss her, but it fills me with so much joy, *so* much joy, to know that she's still with me, in my heart, and that she's no longer in pain."

Austin pressed a few more kisses into the top of her head. "You are an amazing woman, Sommer Hayes," he told her. "And I'm with you every step of the way."

She squeezed him tighter and cried into his shirt. Austin laid his cheek on top of her head and let her grieve without saying a word. This was what she needed, a rock to support her when the weight on her shoulders became unbearable. She didn't need fumbled words of consolation. All she'd needed was to hold on to something that wouldn't move and would never leave, no matter what life threw their way. No matter what curveball fate had in store for them.

However, he could have never planned for the curveball, the distortion of his past, that would come barreling their way.

Chapter Twelve

The year was 1954.

It was a raging Friday afternoon in Montgomery, Alabama with temperatures exceeding the high nineties for the fifth day in a row. Four boys sat in the Montgomery County Courthouse in white collared shirts and tailored black jackets, none of them older than the age of sixteen. Curious onlookers filled the streets, divided, some with furrowed brows of perspiration and others with looks of hope and righteousness.

Inside, the courtroom was packed to the hilt. Twelve jurors sat complacently in the juror's box as the verdict was delivered to presiding judge Theodore Walcott. With a pert nod, the judge turned his attention to the foreman and the rest of the room followed suit. Breaths were hushed and the room was so still that the racing thumps of the four boys' hearts could be heard reverberating around the room.

"And what say you, foreman?" Walcott asked.

"We, the jury, find the defendants not guilty, your honor."

The room erupted in cheer. On the street, those who previously sported looks of hope were now awash with indignation.

A lone cry pierced through the sky.

Four men rushed to the aid of the woman who fell, her face hidden beneath beads of sweat, grief, and sorrow. Her name was Helena Cartwright, a thirty-four year old widow from New York City who had moved to Alabama with her ten-year old son to live with family after her husband died from tuberculosis.

The next day, Saturday morning papers sported that justice had been served. However, justice was nowhere present in that courtroom for Helena Cartwright. You see, the four boys who pleaded and streamed tears of innocence in the courtroom were on trial for the murder of her young son, Henry Cartwright. The ten-year old was last seen on the morning of October 10th, 1953 playing in the street in front of his grandmother's house.

Turning her back for a brief second, Helena had stepped inside to retrieve a coat for her son, but by the time she'd come back to the front, Henry had already gone missing.

Henry's body would turn up four days later.

The only witness, a shut-in named Frances Tyler, claimed that he'd seen Henry playing when four boys came up to him and asked him if he'd like to join them. Only ten at the time, Henry had been intrigued by the older boys' invitation and had followed them down the street in the direction of the wooded area where his body was later found. Frances identified the four boys as Charles "Charlie" Mason, John Cronar, James Faveratti, and William "Willie" Riley.

Gary looked up from his newspaper when the reporter recited the last name.

William "Willie" Riley is none other than the father of Dallas Quarterback Austin Riley. The same William Riley that Austin led us to believe had died. However, the man is still alive and well, and living somewhere deep in the recesses of the same Alabama neighborhood that rallied around his indiscretions sixty years ago.

THE GAME OF LOVE

Gary picked up his phone. "Selina?"

"I see it," Selina Mercado answered. "Where's Austin? Is he seeing this?"

"No," Gary answered. "He's in North Carolina. At a funeral."

Why is this news, you ask? Well, just a few days ago, Austin Riley revealed to the world that he was the father of a precious, chubby-cheeked baby girl. Searches surged the next day for the mother in question, mostly because the girl shared only two traits with her father: his unusual eye-color and his dark hair. However, as the QB's long, bandaged finger stroked his daughter's cheek, there was a marked difference. Olivia Camden Riley's skin is the color of a creamy latte and obviously, quite a bit darker than her father's.

This can only mean one thing: little Olivia's mother is a black woman. So why, we ask, wasn't this woman there? Why didn't Austin present his child and his daughter's mother to the world after his triumphant win? Also, why is it that just minutes before he was purported to talk about Olivia's mother live with Wendy Carter at the Championship parade, he left the set?

That's what the world has been wondering, Austin, mostly because of your high profile and highly visible relationship with Brazilian supermodel, Jessica Costa, and your brief affair with French violinist, Victoria Ellington. Those relationships were unconcealed. Those relationships were public. Why keep this one in the shadows?

The reporter smirked.

Oh, right. William Riley. Your father. The same father that you tried to keep hidden because you didn't want the world to know what you're a product of. You didn't want the world to find out about your roots, a dark heritage we can only assume you still carry in your heart. But, a source close to us has already done the groundwork for you, Austin.

A smiling picture of Sommer appeared on the screen.

177

> Olivia's mother's name is Sommer Hayes. Sommer is also from the same small, distinctively diverse town in North Carolina where Austin grew up. So, as you can see, from her beautiful brown skin to her shining brown eyes, she is a black woman. But that's not the part that I find the most disturbing. It's the part where she's more than that. She's an extremely stunning woman with looks to rival that of, and triumph over, both Jessica and Victoria's. So why, then, would Austin keep her hidden?

The second picture that appeared was Luke's snapshot. It showed a picture of all four boys sitting in a barn. William and John were on the left, Charlie was in the middle, and James was on the right. Charlie was holding up a copy of the newspaper broadcasting their acquittal on the front cover, and on the plain white t-shirt he wore, written haphazardly in black paint, were the words, "We did it."

> While we don't want to jump to any conclusions, Austin, this reeks of shame. It reeks of Emmett Till and similar injustices that are blemishes on the porcelain face of American history. We can't wait to hear your side of the story. But, in the meantime, we'll just let this picture soak in.

Gary picked up his phone and began to frantically dial Austin's number. When the call went to voicemail, his eyes flicked toward the clock on the wall. Sommer's mother's funeral service had begun about a half hour ago, so Austin wasn't likely to turn his phone back on for at least the next hour. In the meantime, that gave a horde of media outlets a head start to Yearwood.

"Selina, I need a jet," he barked into the phone. "Meet me in thirty minutes. We need to get to Yearwood and head this off. In the meantime, prepare a statement for the press."

Selina rose from her desk. "I'm on it, Gary."

"And Selina?" Gary shrugged on his blazer. "Austin told me about Sommer the minute he flew her to Dallas to live with him. He's not what they're trying to make him out to be. He loves her. Keep that in mind."

Selina nodded. "Got it. See you in a few."

Gary ended the call, grabbed his briefcase, and bound out of the door.

~

Twelve reporters had already congregated outside the modest white church before an entire hour had passed. Cameras were still in the process of being set up, and men and women with microphones in hand were being prepped to begin shooting live. Behind the congregation of reporters, vans, and manmade blockades, a crowd formed. Some were passing by and stopped at the sight of the commotion while others, after seeing the report on the news, had come to either show their support for the couple, or their contempt: for Austin, and how he had kept Sommer a secret as though ashamed of her, or for Sommer and how she'd shamelessly allowed herself to be subjugated by him.

Inside the church, none was the wiser until Caleb Yearwood, the youngest of the town's family namesake, received a notification on his phone. As he bent to quickly read the message, a man in a brown suit walked by one of the lancet windows of the church, causing half of those in attendance to look up. A woman in a dark blue suit followed him, the news logo on the microphone in her hand clearly visible.

Murmurs soon drowned out Reese's eulogy at the front of the room as more checked their phones, gasping when they read the news story. Dozens of eyes went to where Austin and Sommer sat in the front row, his long arm draped across the back of the bench and around her shoulders. As the weight of the stares began to grow heavy, they both turned.

"What's going on?" Austin asked, his eyes connecting with numerous gazes around the room.

"You're not going to like this," Caleb warned, moving over to the aisle where they sat. He handed his phone to Austin.

"What is it?" Sommer peered at the phone's screen. Instinctively, Austin moved the phone out of her line of sight, but as more people began to shadow the windows around the building, he realized she was going to find out anyhow. It was better that she found out from him than from the slew of reporters waiting to greet them outside.

He handed her the phone. "I'm sorry."

Sommer only needed to read the first three sentences before she felt as though the floor of the church had dissolved beneath her feet.

She handed the phone back to Caleb, hand trembling. Austin reached for her, but for the very first time, she pulled away. Then, she mechanically scooped Olivia out of Emma's arms and walked to the front of the room where Reese stood. Unsatisfied, Austin started after her, but she sent him a look that told him not to come any closer.

"Not a good time," she cautioned.

"Sommer, I didn't know that any of this was—"

"Not a good time," she repeated, louder. "I'm standing in the middle of my mother's funeral, for one, and I was about to unknowingly walk into a crowd full of reporters ready to rush me, denigrate me, and," she gestured toward Caleb's phone, "ask me about how I feel about being compared to Sally Hemings. *This is not a good time.*"

Austin's chest felt as though it was being crushed beneath a heavy weight. "You can't put all of this on me, Sommer."

"What am I supposed to do here, Austin?"

"Not put all of this on me," he repeated. "I wanted everyone to know about us when you were still pregnant with Livvie. You were the one who didn't want me to say anything."

"Because of this, Austin. I was afraid that something like this would happen. Kyle was right. You're the darling of Texas. People have been waiting for the right moment to wrap you in a scandal, and—"

"Sommer," he yelled, cutting her off. "I don't give a damn what those people think. I never have. You matter. Olivia matters. You don't get to dismiss me just because you're upset. You only get to do that if you can tell me the last time I put the needs of the *media* before yours. Or, if you can tell me about the times I wasn't there for you. You only get to dismiss me if you can tell me about the times I told you I loved you and didn't mean it."

Sommer clenched her jaw. She didn't have to search her mind for an answer as he'd never done any of those things. However, the thought of him being anywhere near her at that moment made all of her hairs stand on end. Together, they created catastrophe and she was hanging on by a thread. She *couldn't* handle this right now.

"Didn't think so," he said, resolute. "So, why are you pushing me away right now?"

He stepped closer and again. Reese shook his head to indicate that he didn't want him any closer to his niece.

"I need a moment," Sommer answered.

"And you can't take a moment with me?"

"A moment alone. Just to step away from this. To step away from everything."

"Sommer," he closed his eyes, "it's not just you and me anymore."

Sommer glanced down at Olivia. "I know."

"So what are you saying?"

"Don't make me say it, Austin."

The pressure in his chest increased. "Wait, are you actually saying that you don't want us to be together anymore?"

She looked away. She didn't know what she was saying but them together, at least right now, didn't feel like the right answer. If she listened to her heart, Austin was the solution to everything, but her heart was still blackened, not yet recovered from losing the first love of her life. Her mother.

"Answer me, Sommer, because I *know* you're not saying that you're prepared to throw away everything we've worked for and worked toward because of some false accusation."

"Sweetheart." Emma reached for her son's elbow, but he shrugged away.

"Sixty-seconds?" Austin asked. "A few nights ago, you told me about the things that your mother gave you. A chance at a family. The chance to let yourself fall in love with me. And now, all it took was sixty seconds for none of that to mean anything anymore?"

His shimmering eyes darkened to an even matte.

"Why did you bring Olivia out?" Sommer asked. "Why didn't you talk to me first? Do you understand how big of a mess this is? How big of a mess we seem to cause?"

Austin reached into his pocket, pulled out a small black box, and tossed it to Reese.

"I've been carrying that box around ever since the game," he explained. "The reason I didn't talk to you first is because you were supposed to be on the field with me. Ma and Amelia were supposed to bring you and Livvie down."

Reese opened the box and several people in the crowd gasped. Sommer's angry front crumbled when she saw the crystal clear, princess-cut, diamond solitaire engagement ring.

"Then, there on national TV, in front of millions of viewers, I was going to ask you to be my wife." He turned to the room. "They're going to want to interview as much of you as possible, and while I don't really care what you say about me or my father, don't you dare drag Sommer's name through the mud. I have *never* been ashamed of my feelings for her. Understand that."

The double doors in the back of the church opened and Gary walked in with Selina on his heels. The duo shook their heads and tossed out rehearsed lines to reporters who tried to push past them, then closed the doors on the chaos.

"The version of me that has to live without you doesn't exist, Sommer," Austin added, glancing back to Sommer. "I won't let you run."

Gary's eyes landed on Selina. "Before we go out here and take on these reporters, get someone to take Sommer, Olivia, and Emma out through the back and away from all the cameras. Also, have someone secure the burial site. Funeral services aren't seen as sacred to those hounds out there sniffing around for a good story, so make sure Sommer still has the chance to give her mother a proper goodbye."

Selina nodded and lifted a phone to her ear. Seconds later, two large men entered the church through the back entrance, and two more guarded the doors at the front.

"The usual lines?" Austin asked, loosening his tie and walking past Gary to the doors.

"Family privacy, difficult time, yada yada," Gary rehearsed, following him. Selina brought up the rear and the minute they walked through the double doors, all three were engulfed by reporters.

When the doors closed, Sommer drew her attention back to the room. She noticed phones discreetly being tucked away, having already captured the scene that had occurred just a few minutes prior. Soon, videos would be plastered all over the internet and she hoped they'd recorded the essence of what Austin had said, and the way he'd bared his feelings in front of a room full of people without a care about who knew how he felt.

The true Austin.

She also hoped they'd missed the way she'd shied away from him whenever he tried to come closer as though he'd been the one to blame for all that was happening.

He'd been right.

If she hadn't been so afraid of *everything*, none of this would have happened. Even if people had made remarks about who he'd chosen to love and start a family with, if they had only come out in the beginning, the press would have never been able to spin the story to the extreme where Austin came out looking like a bigot.

"Who wants to leave can leave," she announced. "Who wants to stay, we're proceeding to the burial site. You can either choose to pay your respects or talk to reporters. It's up to you. My choice is to say goodbye to my mother and lay her to rest. In peace."

She and Emma trailed the two men through the back of the church, and Caleb stood in for Austin as pallbearer. Everyone in the congregation followed.

"Sommer," Reese called, tossing over the ring box. She caught it and held it firmly in her grasp.

"Don't be stupid," he encouraged.

Nodding, she slipped the box into her purse before disappearing through the back doors.

Chapter Thirteen

William let the brown vinyl blinds fall one by one from his finger as he turned away from the window. Three weeks. It had taken them three whole weeks to find him out there in rural Alabama when he'd practically gift-wrapped everything for that reporter Luke Maisley. Granted, he probably hadn't been the easiest person to locate, but he'd seen the news media track down criminals who'd been on the run for decades. Hell, he wasn't Jimmy Hoffa's remains.

He stood in the mirror and straightened his tie. The salesgirl at the mall had been right when she'd suggested that he wear the red tie against his white shirt and navy blazer. Adding khaki pants, he didn't look like a man who'd spent the last decade of his life in a tortured relationship with Jack Daniels and Jim Beam.

Smoothing back his hair one final time, he opened the door and was greeted by the hot, white flash of a camera lens. Additional news vans raced down the street and soon, the entire avenue had been blocked off. Inwardly, he was smiling, but outwardly, William expertly fabricated an expression of pure shock. He wildly glanced around at all the cameras and shielded his face as reporters ran forward.

"William Riley?" they all seemed to ask in unison.

"Yes, I am William Riley," he said. "What is all of this?"

"Haven't you been watching the news, William?" a woman in a black blazer and purple top asked.

"Do you know Sommer Hayes?" a slightly older gentleman asked.

William's eyes settled on the woman. He knew how these things worked. For the last two weeks, he'd seen how the world could go from loving someone, namely Austin, to turning him into a martyr. And although he loved his son, this was the very thing he'd warned the boy about.

History was like a bell curve. Just because people were now accepting mixed relationships and gays could marry, it didn't mean that things would not eventually return to status quo. Gays once ran rampant beforehand in the land of Sodom and Gomorrah, but look at what had happened there.

His eyes trailed over the woman's brown skin and long lashes. "I'll talk to you," he said, turning to the gentleman. "What do you want to know?"

The man smiled triumphantly. "Good to hear. Richard Morrison from Sports Tonight. First, have you been watching the news?"

"I have," William replied, twiddling his thumbs. "Can't say I too much like what you all have been saying about my boy."

"But that same boy of yours had us all convinced that you were dead. Do you have any comments about his relationship with the woman now identified as Sommer Hayes?"

"Like what?"

"Like, did you know about it?"

"I haven't talked to Austin since he was about thirteen years old."

Richard seemed surprised. "Is it because he found out about the conviction?"

"I was never convicted, so get your facts straight. And I'm not sure when he found out about that. We haven't talked since I was run out of Yearwood."

"What do you mean run out of Yearwood?" Richard continued to question.

"I mean, it just so happened that a relative of the mother of the boy who died lived in Yearwood and recognized me one day at the market. She threatened to blow the story wide open if I didn't leave town, saying something about how she couldn't stand living just a few streets over from me. By then, me and my ex-wife had already filed for divorce."

Richard's brows came together. "Henry Cartwright."

"What?"

"The boy who died, his name was Henry Cartwright."

"Anyhow," William waved away the assertion, "I don't have anything more to say at this time. I'll only tell the whole story if I get the chance to sit down with my son, daughter, and ex-wife."

"And what about Sommer Hayes?"

William scrunched his nose. "I don't need to talk to her."

"But, she's the mother of your grandchild."

"Allegedly."

Richard's face flushed. He struggled to quell his anger. "If I can ask one more thing, Mr. Riley?"

William nodded.

"Austin has been mum about this issue for three weeks. Since his request for privacy outside of the church in Yearwood, his camp has been trying to appease us with rehearsed responses. Sommer Hayes has also seemingly disappeared. No one has been giving us a straight answer. In your opinion, why do *you* think Austin failed to introduce the world to his daughter's mother, but readily did so with his daughter?"

William stuffed a hand into his pocket and pretended to think for a minute. He knew that his next few words were crucial, so he decided to choose them wisely.

"Well," he began, "even though we haven't spoken in over fifteen years, I still know my son. I know my boy. He's a man cut from the very same cloth that his father was cut from. I mean, these things are delicate in this day and age with Civil Rights and Affirmative Action and whatnot. And men, we were made to procreate. To spread our seed. Sometimes, one of those seeds take root. You can't help who it's with. But you've seen the baby. Olivia. She's a doll. She's a part of him. He had to show *her* off."

Richard further suppressed his disdain for the man standing in front of him. "So, are you saying that Austin is ashamed of Sommer's race?"

William held up a hand and headed back toward his front door. Richard started after him, but William whistled through his teeth, bringing a snarling Gus to the front of the house.

"No more questions," William restated. "Like I said, I won't answer anything else unless I can talk to my family. Any further questions can be answered through my lawyer. At least, once I get one."

He ushered Gus inside and then slammed the door shut behind him. Never did he think that answering a few questions could result in this type of a rush, but even his hands were shaking. Now, all he had to do was wait.

Years ago, when Austin was in middle school, he'd gotten detention for some foolish display of reciting poetry and tossing a rose at Sommer's feet. Clarita Waters, Austin's teacher at the time, had called the house to let William and Emma know about Austin's behavior, and that Austin had stolen the rose from her cherished anniversary bouquet. Emma had actually found the display "cute," which had been her exact terminology, but he'd been furious.

So, that day after school while Emma and Arielle were away, he'd taken Austin out back to teach him a lesson. Then, he'd explained to him about the complexities of the world and that, although it might feel uncomfortable to think about at first, having feelings for someone like Sommer would ruin his chances at ever being successful, as well as his chances for upward mobility.

He'd assumed that the boy had listened to his advice when, during draft day, it had only been Arielle and Emma there with him. He was even more proud when he'd seen the relationship between Austin and Jessica as Jessica had been an exceptional choice for a mate. But now, he'd gone and messed up. He'd fallen back into Sommer's trap and had let her use him in an attempt to raise her social status.

William looked down at Gus. "They'll get me that interview with Austin, Arielle, and Emma. The news people, they just have a way of working these things out. Maybe then I'll be able to get Austin to put his head back on straight to provide financially for his daughter, but then move on to build a real family. Arielle didn't listen and ended up having four half-breed children with that boy, Justin. Bet he's not doing a damn thing with his life right now."

He scratched behind Gus' ear.

"I tried to warn those kids, but they're hardheaded just like their mother. You'd think a little bit of education would help, but just like all those years ago, they think they know everything. Now, look at how everything is unfolding, Gus, and tell me, who do you think was right?"

Gus whimpered, walked to the other side of the room, flopped down onto his bed, and placed a paw over his nose.

～

"THANKS FOR PICKING US UP ON SUCH SHORT NOTICE, WALT," Sommer thanked, slipping into the black Town car.

"You don't have to thank me, Sommer." Walt waved in the rearview mirror at Olivia who was wide awake and strapped into the car seat next to her mother. "I'm just relieved that you were able to avoid those reporters. Those people are too nosy for their own good. They need to leave you and Olivia alone."

"I wish they would too," Sommer agreed, "but Austin hasn't released any further public statements and I've been hiding out at Arielle's for the past three weeks. The only thing that prevented them from finding me there was Arielle's sharp tongue and Justin's law degree. That didn't mean they still weren't parked on the street like a police protective detail."

Walt shook his head. "So, are you telling me that you weren't able to even go outside while you were at Arielle's?"

"No sir," Sommer answered with a sigh. "If it weren't for the huge trees in their backyard, we wouldn't have even been able to go out back. Three weeks and you'd think these people would have had their fill, but it's as if the wound is only being dug deeper."

Walt started the engine. "They want blood. They want Austin to come out and explain himself. But, I don't think that this is such a bad thing."

Sommer's brow shot up. "How's that?"

Walt peered into the side mirror as he pulled out into the departing lane. "I think that what you and Austin have is a chance to spark some important dialogue in this country. For people to look at themselves and wonder either why they can't accept that Austin genuinely does love you, or why they are disturbed by your relationship. I have lived a lot of years and I've seen plenty of things, but sometimes I still have to find a newspaper somewhere to make sure that I'm truly living in the twenty-first century."

Sommer looked out onto the moving landscape. "I can only imagine what you've seen, Walt."

"And there's even more world for your eyes to see, yougin,'" he added with a chuckle. "Then even more for Olivia who hasn't seen a full year on this Earth yet. Muhammad Ali once said that 'it's not the mountains ahead to climb that wear you out; it's the pebble in your shoe.' Now, think about the world that you'd like for Olivia to grow up in. Ask yourself if you would rather toss that pebble into a river and watch as it creates ripples, changes throughout the current and throughout time, or would you prefer that it stay in your shoe, bothering you for years to come?"

He briefly met her eyes in the rearview mirror and Sommer swallowed tears as she studied the sheer innocence of her daughter's face.

"Thank you, Walt," she answered with a grateful smile.

Walt returned the gesture, winked at her, and turned his attention back to the road.

∼

"So, you're telling me that Alexandrina told you about Sommer, and then you told Kyle?" Austin asked Jessica from across his kitchen counter.

"Yes," Jessica answered with a pert nod.

"And you think that Kyle was the one who told that tabloid reporter, Luke Maisley?"

"Luke is always writing stories about Kyle, some of which I'm sure Kyle handfed to him."

Austin paused to piece the information together. "It makes sense since Kyle is from Yearwood and would definitely know that my father's still live. What doesn't make sense is the connection between you and Kyle. How do you two know each other?"

Jessica lifted the steaming cup to her lips. Even after everything she'd done to him, Austin had still been enough of a gentleman to offer her a warm cup of tea.

"We did a magazine shoot together a couple of years back. He asked me out a few times, but I turned him down. Kyle, he is...aggressive. Plus, he is the type that wanders."

Her gaze fell into her cup. She prepared herself for a rebuttal about her also being the type that wandered. However, it didn't come and she found that slightly disappointing.

"But why would Kyle want that information to come out?" Austin asked. "We've never had any bad blood, so I don't get why he'd mastermind an entire smear campaign against me."

Jessica shrugged. "I can't answer that either, but he seemed pretty upset when I mentioned Sommer's name. Did they date, maybe?"

Austin shook his head, but then realized that he wasn't certain.

He'd assumed that Kyle's flirtation toward Sommer and his defensiveness that night at her mother's house were part of Kyle's Lothario-style personality. The man wanted nearly anything with breasts. However, there was a possibility that it could have gone deeper than that.

Austin's mind then ran to Sommer's words that night on the beach. About being used up and tossed aside like trash.

"I'll get to the bottom of everything," he said. "But is that the only reason you came here tonight? To tell me that?"

When Jessica looked up, she saw a flash of desire flicker in his eyes and nearly choked on her sip of tea. She'd read him all wrong. He *did* still want her.

"Maybe." She placed the cup on the marble countertop. "Unless there's something else that you have in mind."

"You don't have a moral bone in your body, do you?" Austin spat.

"But I thought—"

"What'd you think, Jessica? That I still wanted you? You're no different from the people out there claiming that I can't possibly really love Sommer because we have different complexions."

"That's not true," she argued. "I just don't like thinking that there's no possibility for you and me anymore."

"You may not like thinking it, but it's true."

"I know it's true." She pushed the mug out of arm's reach. "I mean, people have dragged me into this too. Asking me if your affair with Sommer was the real reason for my tryst with Walter Remos, and if it's been going on for longer than speculated."

"And you've been handling that pretty well," Austin said, surprising her. "I appreciate that you didn't take this as a chance to drag either one of our names through the mud. Thank you, for that."

She tugged on the sleeve of her pullover sweater. "When I ran into you and your sister at that burger restaurant, I knew that what you said was true. That you were in love. I was not ready to accept it yet, but I never questioned what you said."

Austin sighed and clasped his hands behind his head. Three weeks had been too long for him to be without his family, but he also knew that Sommer had needed that time. She'd been thrust into the spotlight in the most negative of ways and during one of the most vulnerable periods of her life, so he'd taken a step back to give her a chance to piece everything together. But time was now up. He missed his daughter, and he missed his woman.

"Jessica?"

Both he and Jessica looked up and in the direction of the voice.

Austin took Sommer in as if he expected her to float away. She looked absolutely gorgeous dressed comfortably and casually in a pair of jeans and one of his college FSU hoodies. Olivia was attentively looking around the room and he wondered if his curious daughter ever slept.

He crossed the room and crushed their lips together for what seemed like an eternity. When he finally let her up for air, he brushed a finger across her jaw and lifted Olivia from her grasp and into the air. When he brought her down, he pressed raspberry kisses against her cheeks.

Sommer's eyes flickered over to Jessica and for a split second, she actually felt sorry for the woman. Even with all of Jessica's money and good looks, she was still the woman across the room with that hollow look in her eyes as she watched on, excluded from a moment of happiness. Unfortunately for her, Austin was one piece of happiness that Sommer was never going to get back.

"I guess I should go," Jessica said, retrieving her purse.

"I'll walk you out," Walt offered, appearing in the hallway. "Austin and Sommer have some talking to do."

With a brief nod, Jessica followed Walt out the door and Austin lifted Olivia into the air once more. Sommer watched them in delight before making her way over to the refrigerator.

"She cried for five nights in a row," she told Austin, putting away a generous portion of brownies that she, Arielle, and Arielle's two older daughters had made. Thinking about the way they'd looked in the kitchen, Aria with a face full of flour and Isabela tumbling with laughter whenever Aria smudged cocoa on her nose as she tried to get it off, had made her heart long for Austin in a way she hadn't even known was possible.

Not having him around had only magnified the loss of her mother, and she realized then how stupid she'd been to think that not having him in her life could have ever been a solution. To anything.

"Baby girl, why were you crying?" Austin cooed, taking a seat and holding Olivia up to face him. "Did you miss Daddy?"

Sommer unwrapped one of the brownies and took a bite. She'd missed Daddy too.

"How about Mommy? Did she miss Daddy too?" Austin said, echoing her thoughts. "Was she tossing and turning at night because she realized she can't live without Daddy either? Did Mommy really think that Daddy would let more than three weeks pass before he came looking for his ladies again?"

Olivia beamed and it lit up his heart.

"You're corrupting our child," Sommer teased, crossing the room. She took a seat next to him and held up the brownie to his mouth.

"I missed you," he said, taking a bite and lowering his voice.

"Austin, don't do that."

"Do what?"

"Be all sweet and use your Barry White voice at the same time. It confuses me."

He tossed his head back and laughed.

"I missed you too." She leaned into his side.

Austin rested his cheek against the top of her head. "I would've come for you," he assured. "Not having me in your life was not an option."

She reached up and touched the side of his face. "I love you, and I'm sorry."

"I love you too, and don't worry, you're going to make it up to me."

She leaned forward and took his mouth, this time letting her lips linger even longer against his. She welcomed his tongue and used her own to play back, then slipped her hand behind his head to pull him closer. She ended the kiss by nibbling on the sensitive spot she'd found on his lower lip.

Austin glanced down at Olivia and then cradled her in his arms. "*Rock-a-bye baby, on the treetop.* Come on, baby girl, it's time for you to sleep. Mommy and Daddy have some making up to do."

Sommer covered her ears. "I guess that's where the similarities between you and Barry White end."

Austin laughed and continued to sing as he carried Olivia up the stairs, and Sommer made her way to the master suite on the ground level. The minute she walked in, Austin's phone began to vibrate wildly in the middle of the bed. She leaned over to see several missed calls from Gary, which usually meant bad news.

She returned to the kitchen to search through Olivia's baby bag and found a few missed calls from Emma and Arielle, her phone still on do-not-disturb since their connecting flight in Atlanta. There was a single message from Arielle instructing her to turn to the sports channel, so she turned on the TV in the kitchen.

The featured story of the night was none other than William Riley, and viewer comments and responses followed the image of a face older than Sommer had remembered, with a head full of hair that had been obviously dyed brown. The reporter shook his head in disgust as he read a quote that was highlighted on a blurred background:

"I mean, these things are delicate in this day and age with Civil Rights and Affirmative Action and whatnot. And men, we were made to procreate. To spread our seed. Sometimes, one of those seeds take root. You can't help who it's with."

Anger simmered beneath Sommer's surface. William Riley had actually had the audacity to say that she'd just been a receptacle for

Austin's *seed*. That Olivia, their daughter, was the result of some sort of uncontrollable, instinctual penile curiosity.

"Where'd you run off to, baby?" Austin called, his voice coming from the direction of the bedroom. When he appeared in the kitchen entryway, he grinned seductively when he saw her standing there, but the grin faded when he followed her eyes to the TV.

"Austin," she said, turning to face him. "I'm done running from this."

"What the hell is this?" Austin crossed over to the TV in a few strides.

He grabbed the remote to increase the volume, then stood with his hands folded and legs shoulder width apart as William's story was replayed for what was probably the umpteenth time that night.

Dressed in his traditional navy and khaki, Austin was sure that his father had assumed he'd looked professional, but new clothes couldn't hide the aging lines that had been etched into the man's face. Nor could they hide the slight yellow tinge to his eyes indicating early liver problems after a life enslaved to alcohol. Even as William tried a smile, his face had only twisted into a villainous smirk that clearly revealed a man that could not be trusted. Yet, the reporters hung onto his every word. They'd even had the audacity to give credence to those words, and think that they represented anything that Austin had ever believed.

"We have to get in front of this, Austin," Sommer said. "As much as we'd like for it to, it's not going to go away. The more we try to brush it off or avoid it, the more the media gets to add their own spin to it and turn us into people we're not."

Austin tracked his father's movements across the screen. It had been nearly two decades since he'd last seen the man and just like back then, he'd hated him. However, there was no longer a son's underlying need for unconditional acceptance from his father living somewhere in that hate.

Back then, he'd tried everything he could think of to get his father to accept him just the way he was, as well as accept who he chose to befriend. But, as he watched as William answer questions in the middle of his front lawn and in front of a house that should have been destroyed years ago, that need for acceptance was nowhere to be found. It had been engulfed by pure contempt.

"You're right." He turned to face Sommer. "I'll call Gary and give old Willie Riley his interview. But first, I have a question. Jessica told me that she thinks Kyle is the one who leaked that my father was still alive and gave your name to the press. That night we went to Louie's, you said something about being tossed aside like trash by somebody. Was that person Kyle?"

Sommer nibbled on her bottom lip and carried her gaze over to the stovetop. "I was talking a little bit about Kyle, and a little bit about my father."

"I know about your dad, but what did Kyle do?" Austin prodded. "Whatever the problem is that he has with me, it seems to be related to you."

Sommer shifted her weight onto her other leg. "Well, the four years me and Kyle spent together at NC State, we became pretty close. Really good friends. Somewhere along those lines, his view of our relationship got blurred and he started seeing me as his property, rather than just his friend. Kyle's always been the possessive type. The formulaic only-child used to getting whatever he wants."

She stopped and Austin tilted his head, indicating that he knew her story wasn't over.

Sighing, Sommer climbed onto a bar stool. "After we graduated, I started working at a small PR firm in Charlotte and he moved to Miami. We kept in touch, and it was through those conversations that he found out about the crush I'd had on you for all those years. Once he found out, he started showering me with gifts that I would politely return. When that didn't work, he introduced me to all of his girlfriends and told me about how wonderful they were. Each time, I'd only be happy for him. When *that* didn't work, everything went back to normal...until I got offered the job at that firm in New York. It was short notice so when I told him, he offered to let me stay at a place he'd bought out there. I accepted because I needed something quick, and told him that it would only be for a few months until I got everything figured out."

She squeezed her forehead and Austin already didn't like where the story was headed.

"So, I moved to New York and everything was perfect. The job was perfect, the place was perfect. It was wonderful. Then, on a whim, I decided to buy a ticket to the game Dallas was playing in New York. Kyle called the same night I bought the ticket and I told him, not thinking anything of it because we were *just friends*. He said that it was his team's bye week so he'd come along. I didn't think anything of it until that night in bed when I felt someone climb in next to me."

Austin's jaw clenched and he sat in the stool across from her, never breaking his gaze.

"Even though I was scared out of my mind," Sommer went on, "once I realized it was Kyle, the terror waned some. I was more confused as to why he was in bed with me. He then explained that he didn't like the fact that, even after all these years when he'd been there for me, I still kept an image of you hanging like a shadow over 'our relationship.' That was when I first realized that he'd seen our relationship completely different than I did."

She closed her eyes.

"I made the mistake of telling him that he and I had never been in a relationship, and pointed out that I'd dated several men since college, all of which he'd known about. His answer to that was that those were regular men. Middle-class men. He would always be better than them and I would have always come back to him. But you, he saw as a threat."

"Because he knew how I felt about you," Austin filled in. "Me and Kyle didn't see each other much, just those times when we played on the same field, and each time I would ask him about Yearwood. Then,

I would ask him about you. Even when I was seeing Jessica, I would ask him about you. Or I'd ask my mother about you. I'd even ask Arielle about you."

Sommer's face flushed. As it seemed, regardless of their fears or circumstances, fate had made sure that there would be a way for them to be together.

"Well, when I told Kyle that there'd never be anything between me and him, he went crazy," she continued. "He broke my laptop in half. Destroyed lamps and pillows. It was literally like a spoiled child's tantrum. So, I let him throw his tantrum and when he was done, he fell to his knees in front of me and apologized. I told him that it would be okay and tried not to sound too scared, looking at all the destruction he'd just caused. After that, he left. The next day, on my way home from work, I came back to changed locks, a note on the door telling me that I'd been 'evicted,' and directions to the storage facility where I could pick up my things. Then, I got a call from my uncle about Mom's breast cancer. That's how I ended up moving back home. I'm not proud to admit it now, but I literally just gave up on everything."

"You ran," Austin surmised.

"I ran."

"Well, we're going to stop running, Sommer."

They both turned to look at the TV. Yet again, another loop of William's statement was displayed on the screen. This time, it also included commentary from a few other players across the league as they weighed-in with their opinions on the matter. So far, Austin had garnered nothing but support from his colleagues, another thing for which he'd been extremely grateful. His father had assumed that, at the center of everything, the world had remained the same from the days when his bigotry was the norm. Now, they were going to demolish that entire ideology by showing him exactly how much everything had changed.

"One more thing." Sommer reached into the front pocket of the sweatshirt and pulled out the ring box. "About this—"

"What about it?" Austin asked, challenging her with his eyes.

"We're you really going to propose to me on live television?"

"Yes." He slipped the box from her fingers. "I had it all planned out. I was going to bring you and Livvie up to the platform. Then, I was going to introduce Livvie, just like I did, and hand her off to Ma. Do you want to hear the speech I had planned?"

Sommer placed a hand on her chest. "You wrote a speech? I'd love to hear it."

He turned off the flat-screen and walked her by the hand out to the living area. Sommer sank into the sofa.

"Well, after Ma took Livvie," he began, "I was going to turn around and say: 'Today is probably going to go down as one of the most memorable days of my life. As kids, we spend most of our time dreaming about the things that we want to accomplish. These things might change as we get older, but at the end of the day, our goal revolves around our own version of a perfect life. For me, I can say that I'm one of those lucky kids who had the chance to live my dream. Ever since I was nine years old, I knew that I wanted to be a quarterback, buy my mother a BMW, secure the financial future of my family, and get a Super Bowl ring. Ever since I was nine years old, I also knew that I wanted to marry Sommer Hayes.'"

Sommer lowered her eyes and smiled. He responded to her embarrassment with a boyish grin.

"'She was my number one enemy,'" he went on. "'If I was fire, she'd have to be ice. If I was scissors, she was always rock. We'd argue over everything and scream how much we hated each other, but if a bee had so much as threatened to try and sting her, I would have probably taken down the whole hive. I was the only one with permission to hate her because I knew, deep down, I truly didn't hate her. It would be nearly twenty years before I found out that she'd felt the same way.'

"Then, I was going to turn to you and get on one knee," he explained, demonstrating. "After that, I was going to say, 'Today, I'm standing here as a professional quarterback. Check. I just bought my mother a 5-series, my family's future is secure, and Dallas just won the Championship. Check. I guess the last thing I need to check off the list is marrying Sommer Hayes,' so," he opened the box and the sight of the ring again took Sommer's breath away, "will you marry me, Sommer?"

Sommer stood and clapped her hands. "That was amazing, Austin. That would have been an excellent speech."

He didn't move.

"So, will you, Sommer?"

Sommer's fingers went ice cold. "Will I what?"

"Marry me. Be Mrs. Sommer Riley."

"Mrs. Sommer *Hayes*-Riley," she said, her eyes brimming with tears. "And yes, of course I'll marry you, Austin. Of course, of course, of course."

He finally got the chance to slip the ring onto her finger, and it fit perfectly as though it was designed to be nowhere else. He then stood and lifted her into his arms, kissing her as he walked them back to the bedroom. He placed her in the center of the bed and hovered over her body.

"You and that damn hyphenation," he teased with a grin, filling his senses with her taste and smell, and his hands with her heated skin and the soft mounds of flesh he released from their enclosure.

He tortured her with impassioned lovemaking which she returned with the same intensity. She stroked and tasted him. He ran his tongue, agonizing and slow, over her naked body and then inside of her, licking and gently tugging her into frenzied fits of ecstasy. He filled her with restrained urgency, and she cried his name into the walls. She rode him and he took her from behind. Although he made love to her all night and well into the next morning, she'd finally given him the chance to love her much longer.

Chapter Fourteen

Wendy found that she couldn't tear her attention away from Austin and Sommer as they sat in a plush sofa on the other side of the studio. Austin was ridiculously handsome in a crisp suit, tie, and vest combination. Sommer sat in his lap in a coral colored top and cream pencil skirt, looking nothing like a woman who'd just given birth a mere two months ago. The two were talking and laughing like old friends, an obvious indication of how long they'd known each other.

"Ms. Carter?"

Wendy looked up.

"Do you want to do a red lip or nude lip?"

The woman standing in front of her swirled a kabuki brush across her cheeks, and then pointed to the lipstick palette next to her. Wendy mechanically looked at the palette, but her gaze slipped to Austin and Sommer again, then up toward Arielle, her husband, and Emma Riley just arriving on the set.

"Ms. Carter?"

"Red," Wendy answered. "Let's stick with red. That's my power color."

In just a few minutes, she was going to give one of the most important interviews of her life. But, it suddenly started to trouble her that her goal had been to try to show everyone in the nation that Austin truly *didn't* love Sommer. To prove that he'd hidden her because he was afraid of what the world would think about his daughter's mother, and how their relationship would affect his career.

Usually, whenever she interviewed couples on her show, she was instantly able to determine at which point they were faking. If it wasn't the way they seemed to avoid each other while walking around the set, it was the way their affection seemed overdone as if they were trying convince themselves, along with everyone around them, that they actually tolerated each other.

This couple was different.

Austin was relaxed in the chair with one arm around Sommer's waist, and they were sharing a cream cheese-filled croissant from the breakfast table. Sommer broke a piece with her fingers before slipping it into Austin's mouth, and if any of the pastry happened to get on his face, she'd remove it as though touching his face was the most commonplace thing in the world.

Their exchange was so intimate that Wendy felt like a voyeur, as if she was watching them in secret. So why was she so ready to discredit that? What was it about Austin's relationship with Sommer that made her believe that the love she was currently witnessing between them was false?

"Where do I get my makeup put on?" A towering voice bellowed from behind her chair. When she spun around, this time dressed in a charcoal gray suit and yellow dress shirt, sauntered in the controversial William Riley.

∼

THE ROOM FELL QUIET AND AUSTIN'S GRIP AROUND SOMMER'S WAIST tightened as though an enemy had walked in. When Sommer turned toward the voice that had just exploded into the room, she realized that one had.

Arielle slipped her hand into Justin's, and Emma held the gaze of the man she loathed more than anything else in the world, despite the fact that he was father to her two absolutely wonderful children.

"Is this a funeral?" William strolled over to the breakfast table with a hand in his pocket. He picked up a cube of cheese and popped it into his mouth. "This must be what rich, fancy people eat for breakfast. No wonder you TV broads stay so skinny."

When no one responded to his quip, he chuckled to himself and moved over to a bunch of grapes sitting on a tray next to the cheese.

"You know, there are utensils that you can use to pick those up," Justin spoke up, already annoyed by the man's presence. "We all pretty much have access to that buffet. It would be nice if your fingers weren't in it."

William continued to pluck grapes off the stem as though no one in the room had spoken.

"Alright people, we're on in three minutes," the director announced. "Mr. Riley, if you'd come over here, I'm going to show you where to sit."

"I'm only sitting next to my son," William asserted.

"Don't put that man any less than two feet away from me," Austin warned. "Unless you want this civilized show to turn into an episode of Jerry Springer."

The response only seemed to amuse William.

"Alright, fine," William conceded. "Then sit me next to my lovely wife. How have things been with you these days, Emma? You are still as beautiful as ever. My bed has been mighty cold without you in it."

Emma's eyes bore into his, but she didn't offer a response.

William chuckled again, rubbed his hands together, and then turned to the director. "Where do I sit, now?"

Three minutes later, with the exception of Justin, they were all situated in front of the camera. William sat alone on Wendy's left side while the other four sat to her right. Austin kept a tight grasp on Sommer's fingers as though he expected William to spring forward and grab her, and William refused to take his eyes off his son. He was even more proud of the specimen Austin had become now that he was looking at him in person.

"It's the interview that everyone has been waiting for," Wendy announced, looking at the camera. "Today, I'm here with future Hall-of-Fame quarterback Austin Riley, his sister, Arielle Wells, his mother, Emma Riley, and the woman we've all been waiting to meet, Sommer Hayes. Also with us today is William Riley, the father that everyone once thought was dead." She turned to William. "The first thing I want to address is the controversial statement you made on national TV a few days ago."

"What's so controversial about it?" William brazenly asked. "Look, I understand that these things can be sensitive to talk about, but what did I say that was wrong?"

Austin's fist clenched.

"Are you racist, Mr. Riley?" Wendy asked.

"Of course not. I think you all are taking what I said out of context. I'm not saying that Sommer shouldn't be married or have children one day. I'm just saying that it should be with someone other than Austin."

"And what kind of someone is that?" Arielle cut in.

William smiled at the little girl he used to carry on his shoulders. "Someone that looks more like her."

Austin's grip went even tighter and Arielle took a quick glance over at Justin.

"So, what about me and Justin?" Arielle asked. "What about our children? We have four of the most perfect, precious, and wonderful children in the world. What do you say to that?"

William smiled again. "I'll be honest and say that half-breed children are nice looking. Just look at that Halle Berry woman. And Derek Jeter."

Arielle started to rise from her seat, but Austin grabbed her with his other hand.

"Mr. Riley," Wendy interjected, "did you really just call your grandchildren half-breeds?"

William shrugged as if there'd been no problem with the way he'd answered the previous question.

Wendy stared at his face in disbelief for a few seconds before she continued. "If we took a poll right now, Mr. Riley, do you think America would think you're racist?"

William shrugged again. "Everybody's trying to be politically correct these days. They would answer in a poll that they think I am, but it would be a different story if we had a one-on-one conversation."

Arielle began to move forward again, but Austin held her tighter.

Wendy turned to Emma. "Mrs. Riley—"

"Emma," she cut off. "Please, call me Emma."

Wendy nodded. She completely understood the need to not be associated with a man as vile and contemptible as William Riley.

"Emma, how did you stay married to this man?"

Emma smirked. "The minute I found out who *this man* really was, I immediately divorced him. I was not content living with a man with Mr. Riley's predilections, especially when I raised my children to love whoever they wanted to love as long as that person genuinely loves them back."

William leaned forward. "She put me out as soon as she found out about that kid in Alabama. I couldn't even get a word in edgewise. Couldn't even explain myself."

"For God sakes, William, his name was Henry Cartwright," Austin lashed out. "He's not just some *kid* from Alabama. He's a kid whose death you and your friends are responsible for. Don't you think his family is watching right now? Don't you have any respect for human life? Out of the four men responsible, you are the only one that's still living. You could have taken this opportunity to give Henry and his family the respectful apology that they deserve."

Again, William acted as if he'd said nothing out of place. He was happy, however, that Austin had actually directed some sort of comment toward him.

Wendy's eyes darted between Austin and William. She'd come back to this later. Not only did she want to get to the bottom of what had happened that day in 1953, but she also wanted the people to witness Austin's ire toward his father. She'd been mistaken. Austin was nothing like the old bigot sitting across from him.

"I understand that you and Sommer's mother were best friends," Wendy said, turning back to Emma. Her hand then lovingly covered Sommer's wrist. "I'm so sorry about your loss."

Sommer's smile revealed a woman that was still grieving, but was putting on a brave front for the sake of her family.

"Sommer's mother and I shared a love of helping people," Emma answered. "We loved gardening, gabbing, and baking together. A lady couldn't find a better friend than Caroline Hayes. She saw me through some very difficult times, and I was with her through both of her bouts with cancer, every step of the way. I saw her as a woman who was my best friend and nothing else, but it wasn't until William's past came out that I found out that he was always uncomfortable with having her in our house. Or that he threw out the cups she used."

Sommer's eyes widened. "Come again?"

"He threw out anything she ate from," Emma reiterated, tears in her eyes. "I thought I was going crazy for a minute, losing cups, plates, and utensils. Then, when I found out, I just couldn't believe it. I mean, she was my best friend and he knew that. I couldn't understand how someone could be so depraved."

She hung her head and dabbed at the tears now flowing from the corners of her eyes.

"You threw out my mother's cups?" Sommer asked, anger scorching the back of her throat.

"Yes, but it's not what you think," William attempted to justify. "I didn't throw them out because she's black. That's just ridiculous. I threw them out because she had cancer. I read somewhere online that cancer was contagious."

Sommer closed her eyes and said a silent prayer. Wendy, however, was looking at William with narrowed brows. She'd never come face to face with this kind of ignorance before and it was utterly repugnant. Her stomach was literally turning.

Austin placed a kiss against Sommer's temple and then whispered a few reassuring words in her ear. He wanted neither her nor Arielle's anger to be bolstered by his father's ignorance. He was going to take it all for them.

"This is not fair," William argued. "I agreed to come on here to see my kids and for you all to see that Austin's just like me, not for you all to gang up on me like this."

"I'm nothing like you," Austin shot back.

"I want to switch gears here a minute," Wendy interrupted, turning to face Austin. "Austin, I just have one question. Are you ashamed that you have a daughter with a black woman?"

Austin's eyes squared on Wendy. "I'm not ashamed to say that I have a daughter with black woman, that I'm in love with a black woman, or that I'm marrying *this* black woman."

A woman somewhere off set yelled and clapped her hands in support.

"Well, you could've fooled us," Wendy came back. "You could barely turn a channel without seeing intimate video or photos of you and Jessica Costa when you two were together. Your relationship with her wasn't hidden."

"And who took those videos and photos?" Austin asked.

"Well, the paparazzi, I'm guess—"

"So, *I* never actually plastered pictures of us all over the internet, did I?"

Wendy attempted to respond, but couldn't find the words.

"How long did it take before your people found out that Jessica and I were together?" he added.

Wendy shrugged. "Almost immediately."

"Jessica and I had been dating for three months before our relationship became the public's business. I didn't want the cameras in the middle of it, but she claimed that she wanted everyone to know that she was in love."

Wendy shook her head. "Well, what about Victoria Ellington?"

"I never dated Victoria."

She pointed to a photo that was now displayed on a large LED screen behind them. "Isn't that you with Victoria at a formal, black-tie event?"

"What other pictures of Victoria and I together do you have?"

"None at this time."

"Because there aren't any. I escorted her to the event and that was that. Stop trying to paint me out to be someone I'm not."

Even though she'd begun to doubt herself, Wendy was still determined to get to the bottom of Austin's actions.

"So, why not come forward with your relationship with Sommer?"

"That was my doing," Sommer spoke up. "I want to come clean and say that Austin never wanted our relationship hidden. He never had a problem with people knowing that we were together. I was the one who had the problem with it."

Wendy did her best to hide the surprise from her face. If she'd been dating Austin Riley, she'd tell everyone from Texas to Guam.

"Why is that?" she prodded. "Were you afraid of how people would react when they found out that you were black?"

Sommer looked at Austin. "Back home in Yearwood, I was mostly concerned with what people would say. You know, small town talk. Austin hadn't been home in ten years and all of a sudden, I'm all over him? I was afraid that they would think it was because of his money, which led me to be afraid that Austin would think the same thing."

William made a noise in the back of his throat which the room actively ignored.

"But, it wasn't until a conversation that we'd had with Kyle Stallworth that I realized that here in Texas, Austin is pretty much revered," Sommer continued. "He's to Texas what Peyton Manning was, and still is, to the city of Indianapolis. That's when I started thinking about how people would regard me. Here I was, just this ordinary girl from this speck of a town, and I wasn't a redheaded, blue-eyed musician, a Brazilian model, or even the heir to some obscure fortune. And don't get me wrong, I have had the opportunity to read some of the things that I already knew people would say about me, and even about Olivia. How much less the championship meant to them when they found out about who I was, things like that."

She touched the side of Austin's face, enjoying the way his rugged cheek felt against her palms. He smiled at her and held her gaze, the glowing eyes she loved more than life itself cocooning her in their blanket of warmth. In them, she could see it. He loved her just as much, and maybe even more.

"That's when I realized I'd been worrying about the wrong thing." She reluctantly tore her gaze away from Austin to settle them onto William. "What other people would think isn't as important as what I feel for this man."

William rolled his eyes, but Sommer's gaze didn't waver. Even though she was looking at him, her next statement was directed at all the viewers who'd been first in line to say that their relationship was a farce.

"Ask yourselves what love can do, what it can conquer. What it can accomplish. Then, if you come up with an answer other than the word *anything*, you need to challenge your convictions."

Wendy felt a quake of guilt start as an unsettling tremor in her toes. There was something about the certainty in Sommer's eyes that made her finally realize that she *hadn't* been any different from the people who'd jumped to the internet to spread their disdain or ignorant accusations about the nature of Sommer and Austin's relationship. She'd been so sure that she could get the truth out of him—the truth which she'd assumed was that Austin had been no different from some of the other ball players she'd met who kept certain women under wraps. Whether the woman was not from the best family, not the most attractive or physically fit, of a different ethnicity...she'd seen it all. But oh, how wrong she'd been. This wasn't that. This was the complete opposite. Austin had wanted to sing his girlfriend's praises and proverbially shout their love from a mountaintop, but it was Sommer who'd been reserved, calculated, and scared, not of what it would do to his career, but how people would view the man she loved.

"Do you get it now?" Austin asked his father. "Arielle and Justin. Me and Sommer. Tons of couples around the world. Do you get it now? This isn't the 1950s anymore, and while I will argue that there are still tensions from your time period festering away sixty years later, this is not the same world that you keep in your head."

"So you mean that this is not the same world where a man gets to go home after killing a kid?" William goaded with a smirk. "I beg to differ."

"So you admit that you killed Henry?" Austin asked. "This isn't some photograph of four kids admitting to their guilt, William Riley. This is national TV. Millions of viewers. Are you finally admitting your guilt today?"

When Austin grinned, William realized what was happening. His son hadn't taken this interview solely to put the rumors about him and Sommer to rest. Austin intended to air out the dirty laundry he'd kept hidden for the last six decades.

Suddenly, a group of people arrived on set and William recognized one of them as the woman he'd spotted in Yearwood. The one who'd recognized him. Henry Cartwright's cousin. It didn't take much longer to figure out that the other people with her were also Henry's relatives ranging from the old to the very young.

"I'm not standing around for this," he declared, standing and reaching around to detach his microphone.

Austin stood and faced him. "You're either going to sit or stand for it, but you're not going anywhere. Now, answer my question. You hide behind your double entendres and your moronic rants, but what happens when things are shoved into your face, William? When you're forced to be a man for the very first time in your entire god damn life? A man who didn't even know what it had meant to be a father?"

William's face flushed and anger tugged the corners of his mouth south. His eyes darted around the studio only to find that all eyes were on him, and his chest heaved as his temper flared into a rumbling boil.

"What did you expect me to do?" He tossed up his hands. "I was just a kid. A kid in the fifties. All sorts of tensions were high back then, and I wasn't old enough to know what was right from what was wrong. So, when Charlie suggested that we trick this little black boy into coming into the woods with us and leave him there, I had no choice but to go along with it." He jerked his hand toward the family. "Is this what you want to hear? How Henry screamed for his mother while me, James and John watched Charlie choke him to death? How Charlie's father had seen the killing as a 'rite of passage' for his boy? Is that what you want to hear?"

A woman placed a hand over her throat and the man standing next to her comforted her.

"You still make me sick," Austin told his father. "How could you, as a human being, see something so inhumane and then decide to live your life the way you did? Even going so far as trying to convince your children that they should be the same way too?"

"To help you," William growled. "Look at Arielle. With all of her smarts, she ended up with a nobody like this Justin kid. And you, Austin? Do you think that you and Sommer will still be together ten years from now? Do you really think that all of your sponsors and endorsement contracts will remain intact now that your little whore has been rev—"

Austin's fist went to his father's face before he had a chance to finish his sentence, and William stumbled over his chair before he crashed to the floor. No one rushed forward to impede Austin's path to his father, and even as Arielle moved forward to calm her brother, both

Emma and Sommer stopped her. Sommer, remembering the look in Austin's eyes when they first found out that they were having a little girl knew that he needed this moment.

"First of all, I let no one degrade Sommer. No one. It's been that way since we were kids, and it's always going to be that way. Second, Justin is a partner at a very successful law firm. Hardly a nobody. If you'd pick up a book and read sometimes, you would know that. Lastly, I never want to see you again. Ever. Although people change every day, you're not one of them. You never will be. So, I highly suggest that you no longer consider yourself tied to me, Ma, or Arielle in any way. Just as it has always been, I have no father. I hate you and have no respect for you."

William's eyes widened and he touched his lip. He grimaced at the pain and drew back a finger dotted with blood. Yet, even though the pain was only increasing as the area swelled, Austin's words had felt much worse. All this time, the image of the son he thought he'd had was wrong. He'd held out hope that Austin really had been just like him, cut from the same cloth, but the man standing in front of him wasn't even an eighth of that. Austin really was more of a man than he could ever hope to have been, no thanks to him.

"Are you okay, Austin?" Sommer asked, rising and walking over to where Austin stood. He nodded, pulled her into his arms, and kissed the top of her head.

"I'm good, baby." Then, he turned to Wendy. "Are we finished here?"

Wendy motioned for someone to come and help William off of the set.

"Not yet," she replied. "I want to apologize to you two first. I want to also especially apologize to you, Austin, for the assumptions I made. I'm woman enough to admit when I'm wrong, and looking at the two of you gives me hope that my prince charming is still waiting for me somewhere out there."

Her eyes flicked up to Austin. As delicious as he was, and despite the seven years she'd spent trying to get him to creep between her sheets, this one was definitely off the market. Austin only had eyes for one woman.

She motioned to the director. "I don't want to edit any of that out. I want to do a final shot with Austin, Sommer, and Olivia, and then my closing remarks."

The director nodded and then signaled that everyone had a five-minute break. Austin made his way over to the Cartwright family.

"Since my father won't do it, I want to apologize for the grief that his maliciousness caused your family," he expressed.

The family members parted to reveal an elderly woman in a wheelchair, her face still moist from tears and the tissue she held in her hand dampened. Austin offered her the square from his pocket, and she smiled as she motioned for him to come closer. He knelt next to the chair and she brushed a finger over his cheek.

"Mrs. Cartwright?" Austin guessed.

"Call me Helena," she reassured. "And I just wanted to say thank you, young man, for what you did here today. It tormented me for years, wondering what was going through the minds of the boys who killed my son. I even found myself getting upset with Henry at times over the fact that he'd gone off with strangers, something that I was always sure to remind him not to do in New York. But, he was just ten years old. All he saw was boys who wanted to play with him. He wasn't privy to the things that were going on during that time. That's just the kind of kid he was."

She called Sommer over.

"You two may not realize it," she continued, "but you set a precedent here today. And it's not only because of the couple you are, but it's because you asked people to challenge their convictions. To open their eyes and to look at love bare, stripped of the unsavory things we attach to it—jealousy, deceit, and lies. At its base, you'll find unconditional and undying affection between two people, no matter their creed or origin." She pulled Austin in for a loving hug, and then did the same for Sommer. "Those are my wishes for you as you embark on this journey together."

"Ten seconds everyone," a man behind them shouted, and after another hug, Austin and Sommer took their place beside Wendy, and Emma brought out Olivia who was dressed in a pair of overalls and pink socks. When the cameras started rolling, Wendy flashed a grin.

"There you have it, folks. Austin Riley and Sommer Hayes. Just another part of the game of love." She turned to Sommer. "So, tell us about those wedding plans, Future Mrs. Austin Riley?"

Chapter Fifteen

The dense fog that Sommer and Austin had been living in for the past few weeks was finally starting to dissipate. After the interview, the support for their relationship increased ten-fold, along with nearly unanimous contempt for William Riley after seeing how deep the old man's prejudices went. A petition had even begun requesting that federal officials try his case in a higher court. And although garnering that support was exactly what they'd needed to ease their lives back into some sort of normalcy, Austin was just relieved to finally have the ability to share the woman that he loved with the world, and that people had a chance to witness the love that he had for his family.

He was also relieved to know that when Olivia got older and was eventually exposed to what had happened, she'd be able to take pride in the way her parents had handled the situation, and the small step they'd taken in creating a better world for her existence.

A sudden gust of cool wind whirled through the trees, and Sommer hugged her sweater closer to her body. Spring had descended upon North Carolina, which was evidenced by signs popping up around town for the Yearwood Founding Festival that was held every March. The days were finally sweater friendly, ponds were now bursting with wildlife, and the violets that welcomed visitors and residents at the entrance to the city were in full bloom. Life was moving on, which was something that Sommer found strange, yet accepted. As she read her mother's headstone a fourth time, she could accept that life would move on because it needed to, but it was still strange that the concept didn't hold true for all. Some people would never move on again.

"I think she would have been extremely proud of you," Austin encouraged as he placed a bouquet of flowers on Caroline's grave. "As hardheaded as you are, you still allowed all the things she wanted for you to come to fruition."

She smiled up at him. "You just had to throw the hardheaded part in there, didn't you?"

Austin shrugged and pulled her into his arms.

"Want to hear something weird?" she asked. "The other day when I was giving Livvie a bath, I noticed that she had a birthmark right down near her ankle."

"Like her mother," Austin pointed out.

"And her grandmother." Sommer's eyes went back to the headstone. "Some of my mom's features, I see in Livvie, and that somehow makes me feel a million times better. Then, when I came back here and saw everyone outside the bakery..."

Her voice trailed off as her throat swelled with emotion.

They'd arrived in Yearwood earlier that morning to handle some business with the bakery only to find nearly the entire city inside the café and spilling out into the parking lot.

They were bombarded with hugs, kisses, and congratulatory pats as they made their way through the crowd. Reese and Marcie had been standing at the counter with the new girl, Faye Westwood, a transplant from New Orleans. According to Reese, Faye had fit in perfectly with the customers, staff, and seemed to have caught the interest of Cameron Yearwood, the middle son of the town's family namesake. Cameron had stopped in to the bakery nearly every day since Faye arrived, and Sommer had made a mental note to warn the girl against succumbing to a man who'd had a "Playboy Certificate" created for him by a few women he'd dated.

Reese, Marcie, and Faye had stepped aside to reveal a beautiful, three-tiered cake congratulating Sommer and Austin on their engagement. Next to it was a smaller photo cake of a picture that Sommer had taken with her mother and a then three-day old Olivia. Sommer had burst into tears and received hugs from the congregation of townspeople before being wrapped up in Austin's familiar and welcomed embrace.

It had been the perfect way to be welcomed home, and although her life was now in Dallas, Yearwood would forever be at the center of her heart.

"Austin, Sommer."

Kyle appeared behind them in a camel-colored pea coat and matching Armani scarf. A wool cap was pulled down over his ears.

"How's it going, Kyle?" Sommer asked.

"Good," he answered with a nod. "Do you guys have a minute?"

His eyes flicked to Austin who had yet to say a word.

"Sure, why not," Sommer answered.

Kyle rubbed his gloved hands together as though unnerved by something. "I want to make a confession first," he began. "I just wanted to say that I was the one who told the press that your father was still alive, Austin, and I was the one who gave them your name as Olivia's mother, Sommer."

"Why?" Austin finally spoke up. "What made you even think to want to do that?"

"Because you always get what you want, even when I want the same thing," Kyle revealed. "Your pathway has always been paved with gold. Plus, I remember you telling me and Darrell about your dad so I figured Sommer had to be a brief case of jungle fever for you. She wouldn't have been for me."

"Kyle, you've known me ever since your family moved here from Detroit when we were in the third grade," Austin reminded. "You were one of the only who knew, truly knew, how I felt about Sommer. You were also the only person I told about my father and what he did. You were even there that day when we were throwing his stuff into boxes and found that picture. You're the last person I would expect to think that I was somehow faking my feelings. So, what were you trying to do by sending a reporter out to Alabama? Do you have a problem with me?"

"Not with you." Kyle gestured between them. "But with this. You two. I have feelings for you, Sommer. And Austin, I thought that, deep down inside, you were like your father and I didn't want Sommer to end up getting hurt when she realized that you didn't really care about her."

"But you're using the past tense," Sommer acknowledged. "Are you saying that you don't think that anymore?"

His shoulders fell. "I watched Wendy's show. Just like everybody else, I tuned in expecting that I'd see evidence of what I'd thought. Evidence of the truth. But the show only made me angrier with each passing minute."

He clenched and unclenched his fists.

"You really do love her, don't you, Riley?"

Austin laughed. "That's not obvious yet?"

Kyle turned to Sommer. "I'm not used to not getting what I want," he confessed. "You know that. My father sold his business for millions at forty and then retired in Yearwood with my mother, who was only twenty-five at the time. I was an only kid until my cousin Andrew came to live with us, and even then I was still the center of attention because Drew's six years older than me. I was spoiled, but that doesn't mean I don't know when to quit."

Sommer begged to differ, but she kept her thoughts to herself.

"And I never chase women, not even you, Sommer," he added. "So, first off, I want to apologize for any harm that my actions might have caused. I wasn't thinking straight. AndI want to apologize to you, Sommer, for what I did to you back in New York. That was childish,

I'll admit, but I thought that putting you out would make you come crawling back to get into my good graces. Guess I was wrong there."

"Dead wrong," Sommer emphasized.

Kyle's jaw clenched, but with Austin's eyes on him, he relaxed the muscle and took a silent breath.

"I realize now that there's no hope for us, Sommer," he conceded, "so I'll go ahead and leave you alone. I'll leave you two alone. But—"

"Don't say that you'll be there for her if things don't work out between us," Austin warned. "This has been meant to be for almost three decades. It's not going anywhere."

Kyle took another silent breath. "Fine. I wish you guys the best." His eyes darted to the headstone. "And I'm sorry for your loss, Sommer. Mama Hayes will be missed by everyone."

Sommer nodded toward him in appreciation, and with a slight wave, he walked away. When he'd disappeared down the street, Sommer squeezed her forehead.

"I think scientists should study Kyle to find out the root cause of where headaches come from," she suggested. "People always seem to get them when he's around." She wrapped both arms around Austin's midsection. "How were you ever friends with him?"

"Kyle, I was friends with," Austin clarified. "I don't know who the hell that was that just walked off."

She laughed and squeezed him tighter. Standing there with him felt so amazing, she knew there would never be anyone else for her.

"By the way, will you go to the movies with me tonight, Sommer Hayes?" he asked. "Check yes or no."

Sommer laughed again and they held hands as they made their way back to the car. "I'll go anywhere with you, troublemaker."

"How about to Spain?"

She looked up, surprised. "What do you mean?"

"I distinctively remember a certain someone telling me that she wanted a Spain wedding. And from here on out, I plan to try to give you any and everything your heart desires."

Still in shock, Sommer's eyes misted over. "All I need is you, Austin."

He pulled her in for a kiss whose taste he knew would never grow old. "And I'm yours, all day and every day. I don't want you to forget that. Ever. But," he reached for his phone, "I guess I'll go ahead and call the wedding planner to cancel that Spain wed—"

"Hold on," Sommer interrupted.

"Oh, wait, what was that?"

"Let's not completely do away with that Spain wedding idea."

Austin laughed and pulled her in for another kiss. The softness of her lips, the familiarity of her scent, and the silkiness of her skin once again intoxicated him.

Just like that day outside the bakery, all those years ago, he'd been mesmerized by Sommer Hayes. And now, he'd be able to wake up next to her every day only to be mesmerized...over and over again.

About the Author

K. Alex Walker is the author of several bestselling novels, including the well-known *Angels and Assassins* series. She was born and raised in the West Indies, spending half of her life between the beaches of St. Thomas and Antigua before relocating to Florida.

When she is not spending hours crafting stories in front of her MacBook or sprinting to her phone to jot down book ideas, she can be found hanging out with her nephews and nieces, reading HGTV magazines, watching Marvel movies or Star Wars, and being a voice for animals and the underserved.

Made in United States
Cleveland, OH
20 April 2025